gossip girl

psycho killer

gossip girl
psycho killer

by
Cecily von Ziegesar

poppy

LITTLE, BROWN AND COMPANY
New York   Boston

Poppy
Hachette Book Group
237 Park Avenue, New York, NY 10017
For more of your favorite series and novels,
visit our website at www.pickapoppy.com

Poppy is an imprint of Little, Brown and Company.
The Poppy name and logo are trademarks of Hachette Book Group, Inc.

The publisher is not responsible for websites
(or their content) that are not owned by the publisher.

First Edition: October 2011

The characters, events, and locations in this book are fictitious. Any similarity to real persons, living or dead, is coincidental and not intended by the author.

Haikus on pages 159, 186, and 188 © 1994 Robert Hass. Extracted from *The Essential Haiku: Versions of Bashō, Buson, & Issa*, edited and translated by Robert Hass, New Jersey: The Ecco Press, 1994.

"Sexyback" by Nathaniel Hills Floyd, Timothy Z. Mosley, Justin R. Timberlake (Tennman Tunes, Universal Music-Z Tunes, LLC, Virginia Beach Music, WB Music Corp.). All rights reserved.

"Le Freak" by Bernard Edwards, Nile Gregory Rodgers (Bernard S Other Music and Sony/ATV Songs LLC). All rights reserved.

"Whip My Hair" by Ronald M. Jackson, Janae Liann Ratliff (Dime 4 My Jukebox, EMI April Music, Inc., The Levite Camp Music, Universal Music Corporation). All rights reserved.

"Ballad of Sweeney Todd" by Stephen Sondheim (Revelation Music Publishing Corporation, Rilting Music, Inc.). All rights reserved.

"Emotional Rescue" by Michael Phillip Jagger, Keith Richards (EMI Music Publishing LTD). All rights reserved.

alloy**entertainment**

Produced by Alloy Entertainment
151 West 26th Street, New York, NY 10001

Cover and book design by Liz Dresner
Cover photo by Jill Wachter
Illustrations by Jeanne Detallante

ISBN 978-0-316-18509-7
10 9 8 7 6 5 4 3 2 1
CWO

Printed in the United States of America

The Gossip Girl novels:

Gossip Girl
You Know You Love Me
All I Want Is Everything
Because I'm Worth It
I Like It Like That
You're The One That I Want
Nobody Does It Better
Nothing Can Keep Us Together
Only In Your Dreams
Would I Lie To You
Don't You Forget About Me
It Had To Be You
I Will Always Love You
The Carlyles
You Just Can't Get Enough
Take A Chance On Me
Love the One You're With
Gossip Girl, Psycho Killer

There's blood on thy face.
　　　　　　　　　—*Macbeth*, William Shakespeare

gossipgirl.net

Disclaimer: All the real names of places, people, and events have been altered or abbreviated to protect the innocent. Namely, me.

topics   sightings   your e-mail   post a question

hey people!

Ever wondered what the lives of the chosen ones are really like? Well, I'm going to tell you, because I'm one of them. I'm not talking about models or actors, royalty or reality show stars, cult leaders or the undead. I'm talking about the people who are *born to it*—those of us who have everything anyone could possibly wish for and who take it all completely for granted. The ones who literally get away with murder.

Welcome to New York City's Upper East Side, where my friends and I live, and go to school, and play—and sometimes kill each other. We all live in huge apartments with our own bedrooms and bathrooms and phone lines. We have unlimited access to money, booze, antique weaponry, apocalyptic poisons, the best carpet cleaners, bespoke luggage, Town Cars, and whatever else we need. Our parents are rarely home, so we have tons of privacy and unlimited opportunities to commit outrageously messy crimes. We're smart, we've inherited classic good looks, we wear fantastic clothes, and we know how to party. Our shit still stinks, but you can't smell it because the penthouse is decontaminated hourly and then sprayed by the maid with a refreshing scent made exclusively for us by French perfumers.

It's a luxe life, but someone's got to live it . . . until they die.

Our apartments are all within walking distance of the Metropolitan Museum of Art on Fifth Avenue, and the single-sex private schools, like Constance Billard, which most of us go to. Even with a hangover and a charley horse from last night's killing spree, Fifth Avenue always looks so beautiful in the morning with the sunlight glimmering on the bobbing heads of the sexy St. Jude's School boys.

But something is rotten on Museum Mile. . . .

SIGHTINGS

B shooting daggers at her mother in a taxi in front of **Barneys**. *N* firing up a joint on the steps of the **Met**, his lacrosse stick at his feet. *C* spending a killing on new school shoes at **Hermès**. And a familiar, tall, eerily beautiful blond girl emerging from a New Haven–line train in **Grand**

THE METROPOLITAN
MUSEUM OF ART

Central Terminal carrying a duffel bag large enough to stuff a body into, and a violin case, even though she doesn't play. Approximate age: seventeen. *By the pricking of my thumbs, something wicked this way comes.* Could it be? *S* is back?!

THE GIRL WHO LEAVES FOR BOARDING SCHOOL, GETS KICKED OUT, AND COMES BACK TO HAUNT US, OR WORSE

Yes, *S* is back from boarding school. Her hair is longer, paler. Her blue eyes have the depth and mystery of a closet so full of skeletons the door won't close. She is wearing the same old fabulous clothes, now in rags from fending off bewitched boarding school boys and the stakelike icicles of long New England winters. This morning *S*'s creepily jubilant laughter echoed off the steps of the Met, where we will no longer be able to enjoy a quick smoke and a cappuccino without seeing her waving to us with one of her victims' severed hands from the window of her parents' penthouse apartment across the street. She has picked up the habit of biting her fingernails bloody, which makes us wonder about her even more, and while we are all dying to ask her why she got kicked out of boarding school, we won't, because we'd really rather she stayed away. But *S* is definitely here to haunt us.

Just to be safe, we should all synchronize our watches, warn the doorman, change the locks, and keep a baseball bat or golf club handy. If we aren't careful, **S** is going to win over our teachers, wear that dress we couldn't fit into, eat the last olive, have sex in our parents' beds, spill Campari on our rugs, wrench out our brothers' and our boyfriends' hearts, strangle us in our sleep, and basically ruin our lives and piss us all off in a major way.

I'll be watching closely. I'll be watching all of us as we drop like flies. It's going to be a wild and wicked year. I can smell it.

Love,

gossip girl

like most killer stories, it started at a party

"I watched *Dexter* reruns all morning in my room so I wouldn't have to eat breakfast with them," Blair Waldorf told her two best friends and Constance Billard School classmates, Kati Farkas and Isabel Coates. "My mother cooked him a piece of fried liver. I didn't even know she knew how to use the stove."

Blair tucked her long, dark brown hair behind her ears and swigged her mother's fine vintage scotch from the crystal tumbler in her hand. She was already on her second glass and planned on drinking several more. Anything to ward off the murderous rage that threatened to overcome her. Her forehead got all wrinkly and unattractive when she was mad.

"Which episodes did you watch?" Isabel asked, removing a stray strand of hair from Blair's black cashmere cardigan.

"Who cares?" Blair said, stamping her foot. She wore her new black ballet flats—very bow tie proper preppy, which she could get away with because in an instant she could change her mind, smudge her lipstick, tease her hair, and put on her trashy, pointed, knee-high boots and that murderously short metallic skirt her mother hated. *Poof*: escaped convict meets rock star sex kitten.

Meow.

"The point is, I was trapped in my room all morning because they were busy having a gross romantic breakfast in their matching red silk bathrobes. They didn't even take *showers*." Blair took another gulp of her drink. The only way to tolerate the thought of her mother sleeping with *that man* was to get drunk, very drunk, and imagine them both dying from the Mad Cow bacteria in their fried liver.

Luckily, Blair and her friends came from the kind of families for whom drinking was as commonplace as a bloody nose or a surgical scar. Their parents believed in the quasi-European idea that the more access kids have to alcohol, the less likely they are to abuse it. So Blair and her friends could drink whatever they wanted, whenever they wanted, as long as they maintained their grades and their looks and didn't embarrass themselves or the family by puking in public, pissing their pants, or ranting in the streets. The same thing went for everything else, like sex or drugs or murder—as long as you kept up appearances, you were all right.

But keep your panties on. That's coming later.

The man Blair was so upset about was Cyrus Rose, her mother's new boyfriend. At that very moment Cyrus Rose was standing on the other side of the living room, greeting the dinner guests. He looked like someone who might help you pick out shoes at Saks—bald, except for a small, bushy mustache, his fat stomach barely hidden in a shiny blue double-breasted suit—or someone you'd pay to finish off that filthy rich great-aunt who refused to die. He jingled the change in his pocket incessantly, and when he removed his jacket, there were big, nasty sweat marks on his underarms. He had a loud laugh and was very sweet to Blair's mother. But he wasn't Blair's father. Last year Blair's father had run off to France with another man, who could have been a very handsome psychopath for all Blair knew.

Although the private-label wine they produce at their chateau is excellent.

Of course none of that was Cyrus Rose's fault, but that didn't matter to Blair. As far as she was concerned, Cyrus Rose was a completely annoying, fat *loser* who deserved to die—by strangulation perhaps, after getting his bulbous neck stuck in the cord of his horrible red silk bathrobe.

But not tonight. Tonight Blair was going to have to tolerate Cyrus Rose, because her mother's dinner party was in his honor, and all the Waldorfs' family friends were there to meet him: the blue-blooded Basses and their sons, Chuck and Donald; the tragic widower Mr. Farkas and his daughter, Kati; the 1980s slasher film producer Arthur Coates, his grave-digging wife, Titi, and their daughters, Isabel, Regina, and Camilla; dead English royalty offspring Patty and Roger Scott Tompkinson and their son, Jeremy (who hadn't actually shown his face, but was probably just getting high in the maid's bathroom); Captain "Kill or Be Killed" Archibald, his wife, Mrs. Archibald, and their son, Nate. The only ones still missing were Mr. and Mrs. van der Woodsen, whose teenage daughter, Serena, and son, Erik, were both away at school.

Blair's mother was famous for her dinner parties, and this was the first since her infamous divorce. The Waldorf penthouse had been expensively redecorated that summer in bruised reds and molten browns, and it was full of impressive antiques and artwork cleverly scavenged by her decorator from the estates of recently deceased art collectors before they went to auction. In the center of the dining room table was an enormous silver bowl full of white lilies, petrified scarab beetles, and desiccated pussy willows. Gold-leafed place cards lay on every red-lacquered plate. In the kitchen, Myrtle, the cook, was whisper-shouting Ozzy Osbourne songs to the soufflé, and the sloppy Irish maid, Esther, hadn't dropped her famous blood pudding and Ritz cracker canapés down anyone's dress yet, thank goodness.

Blair was the one getting sloppy. And if Cyrus Rose didn't stop harassing Nate, her boyfriend, she was going to have to go over there, spill her scotch all over his tacky Italian loafers, and bludgeon him to death with her empty tumbler. Not that she'd ever actually kill anyone, but it was fun to imagine it.

Such fun.

"You and Blair have been going out a long time, am I right?" Cyrus said, punching Nate in the arm. He was trying to get the kid to loosen up a little. All these Upper East Side kids were wound way too tight.

Hence the high mortality rate.

"You sleep with her yet?" Cyrus asked.

Nate turned redder than the gore smeared on a butcher's apron. "Well, we've known each other practically since we were born," he stuttered. "But we've only been going out for like, a year. We don't want to ruin it by, you know, rushing, before we're ready?" Nate was just spitting back the line that Blair always gave him when he asked her if she was ready to do it or not. But he was talking to his girlfriend's mother's boyfriend. What was he supposed to say? "Dude, if I had my way we'd be doing it right *now*"?

"Absolutely," Cyrus Rose said. He clasped Nate's shoulder with a red, meaty hand. Around his fleshy wrist was one of those gold Cartier cuff bracelets—very popular in the 1980s and not so popular now—that you screw on permanently and never take off, unless you cut off your own arm.

Or someone cuts it off for you.

"Let me give you some advice," Cyrus told Nate, as if Nate had a choice. "Don't listen to a word that girl says. Girls like surprises. They want you to keep things interesting. Know what I mean?"

Nate nodded, frowning. He tried to remember the last time he'd surprised Blair. The only thing that came to mind was the time he'd brought her an ice cream cone when he picked her up at her tennis lesson. That had been over a month ago, and it was a pretty lame surprise by any standard. At this rate he and Blair might never have sex.

Nate was one of those boys you look at, and while you're look-ing at them you know they're thinking, *That girl can't take her eyes off me, I'm so hot.* Although he didn't act at all conceited about it. He couldn't help being hot—he was born that way. Poor guy.

That night Nate was wearing the moss green cashmere V-neck sweater Blair had given him last Easter, when her father had taken them skiing in Sun Valley for a week. Secretly, Blair had sewn a tiny gold heart pendant inside one of the sweater's sleeves, so that Nate would always be wearing her heart on his sleeve. Blair liked to think of herself as a hopeless romantic in the style of old movie actresses like Lana Turner in *The Postman Always Rings Twice*, Sissy Spacek in *Carrie*, or Glenn Close in *Fatal Attraction*. She was always coming up with plot twists for the movie she was starring in at the moment. And usually some-one wound up dead.

C'est la vie.

"I love you," Blair had told Nate breathily when she gave him the sweater.

"Me too," Nate had said back, although he wasn't exactly sure if it was true.

When he put on the sweater, it looked so good on him that Blair wanted to howl like a werewolf, rip off all her clothes, and jump him. But it seemed unattractive to scream in the heat of the moment—more Janet Leigh in *Psycho* than Marilyn in *Some Like It Hot*—so Blair kept quiet, trying to remain fragile and baby bird–like in Nate's arms. They kissed for a long time, their cheeks hot and cold at the same time from being out on the slopes all day. Nate twined his fingers in Blair's hair and pulled her down on the hotel bed. Blair put her arms above her head and let Nate begin to undress her, until she realized where this was all heading, and that it wasn't a movie after all—it was *real*. So, like the well-trained, civilized girl she was supposed to be, she sat up and made Nate stop.

She'd kept on making him stop right on up until today. Only two nights ago, Nate had come over after a party with a half-drunk flask of brandy in his pocket, gotten into bed with her, and murmured, "I want you, Blair." Once again, Blair had wanted to scream bloody murder, jump on top of him, and smother him with kisses. But she resisted. Nate fell asleep, snoring softly, and Blair lay down next to him, imagining they were the stars in a movie in which they were married and he had a drinking problem and possibly a multiple personality disorder, but she would stand by him always and love him forever, even if he occasionally spoke in tongues and wet the bed.

Blair wasn't trying to be a tease; she just wasn't *ready*. She and Nate had barely seen each other at all over the summer because she had gone to that horrible boot camp of a tennis school in North Carolina where she had tried to poison everyone's Kool-Aid, and Nate had gone sailing with his father off the coast of Maine. Blair wanted to make sure that after spending the whole summer apart they still loved each other as much as ever. She'd wanted to wait to have sex until her seventeenth birthday next month.

But now she was through with waiting.

Nate was looking better than ever. The moss green sweater had turned his eyes a dark, sparkling green, and his wavy brown hair was streaked with golden blond from his summer on the ocean. And, just like that, Blair knew she was ready. She took another sip of her scotch and cocked her fingers around the glass tumbler as if she were firing a shiny .38 caliber pistol.

If only she could take Cyrus out of the picture—*bam!* And everyone else at the party for that matter—*bam! Bam! Bam! Bam! Bam! Bam! Bam!* Then she and Nate could do it right there in the living room, naked, with the whole damned penthouse to themselves, save for the corpses.

She finished her drink and set the tumbler down on a marble side table with such force that both the glass and the marble cracked.

Oh, yes. She was definitely ready.

the end justifies the means

"Keep the change," Serena van der Woodsen called as she stepped out of a cab on the corner of Lexington Avenue and Eighty-fourth Street, three blocks from the Archibalds' townhouse. The trip uptown from Grand Central had gone too quickly. She needed some fresh air, and she certainly didn't need to be spotted right in front of Nate's house. Not today. Of course, anyone who mattered was already at Eleanor Waldorf's autumn soiree. Besides, no one would believe their eyes if they saw Serena van der Woodsen here, on the Upper East Side, when she was supposed to be away at boarding school.

Her scuffed brown Ralph Lauren lace-up paddock boots were silent on the sidewalk as she made her way toward the townhouse, a pair of huge tortoiseshell Céline sunglasses masking her enormous navy blue eyes. A bicyclist paused to let her pass. Park Avenue wasn't as wide as she remembered, and the tulips in the median were long gone. A bored doorman glared accusingly at her as she turned the corner, the green awning above him casting a gloomy shadow across her path. Soon the iron gates of Nate Archibald's stately limestone townhouse loomed before her.

Serena tightened the belt of the translucent brown plaid plastic Burberry trench coat she'd purchased from Bluefly.com in case things got messy—the only item of clothing she'd ever bought online, off-season, and at a discount—took a deep breath, and rang the bell.

No answer. She rang it again and waited. Again, no answer. It was after five o'clock. Hopefully Lourdes and Angel—the couple who served as the Archibalds' housekeepers, cooks, gardeners, handymen, manicurists, hairdressers, masseurs, chimneysweeps, exterminators, launderers, tailors, EMTs, and answering service—had gone home.

Serena donned her taupe cashmere-lined goatskin Sermoneta gloves and dug the key out of her eelskin Dolce & Gabbana Harpoon microhobo—the key Nate had given her the summer before last, when everything had gone so very wrong, or so very right, depending on whose side you were on. The gate creaked open and a black squirrel streaked out of the green hedgerow bordering the walk. Oh, the irony! She just happened to have enough squirrel poison in her bag to kill an entire army of black squirrels. *Are the black ones the juveniles?* she wondered aimlessly, as if trying to distract herself from the true nature of her break-in.

Which is? We're all *dying* to know.

The black and white tiles of the foyer gleamed with clean familiarity. Growing up, Serena had spent almost as much time at Nate's house as she had in her own home. Serena and Blair and Nate—always an inseparable, precocious trio. In first grade they'd doused each other with the garden hose out back. In third grade they'd practiced kissing, determined to get it right before they were all cursed with braces or retainers. In fifth grade they'd stolen half the bottles in the liquor cabinet and mixed cocktails from a recipe book Blair had shoplifted from the Corner Bookstore.

Pushing her sunglasses up onto the crown of her head, Serena mounted the elegant red-carpeted staircase and trotted up to the second floor. She paused in the doorway of the master bedroom, so gilded and nautical with its Louis XVI décor, porthole-shaped skylight over the bed, and red, blue, and gold Persian carpet that had been rescued from the *Titanic*. Looking up, the sky was a torpid turquoise sea. October was weird like that.

Serena continued down the hall and up a narrower staircase to Nate's private floor. There were his boxers on the bathroom tile where he'd left them. There was the rumpled plaid quilt lying askew on his bed. There were his model sailboats and the picture of him and Serena and Blair on the beach behind Blair's house up in Newport. Nate's eyes glittered greener than the ocean behind them. Blair was laughing. Serena studied her own face. She'd had freckles then, and an easy smile. Could she still smile like that?

With a gloved hand she grasped the sleeve of the heather gray Abercrombie & Fitch sweatshirt Nate had worn to play lacrosse that morning and held it to her nose, breathing in the heady soap and sweat scent of him. Nate, her Nate. Blair's Nate.

Again she stared at the photograph. Her carefree twelve-year-old arms were wound around Nate and Blair's shoulders as they laughed. Tiny, happy dimples creased her freckled cheeks. She blinked, and then, just like that, Nate was gone. She'd vanished him from the picture. All she saw was herself and Blair, the two girls. Nate was just a tiny speck, drifting and dissolving as he floated out to sea.

Still wearing her gloves, Serena dropped her bag on the desk and removed the giant syringe she'd procured from the groundsman's shed up at Hanover. Two skulls with Xs through them and the word POISON were emblazoned on the oversized syringe in large black capital letters. She'd smuggled the syringe into the city in a violin case stolen from a Hanover sophomore who used to play first string in the school's orchestra—before he went snowboarding with Serena and had to be air-lifted to the hospital with a fractured jaw, a severed tongue, a punctured lung, and two shattered wrists.

Serena opened Nate's sock drawer and rooted around until she found the pair of balled-up neon yellow polyester Adidas soccer socks where he kept his stash of pot.

"*What a loser,*" she could hear Blair scoff at Nate, her voice pregnant with love and longing. *"I might finally do it with you if it wasn't for those horrible neon things."*

Serena held the marijuana-stuffed socks in one hand and thrust the needle of the syringe into them with the other. The socks grew steadily heavier as they swelled with poison.

Nate's tiny sailboat alarm clock ticked quietly. The silence in the house was excruciating.

Serena had always hated silence, and her time at Hanover Academy in New Hampshire had been full of it. Sure, she'd met some okay people up there, but as soon as she got close to someone, something always happened to spoil it.

There was Jude, for instance. Sweet Jude. One sunny autumn Saturday he'd taken her apple picking at a hilly farm a few miles from campus. It was very romantic. But when they reached the arbor of shiny green Granny Smith apples, she'd thought of Nate. How Nate loved to snack on the crisp, tart flesh of a Granny

Smith. How the green skin of his favorite apples matched the green irises of his eyes. Jude's eyes were a dull gray, not gorgeous green. Jude's hair was thin and straight and auburn, not thick and wavy and golden brown. Jude was from Massachusetts, not Manhattan. And although the apple picking stick in his hand resembled a lacrosse stick, Jude simply wasn't Nate. So Serena had rammed the stick down Jude's throat, catching his tongue and epiglottis in the little metal basket meant for catching apples and killing him instantly.

Then there was Milos from Milan. He'd taken Serena sailing. Big mistake. Milos was still missing, his shark-eaten body floating to and fro in the icy waters between Cape Cod and the Bay of Fundy, in Canada.

Sexy Soren, captain of the ski team, had built her a snowman, just like the snowmen she and Nate used to make in the garden behind Nate's townhouse. When she finally made it back to her dorm, the bloody snowman was wearing Soren's head.

Nate was the only sailor in her life, the only builder of snowmen, the only apple-loving boy. Oh, how she missed him. How she missed New York. The thought of Blair and Nate together in Manhattan without her made her want to kill her roommate, the dean, and everyone else at Hanover.

But the more Serena thought about it, the more she came to understand that three was not a good number. Before Nate showed up in kindergarten, she and Blair had been the inseparable-since-birth twosome, the pair. In preschool, they'd cut their hands with corkscrews and made a blood sister pact. Their friendship wasn't supposed to die, not ever. And they were meant to be together—stopping for scones at Sant Ambroeus on their walk to school and buying the same undies at Barneys—not separated by miles and miles of pretty New England roads. Because without Blair, she was just another beautiful, angry, misunderstood girl.

Try merciless killer freak?

All she'd thought about all year was how to repair their friendship. Eventually it became clear how much easier things would be if Nate were out of the picture—literally. Math wasn't Serena's best subject, but it didn't take a genius to figure out that Nate was the constant variable that fucked everything up:

let Nate = x

$sx + b$ = guilt and shame that drove her away in the first place

$s + bx$ = sorrow, rage, murder, and more guilt and shame

$s + b = 1 + 1$

Thus, x must die.

The notion of eliminating Nate altogether first occurred to Serena last spring, during her Concepts in Political Philosophy class. The class spent an entire week discussing consequentialism. Machiavelli, John Stuart Mill, Henry Kissinger. The theory went like this: Improving the lives of the people was the final goal, regardless of *how* that goal was achieved. A good outcome was a good outcome, no matter how that outcome was attained.

Or who had to die in the process.

The way Serena had come to see it, Nate was the only obstacle. Once he was eliminated, both she and Blair would be happy again. Everything could go back to the way it used to be. They would cut class and lie on their backs in Sheep Meadow in Central Park, watching the clouds drift by overhead. They'd stay up all night dancing in their underwear. They'd watch *The*

Hunger—that oddly addictive classic vampire movie starring David Bowie and Susan Sarandon when they were young and beautiful—and *Cat People*, another good one. They'd get their nails done at J. Sisters together, ordering Waldorf salads from the Waldorf Hotel to the pedicure station just to be super-cheesy because they'd make their appointments under the name Waldorf. Everyone would secretly or not-so-secretly be jealous of them, but they'd both pretend not to notice because they didn't need anyone else when they had each other.

The poison was all gone. Serena withdrew the needle, tucked the syringe back into her bag, and tossed the heavy, balled-up pair of yellow socks back into the drawer. There. Now all Nate had to do was pack a nice big bong hit, smoke it up, and . . .

And?

She'd asked the groundskeeper at Hanover how he kept the school's rodent population under control. He explained in detail how he injected piles of leaves with poison and burned them at nighttime. When the squirrels and rats and moles and ground-hogs inhaled the smoke, the poison triggered a sudden rush of blood to the head, causing the vermin's eyeballs to explode.

Put that in your pipe and smoke it.

Best not to think about that, Serena scolded herself as she made her way downstairs, across the gleaming foyer, and out the front gate.

It was dark out now. Yellow taxis zoomed up and down Park Avenue, ferrying Upper East Siders to their various dining appointments. Fuck walking. Serena raised her hand to flag one down. She couldn't wait to see Blair again.

An occupied cab pulled to a stop directly in front of her. The passenger door opened and a boy she knew well—Jeremy Scott

Tompkinson, one of Nate's St. Jude's friends—stumbled out. Jeremy's parents were cousins of James Hewitt, the polo player who'd had a dalliance with Princess Diana and who was thought to be Prince Harry's real father. They'd come to America after an insurance scandal involving a string of dead polo ponies and a fire at their home in Kent, and had never looked back. Jeremy was a cross between Mick Jagger (skinny, full lips, long hair in his eyes) and Jerry Garcia (perpetually stoned).

"Yo Serena jeez whatcha doing back hope ya didn't get kicked outta boarding school aren't you hot in that coat with those gloves on it's like seventy degrees tonight," Jeremy wheezed. It was safe to presume that he was already high, hence his lack of punctuation.

"Hello." Serena clutched her bag to her chest, afraid he might catch a glimpse of the poisonous syringe. If only she'd bought the regular-sized hobo instead of this stupid *micro*hobo. "May I take this cab?"

Jeremy stepped aside and she ducked into the backseat. He slammed the door closed behind her, swaying in his over-sized khaki pants. His rock star haircut had grown out over the summer into something halfway between a mullet and a Sally Hershberger shag.

"You're really freaking hot," he told her with a stoned leer through the open window. "I just have a quick errand to run, otherwise I'd like, take you out on the town or something."

"Too bad," Serena replied with a wan smile. She pressed the UP arrow on the window control, closing it. "Seventy-second and Fifth," she told the driver.

Her stomach rumbled as the cab eased away from the curb. Hopefully she hadn't missed dinner. And hopefully Eleanor was serving those little red velvet cake petits fours from Petrossian for dessert. The ones with the blood orange frosting were her favorite.

As the cab headed west across Madison, she pressed the DOWN button on the window control and tossed the syringe out onto the avenue, where it rolled silently into the gutter. Closing the window once more, she sat back in her seat, removed her goatskin gloves, and tucked her diaphanous blond hair behind her small, diamond-studded ears. She wouldn't have minded a little ramekin of venison tartare with chilled béarnaise sauce, either.

Nothing like a little murder to whet the appetite.

an hour of sex burns 360 calories

"What are you two talking about?" Blair's mother asked, sidling up to Nate and squeezing Cyrus's hand.

"Sex," Cyrus said, giving her a wet kiss on the ear.

Yuck.

"Oh!" Eleanor Waldorf squealed, patting her blown-out blond bob.

Blair's mother wore the fitted, graphite-beaded cashmere dress that Blair had helped her pick out from Armani, and a pair of black velvet mules. A year ago she wouldn't have fit into the dress, but Cyrus had paid for her to have thirty pounds of fat sucked out of her thighs and waist and she looked fantastic. Everyone thought so.

"She does look thinner," Blair heard Mrs. Bass whisper to Mrs. Coates. "And I'll bet she's had her chin stapled."

"I think you're right. She's grown her hair out—that's the tell-tale sign. It hides the scars," Mrs. Coates whispered back.

Of course, she would know.

The room was abuzz with snatches of gossip about Blair's mother and Cyrus Rose. From what Blair could hear, her mother's friends felt exactly the same way about him as she did . . . minus the fantasies of impaling him with the fireplace poker, ripping out his entrails, and tossing them out the window.

"I smell Old Spice," Mrs. Coates whispered to Mrs. Archibald. "Do you think he's actually wearing *Old Spice*?"

"I'm not sure," Mrs. Archibald whispered back. "But I think he might be." She snatched a warm blood pudding canapé off Esther's platter, popped it into her mouth, and chewed it vigorously, refusing to say anything more. She couldn't bear for Eleanor Waldorf to overhear them. Gossip and idle chat were amusing, but not at the expense of an old friend's feelings.

Bullshit! Blair would have said if she could have heard Mrs. Archibald's thoughts. *Hypocrite!* All of these people were terrible gossips. And if you're going to do it, why not *enjoy* it? Pretending not to be the biggest gossip in the room when you so obviously were was like standing in a room full of slashed-up corpses with a bloody hunting knife in your hand and demanding, "*Who did this?*"

Across the room, Cyrus grabbed Eleanor and kissed her on the lips in full view of everyone. Blair shrank away from the revolting sight of her mother and Cyrus acting like lovestruck teens and turned to look out the penthouse window at Fifth Avenue and Central Park. The fall foliage was on fire—not literally, but figuratively. If it were really on fire she would have tossed Cyrus out into it and watched him burn like fat-streaked bacon. A lone bicyclist rode out of the Seventy-second Street entrance to the park and stopped at the hot dog vendor on the corner to buy a bottle of water. Blair had never noticed the hot dog vendor before, and she wondered if he always parked there, or if he was new, and if he usually stayed there after the sun had gone down.

This hot dog vendor was using a long, sharp knife to spear his hot dogs out of the steaming water. Didn't they usually use tongs, or was it always a knife?

It's funny how much you miss in what you see every day.

Suddenly Blair was starving, and she knew just what she wanted: a hot dog. She wanted one *right now*—a warm Sabrett hot dog with mustard and ketchup and onions and sauerkraut. If Cyrus could stick his tongue down her mother's throat in front of all of her friends, then she could eat a stupid hot dog.

"I'll be right back," Blair told Kati and Isabel.

She whirled around and began to walk across the room to the front hall. She was going to put on her coat, go outside, get a hot dog from the vendor, eat it in three bites, borrow his knife, come back, burp in her mother's face, amputate Cyrus's gross tongue, have another drink, and then have sex with Nate.

"Where are you going?" Kati called after her. But Blair didn't stop. She headed straight for the door.

Nate saw Blair coming and extricated himself from Cyrus and Blair's mother just in time.

"Blair?" he said. "What's up?"

Blair stopped and looked up into Nate's sexy green eyes. They were like the emeralds in the cufflinks her father wore with his tux when he went to the opera. One look into those adoring gems calmed the killer inside her every time.

Well, almost every time.

He's wearing your heart on his sleeve, she reminded herself, forgetting all about the hot dog. In the movie of her life, Nate would pick her up and carry her away to the bedroom and ravish her.

But real life is stranger than fiction.

"I have to talk to you," Blair said. She held out her glass. "Fill me up first?"

Nate loved it when Blair bossed him around. He took her glass and let her lead him over to the marble-topped wet bar by the French doors that opened onto the dining room. He poured them each a tumblerful of scotch and then followed Blair across the living room once more. She didn't stop walking. She was headed for her bedroom.

"Hey, where are you two going?" Chuck Bass asked as they walked by. He raised his eyebrows, leering at them suggestively.

Blair rolled her eyes at Chuck and kept walking, drinking as she went. Nate followed her, ignoring Chuck completely.

Chuck Bass, the oldest son of Misty and Bartholomew Bass, was handsome—aftershave commercial handsome. In fact, he'd starred in a British Drakkar Noir commercial, much to his parents' public dismay and secret pride. Chuck was also the horniest boy in Blair and Nate's group of friends. Once, at a party in ninth grade, Chuck had hidden in a guest bedroom closet for two hours, waiting to crawl into bed with Kati Farkas, who was so drunk she kept throwing up pizza and vodka Jell-O shots in her sleep. Chuck didn't mind the vomit-stained covers, as long as there was a seminaked body underneath them. He was the worst kind of predator, the kind everyone would kill if they could stand to be around him for that long.

Of course, the only way to deal with a guy like Chuck is to laugh in his face while secretly plotting his demise, which is exactly what all the girls who knew him did. In other circles, Chuck might have been banished as a slimeball of the highest order, but these families had been friends for generations. Chuck was a Bass, and so they were stuck with him. They had even gotten used to his gold monogrammed pinky ring, his trademark cream-colored monogrammed cashmere scarf, and the copies of his headshot that littered his parents' many houses and apartments and spilled out of his locker at the Riverside Preparatory School for Boys. Girls threw darts at them and blacked out the eyes with Sharpies.

"Don't forget to use protection!" Chuck called, raising his glass at Blair and Nate as they turned down the long, red-carpeted hallway to Blair's bedroom.

Blair grasped the glass doorknob and turned it, surprising her Russian Blue cat, Kitty Minky, who was curled up on the red silk bedspread. Blair paused at the threshold and leaned back against Nate, pressing her body into his. She reached down to take his hand.

At that moment, Nate's hopes perked up. Blair was acting sort of sultry and sexy and could it be . . . *something was about to happen?*

Oh, something's *always* about to happen.

Blair squeezed Nate's hand and pulled him into the room. They stumbled over each other, falling toward the bed, spilling their drinks and staining the white mohair rug. Blair giggled; the scotch she'd pounded had gone right to her head.

I'm about to have sex with Nate, she thought giddily. And then they'd both graduate in June and go to Yale in the fall and have a huge wedding four years later and find a beautiful apartment on Park Avenue and decorate the whole thing in animal skins, with fireplaces in every room, and have rabid animal sex in front of each one on a rotating basis.

Suddenly Blair's mother's voice rang out, loud and clear, down the hallway.

"Serena van der Woodsen! What a lovely surprise!"

Nate dropped Blair's hand and straightened up like a soldier called to attention. Blair sat down hard on the end of her bed, put her drink on the floor, closed her eyes, and grasped the bedspread in tight, white-knuckled fists—exactly how Carrie's knuckles looked after she was soaked with pig's blood at the prom.

She opened her eyes and looked up at Nate.

But Nate was already turning to go, striding back down the hall to see if it could possibly be true. Had Serena van der Woodsen *really* come back?

Blair clutched her stomach, ravenous again. She should have gone for that hot dog after all, or a whole string of hot dogs with which to strangle the entire guest list, including Nate and Serena. She'd save them for last and do it slowly, with a flourish.

And a little mustard?

s is back!

"Hello, hello, hello!" Blair's mother crowed, kissing the smooth, hollow cheeks of each van der Woodsen. If there were such a thing as sexy skeletons, they were it.

Kiss, kiss, kiss, kiss, kiss, *kiss!*

"I know you weren't expecting Serena, dear," Mrs. van der Woodsen whispered in a concerned, confidential tone. "I hope it's all right."

"Of course. Yes, it's fine," Mrs. Waldorf said. "Did you come home for the weekend, Serena?"

Serena shook her head and handed her plastic Burberry trench coat to Esther. She pushed a stray blond hair behind her ear and smiled at her hostess.

When Serena smiled, she used her eyes—those dark, almost navy blue eyes. It was the kind of smile you might try to imitate, posing in the bathroom mirror, the magnetic "you can't stop looking at me, can you?" smile of a supermodel or a sociopath. Well, Serena smiled that way without even trying.

"No, I'm here to—" Serena started to say.

Kill everyone?

Serena's mother interrupted hastily. "Serena has decided that boarding school is not for her," she announced, patting her hair casually, as if it were no big deal.

Serena's mother was the middle-aged version of utter coolness. In fact, the whole van der Woodsen clan was like that. They were all tall, blond, thin, and super-poised, and they never did anything—play tennis, hail a cab, eat spaghetti, maim an innocent schoolteacher—without maintaining their cool. Serena especially. She was gifted with the kind of coolness that you can't acquire by buying the right handbag or the right pair of jeans. She was the girl every boy wants and every girl wants to be.

Or wants to kill.

"Serena will be back at Constance tomorrow," Mr. van der Woodsen said, glancing at his daughter with steely blue eyes and an owl-like mixture of pride and disapproval that made him look scarier than he really was. There was an old rumor that he had killed a man once. But then again, who hasn't?

"Well, Serena. You look lovely, dear. Blair will be thrilled to see you," Blair's mother trilled.

"You're one to talk," Serena said, hugging her. "Look how skinny you are! And the house looks so fantastic. Wow. You've got some awesome new stuff!"

Mrs. Waldorf smiled, obviously pleased, and wrapped her arm around Serena's long, slender waist. "Darling, I'd like you to meet my special friend, Cyrus Rose," she said. "Cyrus, this is Serena."

"Stunning," Cyrus Rose boomed. He kissed Serena on both cheeks and hugged her a little too tightly. "She's a good hugger, too," Cyrus added, patting Serena on the hip.

Serena giggled, but she didn't flinch. She'd spent a lot of time in Europe, and she was used to being hugged by horny European gropers who found her completely irresistible—and who'd died happily groping her. She was a full-on groper magnet. Lucky for Cyrus, she'd come to the party unarmed.

"Serena and Blair are best, best, *best* friends," Eleanor Waldorf explained to Cyrus. "But Serena went away to Hanover Academy in eleventh grade and spent this summer traveling. It was so hard for poor Blair with you gone this past year, Serena," Eleanor said, growing misty-eyed. "Especially with the divorce. But you're back now. Blair will be so *pleased*."

"Where is she?" Serena asked eagerly, her perfect, bruised peach cheeks glowing with the prospect of seeing her old friend again. She stood on tiptoe and craned her head to look for Blair, but she soon found herself surrounded by parents—the Archibalds, the Coateses, the Basses, and Mr. Farkas—who each took turns kissing her and welcoming her back with the same mixture of rapture and loathing everyone battled in Serena's presence.

Serena hugged them happily. These people were home to her, and she'd been gone a long time. She could hardly wait for life to return to the way it used to be. She and Blair would walk to school together, spend Double Photography in Sheep Meadow in Central Park, smoking and drinking Coke, pulling the legs off ants and splicing earthworms, feeling like hardcore artistes. They'd have cocktails at the Star Lounge in the Tribeca Star Hotel again, which always turned into sleepover parties because they'd get too drunk to go home, so they'd spend the night in the suite Chuck Bass's family kept there, at the risk of being attacked by Chuck. They'd sprawl on Blair's four-poster bed and watch all of Blair's favorite twisted old movies, like *Rosemary's Baby* and *The Shining*, wearing vintage lingerie and drinking vodka and cranberry juice, pretending it was blood. They'd cheat on their Latin tests like they always did: *Pereo, peres, peret*—"I die, you die, s/he dies"—was still tattooed on the inside of her elbow in permanent marker (thank God for three-quarter length sleeves!). They'd drive around Serena's parents' estate in Ridgefield, Connecticut, in the caretaker's old Buick station wagon singing the hymns they sang in school at the top of their lungs and running over already dead roadkill. They'd pee in the downstairs entrances to their classmates' townhouses and then ring the doorbells and run away, barking like wild dogs. They'd take Blair's little brother, Tyler, to the Lower East Side and leave him there to see how long it took him to get abducted or find his way home. They'd make teeny cuts on their hands and rub them together to renew their blood sister pact even though blood was "more dangerous than feces these days," according to the Human Health teacher they'd had in sixth grade who'd been fired for bringing her own fecal matter into school for the class to examine.

Blood sisters once more, they'd go back to being their same old fabulous selves, just like always. And with Nate gone, their friendship would be even stronger. Serena couldn't wait.

"Got you a drink," Chuck Bass said, elbowing the clusters of parents out of the way and handing Serena a tumbler of whiskey. "Welcome back," he added, ducking down to kiss Serena's cheek and missing it intentionally, so that his probing lips landed on her mouth.

"You haven't changed," Serena remarked, accepting the drink. She took a long sip. "So, did you miss me?"

"Miss you? The question is, did you miss *me*?" Chuck said. "Come on, babe, spill. What are you doing back here? What happened? Do you have a boyfriend?"

"Oh, come on, Chuck," Serena said, squeezing his hand with cold, bony fingers. "You know I came back because I want you so badly. I've always wanted you."

Chuck took a step back and cleared his throat, his face flushed. She'd caught him off guard, a rare feat. Serena was like the apple in *Snow White and the Seven Dwarves*—shiny on the outside but poisonous to the touch.

"Well, I'm all booked up for this month, but I can put you on the waiting list," Chuck said huffily, trying to regain his composure.

But Serena was barely listening to him anymore. Her dark blue eyes scanned the room, looking for the two people she wanted to see most, Blair and Nate.

Finally she found them. Nate was standing by the doorway to the hall, and Blair was just behind him, her head bowed, fiddling with the buttons on her black cardigan. Nate was looking directly at Serena, and when her gaze met his, he bit his bottom lip the way he always did when he was embarrassed. And then he smiled.

That smile. Those eyes. That face. She was so glad he wasn't dead yet.

"Come here," Serena mouthed at him, waving her hand. Her heart sped up as Nate began walking toward her. He looked better than she remembered, *much* better. Oh, how could she even think of exploding those gorgeous emerald green eyes?

Nate's heart was beating even faster than hers.

"Hey, you," Serena breathed when Nate hugged her. He smelled just like he always smelled. Like the cleanest, most delicious boy alive. Tears came to Serena's eyes and she pressed her face into his chest. Now she was really home.

Nate's cheeks turned pink. *Calm down*, he told himself. But he couldn't calm down. He felt like picking her up and twirling her around and kissing her face over and over. *I love you!* he wanted to shout, but he didn't. He couldn't.

Nate was the only son of a navy captain and a French society hostess. His father was a master sailor and marksman, but a little lacking in the hugs department. His mother was the complete opposite, always fawning over Nate, and prone to emotional fits during which she would lock herself in her bedroom with a bottle of pills and threaten to hang herself until someone bought her a new boat or a new house or a new fur coat. Poor Nate was always on the verge of saying how he really felt, but he didn't want to make a scene or say something he might regret later. Instead, he kept quiet and let other people steer the boat, while he lay back and enjoyed the steady rocking of the waves. Most people would have ended up with a touch of mental illness after all that repression— raving psychotic episodes, sleepwalking, a bit of burning Mom and Dad in their bed. But not our Natie. He was solidly sane.

At least for now.

"So, what have you been up to?" Nate asked Serena, trying to breathe normally. "We missed you."

Notice that he wasn't even brave enough to say, "*I* missed you"?

"What have I been up to?" Serena repeated. She giggled. "If you only knew, Nate. I've been so, so *evil!*"

Nate clenched his fists involuntarily. Man, oh man, had he missed her.

Ignored as usual, Chuck slunk away from Serena and Nate and crossed the room to Blair, who was once again standing with Kati and Isabel.

"A thousand bucks says she got kicked out," Chuck told them. "And doesn't she look fucked? I heard she had a one-girl prostitution ring up there. The Merry Madam of Hanover Academy," he added with a snigger. "She does it with you, then bludgeons you to death with a hairdryer, and then eats you with chopsticks while you're still warm, like some kind of voodoo sushi."

Getting a little carried away with his own childhood fantasies, is he?

"I think she looks kind of spaced out, too," Kati said. "Maybe she's on heroin."

"Or some prescription drug," Isabel said. "You know, like Valium or Prozac. Or maybe she's been abducted by an alien force and they're like, controlling her brain from outer space."

"She could be making her own drugs," Kati quipped. "She was always good at science."

"What is that on her dress? Campari? Wine?"

"No, blood. Have you seen her fingernails? Disgusting. I heard she really did join some kind of cult," Chuck offered. "Like, she's been brainwashed and now all she thinks about is sex and she like, has to do it all the time. And then she tortures and kills the guys she does it with. Naked."

How convenient. That sounds exactly like his favorite bad dream.

When is dinner going to be ready? Blair wondered, tuning out her friends' ridiculous speculations. Serena was too beautiful and sweet to ever join a cult or torture or maim or kill anyone. Blair even had to do all the dissecting in seventh-grade Biology because Serena didn't want to hurt the poor froggie.

Won't she be pleasantly surprised.

She had forgotten how pretty Serena's hair was. How perfect her skin was. How long and thin her legs were. What Nate's eyes looked like when he looked at her—like he never wanted to blink. He never looked at Blair that way, the fucker. She could kill him for looking at Serena like that. Rip the heart right out of his sleeve and ram it down his throat. If only she didn't love him so.

"Hey Blair, Serena must have told you she was coming back," Chuck said. "Come on, tell us. What's the deal?"

Blair stared back at him blankly, her small, foxlike face turning red. The truth was, she hadn't really spoken to Serena in over a year. For all she knew, Serena really had turned into a cannibalistic brainwashed prostitute slash drug manufacturer.

Not really, but she's getting warmer.

At first, when Serena had gone to boarding school after sophomore year, Blair had really missed her. But it soon became apparent how much easier it was to shine without Serena around. Suddenly *Blair* was the prettiest, the smartest, the hippest, most happening girl in the room. She became the one everyone looked to. So Blair stopped missing Serena so much. She'd felt a little guilty for not staying in touch, but even that had worn off when she'd received Serena's flip and impersonal text messages describing all the fun she was having at boarding school.

Hitchhiked to Vermont to snowboard. Spent nite with hottest guy. Danced his head off!

Bad girl weekend. Head hurts. Boys clothes & shoes on my floor but no boy. Whered he go?

The last news Blair had received was a postcard this summer:

Turned seventeen on Bastille Day. Vive la France!—the most
awesome place to live fast, die young, and leave a beautiful corpse!
Miss you!! xoxo, S.

Blair had tucked the postcard into her old Fendi shoebox with all
the other mementos from their friendship. A friendship she would
cherish forever, but which she'd thought of as over . . . until now.

Serena was back. The lid was off the shoebox, and everything
would go back to the way it was before she left. As always, it
would be Serena and Blair, Blair and Serena, with Blair playing
the smaller, fatter, mousier, less witty best friend of the blond
übergirl, Serena van der Woodsen.

Or not. Not if Blair could help it.

"You must be so excited Serena's here!" Isabel chirped. But
when she saw the murderous look on Blair's face, she changed
her tune. "Of *course* Constance took her back. It's so typical.
They're too desperate to lose any of us." Isabel lowered her voice.
"I heard last spring Serena was fooling around with some townie
up in New Hampshire. She had an abortion," she added. "And
then she started killing guys if they even looked at her."

"Which is sort of hard not to do," Chuck said. "I mean, just
look at her."

And so they did. All four of them looked at Serena, who was
still chatting happily with Nate. Chuck saw the girl whose scabs
he'd offered to pick in first grade. Kati saw the girl she'd gullibly
allowed to shave her arms with a disposable razor during a playdate
in third grade. Isabel saw the girl who'd convinced her to pierce
her own ears, with a nail. Third grade again. Both Kati and Isabel
saw the girl who always stole Blair away from them, leaving them
with only each other, which was too dull to even think about. And

Blair saw Serena, her best friend, the girl she would always love and hate. The girl she could never measure up to and had tried so hard to replace. The girl she'd wanted everyone to forget. The girl she wanted to kill so badly her hair hurt just thinking about it.

For about ten seconds Blair thought about telling her friends the truth: She didn't *know* Serena was coming back. But how would that look? Blair was supposed to be tuned in, and how tuned in would she sound if she admitted she knew nothing about Serena's return while her friends seemed to know so much? Blair couldn't very well stand there and say nothing. That would be too obvious. She *always* had something to say. Besides, who wanted to hear the truth when the truth was so incredibly boring? Blair lived for drama. Here was her chance.

Blair cleared her throat. "It was an accident," she said mysteriously. She looked down and fiddled with the little ruby ring on the middle finger of her right hand. The film was rolling. "She didn't mean to. But she's pretty messed up about it. And I promised her I wouldn't say anything."

Her friends nodded as if they understood completely. It sounded serious and juicy, and best of all it sounded like Serena had confided everything to Blair. If only Blair could script the rest of the movie, she'd wind up with the boy for sure. And Serena could play the girl who falls off the cliff and cracks her skull on a rock and is dismembered and eaten alive by bloodthirsty wolves, never to be seen or heard from again.

"Careful, Blair," Chuck warned, nodding at Serena and Nate, who were still talking in low voices over by the wet bar, their eyes never straying from each other's faces. "Looks like Serena's already found her next victim."

s & n

Serena held Nate's hand loosely in hers, swinging it back and forth. At least she'd have this last moment to remember, after he died.

"Remember Buck Naked?" she asked, laughing softly.

Nate chuckled, still embarrassed, even after all these years. Buck Naked was Nate's alter ego, invented at a party in eighth grade, when most of them had gotten drunk for the first time. After drinking six beers, Nate had taken his shirt off, and Serena and Blair had drawn a goofy, buck-toothed face on his torso in black marker. For some reason the face brought out the devil in Nate, and he started a drinking game. Everyone sat in a circle and Nate stood in the middle, holding a Latin textbook and shouting out verbs for them to conjugate. The first person to mess up had to drink and kiss Buck Naked. Of course they all messed up, boys and girls alike, so Buck got a lot of action that night. The next morning, Nate tried to pretend it hadn't happened, but the proof was inked on his skin. It took weeks for Buck to wash off in the shower.

"And what about the Red Sea?" Serena asked. She studied Nate's face. Neither of them was smiling now.

"The Red Sea," Nate repeated, drowning in the deep blue lakes of her eyes. Of course he remembered. How could he forget?

One hot August weekend, the summer after tenth grade, Nate had been in the city with his dad, while the rest of the Archibald family was still in Maine. Serena was up in her country house in Ridgefield, Connecticut, so bored she'd painted each of her fingernails and toenails a different color, made her own chess set out of corks as she drank her way through the liquor cabinet, stuffed the empty bottles with gasoline-soaked rags, and hurled them at the geese flocked around the swimming pool. Blair was at the Waldorf castle in Gleneagles, Scotland, at her aunt's wedding. But that hadn't stopped her two best friends from having fun without her. When Nate called, Serena washed the feathers and goose blood out of her hair and hopped on a New Haven–line train into Grand Central Terminal.

Nate met Serena on the platform. She stepped off the train wearing a light blue silk slip dress and pink rubber flip-flops. Her still-wet yellow hair hung loose, covering her bare shoulders. She wasn't carrying a bag, not even a wallet or keys. Nate needn't know what she'd done to the ticket collector with his hole punch when he'd asked her to get off the train at Stamford if she couldn't purchase a ticket. To Nate, Serena looked like an angel. How lucky he was. Life didn't get any better than the moment when Serena flip-flopped down the platform, threw her arms around his neck, and kissed him on the lips. That wonderful, surprising kiss.

First they drank martinis at the little bar upstairs by the Vanderbilt Avenue entrance to Grand Central. Serena made Nate laugh by engineering little voodoo dolls out of olives and maraschino cherries and stabbing them with toothpicks and plastic swords. Then they got a cab straight up Park Avenue to Nate's Eighty-second Street townhouse. His father was going to be out until very late, Lourdes and Angel had the day off, and Serena and Nate had the place to themselves. Oddly enough, it was the first time they'd ever been alone together, without Blair or any of their other friends, and without Serena compensating for her forbidden attraction by sneaking into Nate's bathroom when he wasn't looking and stealing the hairs out of his shower drain.

It didn't take long.

They sat out in the garden, drinking beer and smoking cigarettes. Nate was wearing a long-sleeved polo shirt and the weather was extremely hot, so he took it off. His shoulders were scattered with tiny freckles, and his back was muscled and tan from hours at the shore in Maine, hurling boulders into the ocean as he tried to exorcise all horny thoughts of Serena from his mind.

Serena was hot too, so she climbed into the fountain. In the center of the fountain was a marble statue of Morta—a Roman goddess of death, holding the severed head and tail of an unfortunate snake—which the Archibalds had imported from Tuscany to ward off burglars. Serena sat on Morta's feet, giggling and splashing herself with water until her dress was soaked through.

At least it was water this time, not blood.

It wasn't difficult to see who the real goddess was. Nate staggered over to the fountain and got in with her, and soon they were tearing the rest of each other's clothes off. It was August, after all. The only way to tolerate the city in August is to get naked.

And push a few tourists off the Brooklyn Bridge.

Nate was worried the neighbors might see them, so he led Serena inside and up to his parents' bedroom.

The rest is history.

They both had sex for the first time. It was awkward and painful and exciting and fun, and so sweet they forgot to be embarrassed. It was exactly the way you'd want your first time to be, and they had no regrets. Afterward, they turned on the television and watched the coverage of the ongoing serial shark attacks on swimmers in the Red Sea. A single shark had maimed or killed five people standing in shallow water over the course of six days. Holding each other and looking up at the clouds through the skylight overhead, they listened to the narrator until Serena burst out laughing.

"Your shark attacked my Red Sea!" she howled, wrestling Nate against the pillows.

Nate laughed and rolled her up in the sheet like a mummy. Serena marveled at how relaxed she was. For the first time ever, she hadn't had the urge to hurt anyone or set anything on fire. She hadn't even pulled out any of Nate's wavy golden brown hairs for safe-keeping.

Nate ordered a raw eel roll, sea urchin roe, and warm sake from the local sushi place, and they lay in bed and ate and drank. Then Nate bared his teeth and pretended to be a shark, attacking her Red Sea a few more times before they both passed out from exhaustion.

A week later, Serena went away to boarding school at Hanover Academy, while Nate and Blair stayed behind in New York. Ever since, Serena had spent every vacation away—reindeer hunting with her Swedish relatives at Christmas, bone fishing in the Bahamas for Easter, bar-hopping and dismembering and bagging boys throughout Europe over the summer. This was the first time she'd been back, the first time she and Nate had seen each other since the shark attacks on the Red Sea.

"Blair doesn't know, does she?" Serena asked Nate now.

Blair who? Nate thought, with a momentary case of amnesia. He shook his head. "No," he said. "If you haven't told her, she doesn't know."

But Chuck Bass knew, which was almost worse. Nate had blurted out the information at a party only two nights ago in a drunken fit of complete stupidity. They'd been doing shots, and Chuck had asked, "So, Nate. What was your all-time best lay? That is, if you've done it at all yet."

"Well, I did it with Serena van der Woodsen," Nate had bragged, like an idiot.

And Chuck wasn't going to keep it a secret for long. It was way too juicy and way too useful. Chuck didn't need to read *How to Win Friends and Influence People*. He practically wrote it. Although the only friends he had were the people who gave him a standing ovation every time he looked in the mirror, and they didn't actually exist.

Serena didn't seem to notice Nate's uncomfortable silence. She sighed, bowing her head to rest it on his shoulder. She no longer smelled like Chanel's *Cristalle*, like she always used to. She smelled like honey and sandalwood and lilies and something he couldn't identify.

Squirrel poison?

The scent was very Serena, utterly irresistible, but if anyone else tried to wear it, it would probably smell like rotting flesh.

"Oh Nate," Serena sighed, wishing this bittersweet moment would never end. "If you only knew how evil I was, you wouldn't even be talking to me."

"What do you mean? What did you do that was so bad?" Nate asked, with a mixture of dread and anticipation. For a brief second he imagined her hosting orgies in her dorm room at Hanover Academy and having affairs with older guys in French hotel rooms.

Leaving none of them intact. Thank goodness for House-keeping!

"And I've been such a horrible friend, too," Serena went on. "I've barely even talked to Blair since I left. And so much has happened. I can already tell she's mad. She hasn't even said hello."

"She's not mad," Nate said. "Maybe she's just feeling shy."

Serena flashed him a look. "Right," she said mockingly. "Blair's feeling shy. Since when has Blair ever been shy?"

"Well, she's not mad," Nate insisted.

Serena shrugged. Everything would go back to normal once he was dead.

"Anyway, I'm so psyched to be back. We'll do all the things we used to do. Blair and I will cut class and run down to that old movie theater by the Plaza Hotel and see some weirdo film until cocktail hour starts. And then we'll get drunk and pass out and eat a huge breakfast in the morning. And we'll live happily ever after, just like in the movies."

Nate frowned. Where exactly was he in this picture?

"Don't make that face, Nate," Serena said, laughing. "That doesn't sound so bad, does it?"

"No, I guess it sounds okay," he said hesitantly.

"What sounds okay?" a surly voice demanded.

Startled, Nate and Serena tore their eyes away from each other. It was Chuck, and with him were Kati, Isabel, and, last but not least, Blair, looking very shy indeed.

Chuck clapped Nate on the back. "Sorry, Nate," he said. "But you can't bogey the van der Woodsen all night, you know."

Nate snorted and tipped back his glass. Only ice was left.

Serena looked at Blair. Or at least, she tried to. Blair was making a big deal of pulling up her black stockings, working them inch by inch from her bony ankles up to her bony knees, and up around her tennis-muscled thighs. So Serena gave up and kissed Kati, then Isabel, before she made her way to Blair.

There was only a limited amount of time Blair could spend pulling up her tights before it got ridiculous. When Serena was only inches away from her, she looked up and pretended to be surprised.

"Hey Blair," Serena said excitedly. She put her hands on the shorter girl's shoulders and bent down to kiss both of her cheeks. "I'm so sorry I didn't call you before I came back. I wanted to. But things have been *so* crazy. I have so much to tell you!"

Chuck, Kati, and Isabel all nudged each other and stared at Blair. It was pretty obvious she had lied. She didn't know anything about Serena coming back.

Blair's face heated up.

Busted.

Esther had just put a sizzling pot of cod cheek fondue on the side table. Sharp, long-handled fondue forks ringed the pot. Blair could grab one, stab Serena through her annoyingly swanlike neck until the fork came out the other side, grab Nate, and whisk him away to the Pierre Hotel, where they could finally have sex without interruption.

Nate noticed the tension, but he thought it was for an entirely different reason. Had Chuck told Blair already? Was *he* busted? Nate couldn't tell. Blair wasn't even looking at him.

It was a chilly moment. Not the kind of moment you'd expect to have with your oldest, closest friends. It was more like the grisly face-off before a women's wrestling match, minus the tiny bathing suits, fake tans, and inflated boobs.

Serena's eyes darted from one face to another. Clearly she had said something wrong, and she quickly guessed what it was. *I'm so clueless*, she scolded herself.

"I mean, I'm sorry I didn't call you *last night*. I literally just got back from Ridgefield. My parents have been hiding me there until they figured out what to do with me. And I have been *so bored*."

Nice save.

She waited for Blair to smile gratefully for covering for her, but all Blair did was glance at Kati and Isabel to see if they'd noticed the slip. Blair was acting strange, and Serena fought down a rising panic. Maybe Nate was wrong, maybe Blair really was mad at her. She'd missed out on so much. The divorce, for instance. Poor Blair. But the sooner Nate died, the sooner she could make it up to her. Serena would have to start dropping hints to Nate about how much better this party would be if they were both very stoned. Then, hopefully, Nate would run home to get his pot and wouldn't be able to resist doing a quick bong hit on his own. And then . . . bye-bye Natie.

"It must really stink without your dad around," Serena told Blair sympathetically. "But your mom looks so good, and Cyrus is kind of sweet, once you get used to him." She giggled.

But Blair still wasn't smiling. "Maybe," she said, staring out the window at the hot dog stand. She imagined stuffing about fifty of them, complete with buns and sauerkraut and ketchup and relish, down Serena's lovely throat. "But I don't think I want to get used to him."

All six of them were silent for a long, tense moment. What they needed was one more good stiff drink. And a pair of oars or a couple of baseball bats to bash each other's heads in.

Nate rattled the ice cubes in his glass. "Who wants another?" he offered. "I'll make them."

Serena held out her glass. "Thanks, Nate," she said. "I'm so fucking thirsty. They locked the damned booze cabinet up in Ridgefield. And took away all the knives and belts and scarves and shoelaces. Can you believe it?"

Blair remained silent but shrugged her shoulders as if to say, "When you're around, Serena, everyone has to prepare for the worst."

"If I have another drink, I'll be hungover at school tomorrow," Kati said.

Isabel laughed. "You're always hungover at school." She handed Nate her glass. "Here, I'll split mine with Kati."

"Let me give you a hand," Chuck offered.

Before the boys could get started on refills, Jeremy Scott Tompkinson staggered into the penthouse clutching his shaggy head. His face was blotchy and covered with a film of perspiration. In fact, he was a lot worse off than when Serena had bumped into him in front of Nate's townhouse less than an hour ago. He sank to his knees in the middle of the living room.

"Jeremy, what's up?" Nate called. The party had started out so boring, he'd sent Jeremy home to pick up some pot. "You okay?"

Jeremy gazed up at his friends with mournful, red-rimmed eyes. His long hair was matted with sweat and there was a bluish tinge to his lips.

"Serrrrrrreeeeeeeeeeeeeeeeeeeeeeeeee . . ." he slurred nonsensically. He yanked a pair of neon yellow Adidas socks from out of his pocket and tossed them on the carpet.

Serena blanched. Oopsie.

"Dude!" Nate protested. Jeremy had never been one for subtlety.

"Sreeeennnnnnn . . . !" Jeremy wheezed, still clutching his head. His bloodshot eyes were painfully huge.

Blair glanced at Serena. Jeremy was trying to say her name and Serena was just standing there, staring at him like a dumb statue.

"Dude!" Nate said again. This was bad. The pot in the socks was good Thai stick, the best. Should he pick up the socks and implicate himself in Jeremy's mess, or just let it go?

Serena reached for Nate's hand, suddenly grateful that it was Jeremy this was happening to and not him. Nate's eyes were too beautiful and he was too precious to simply poison like some ferret or mole or whatever. Jeremy didn't look very good, but it was too late now. What could she do?

Jeremy's eyes bulged impossibly. Finally, they exploded.

Pop! Pop!

Blood spattered the walls and the furniture. Jeremy collapsed in a blood-soaked heap on the floor.

"Son?" Mr. Scott Tompkinson demanded. "Are we going to have to send you up to Little Silver again?" Little Silver Ranch was a rehab center in Connecticut where Jeremy had spent many a long weekend.

"He can't hear you, dear," Jeremy's mother said. "He's out."

That's one way of putting it.

Kitty Minky slinked out from behind a sofa and began to bat at one of the bloody eyeballs with a soft gray paw. Esther rushed in to usher the guests to the dinner table and close the pocket doors behind Jeremy and his family. It was a good thing Mrs. Waldorf had chosen red and brown for her new color scheme. The blood wouldn't even leave a stain.

Mrs. van der Woodsen touched her daughter's arm. "Eleanor made an extra place for you next to Blair, so you girls can catch up."

Serena cast an anxious glance at Blair, but Blair had already turned away and was headed for the table, sitting down next to her eleven-year-old brother, Tyler, who had been at his place for over an hour, reading *Rolling Stone* magazine. Tyler's idol was Cameron Crowe, the movie director who had toured with Led Zeppelin when he was only fifteen. Tyler refused to use an iPod or even CDs, insisting that real vinyl records were the only way to listen to music. Blair worried her brother was turning into the type of loser who would wind up living in a trailer in the woods, preying on chipmunks and robins for meat.

Serena steeled herself and pulled up a chair next to Blair.

"I'm sorry I've been such a complete idiot," she said, removing her linen napkin from its silver ring and spreading it out on her lap. She felt more at ease now, knowing Nate was still alive, but also a little confused. Plan A had failed and there was no Plan B. "Your parents splitting up must have totally sucked."

Blair shrugged and grabbed a fresh sourdough roll from a basket on the table. She tore the roll in half and stuffed one half into her mouth. The other guests were still milling around and figuring out where to sit. Blair knew it was rude to eat before everyone was seated, but if her mouth was full, she couldn't talk, and she really didn't feel like talking.

"I wish I'd been here," Serena said, watching Blair smear the other half of her roll with a thick slab of French butter. "I went a little crazy last year," she confessed. "I have the most insane stories to tell you."

Blair nodded and chewed her roll slowly, like a cow chewing its cud. Serena waited for Blair to ask her what kind of stories, but Blair didn't say anything, she just kept on chewing. She didn't want to hear about all the fabulous things Serena had done while she was away and Blair had been stuck at home, watching her parents rip each other's hair out and spar themselves bloody with silver candle snuffers.

Serena had wanted to tell Blair all about her exploits at Hanover. About Soren and Jude and how she couldn't stand another winter in New Hampshire. How she just had to come back before she murdered everyone on campus. She wanted to tell Blair how scared she was to go back to Constance tomorrow because she hadn't exactly been studying very hard in the last year and she felt so completely out of touch.

But Blair wasn't interested. She grabbed another roll and took a big bite. Jeremy Scott Tompkinson's eyeballs had just exploded in her living room and she was pretty sure Serena had something to do with it.

"Wine, miss?" Esther said, standing at Serena's left with the bottle. Esther's apron was spattered with Jeremy's blood, but no one seemed to mind.

"Yes, thank you." Serena watched the Côtes du Rhone spill into her glass and thought of the Red Sea once more. *Maybe Blair does know,* she thought. Was that what this was all about? Was that why she was acting so weird? She glanced at Nate, four chairs down on the right, but he was deep in conversation with her father. Talking about sailboats, no doubt.

"So you and Nate are still totally together?" Serena said, gnawing on her bloody thumbnail. "Bet you guys wind up married."

Blair gulped her wine, her little ruby ring rattling against the glass. She reached for the butter, slapping a great big wad on her roll.

"Blair?" Serena said, nudging her friend's arm in desperation. "Aren't you going to talk to me?"

"Um," Blair slurred. It was less an answer to Serena's question than a vague, general statement made to fill a blank space while she was tending to her roll. "I'm not sure I should."

Esther brought out the duck and the acorn squash soufflé and the wilted chard and the lingonberry sauce, and the table filled with the sound of clanking plates and silver and murmurs of "delicious." Blair heaped her plate high with food and attacked it as if she hadn't eaten in weeks. She didn't care if she made herself sick, as long as she didn't have to talk to Serena.

"Whoa," Serena said, watching Blair stuff her face. "You must be hungry." She felt a bit nauseated herself, after the whole Jeremy fiasco.

Blair nodded and shoveled a forkful of chard into her mouth. She washed it down with a gulp of wine. "I'm starving," she said.

"So, Serena," Cyrus called down from the head of the table. "Tell me about France. Your mother says you were in the South of France this summer. Is it true the French girls don't wear tops on the beach?"

"Yes, it's true," Serena said. She raised one eyebrow playfully. "But it's not just the French girls. I never wore a top down there, either. How else could I get a decent tan?"

Blair gagged on an enormous bite of soufflé and spat it into her wine. Was Serena flirting with Cyrus? She imagined them both drowned and bloated, floating on the crimson liquid in her wine glass beside the chunk of soufflé. Then Esther whisked it away and brought her a clean glass.

Serena kept her audience captive right through dessert with

heavily edited stories of her travels in Europe, omitting the parts where people lost limbs or died. Blair finished her second plate of duck, followed by a huge bowl full of chocolate-laced tapioca pudding, tuning out Serena's voice as she spooned it into her mouth. Finally her stomach rebelled and she shot to her feet, scraping her chair back and running down the hall to her bedroom and into its adjoining bathroom.

"Blair?" Serena called after her. She stood up and hurried off to follow.

Several seats away, Chuck nudged Isabel with his elbow. "Beware the shit storm. Heads are about to fly."

Nate watched the two girls flee the table with a mounting sense of unease. He was pretty sure the only thing girls talked about in the bathroom was sex.

And mostly he'd be right.

Blair kneeled over the toilet and stuck her middle finger as far down her throat as it would go. Her eyes began to tear and then her stomach convulsed. She'd done this before, many times. It was disgusting and horrible, and she knew she shouldn't do it, but at least she was only hurting herself, which was more than she could say for some people.

The door to her bathroom was only half closed, and Serena could hear her friend retching inside.

"Blair, it's me," she said quietly. "Are you okay?"

"I'll be out in a minute," Blair snapped, wiping her mouth. She stood up and flushed the toilet.

Serena pushed the door open and Blair turned and glared at her. "I'm fine," she said. "Really."

Serena put the lid down on the toilet seat and sat down. "Oh, don't be such a bitch, Blair," she said, exasperated. "What's the deal? It's me, remember? We know everything about each other."

Blair reached for her toothbrush and toothpaste. "We used to," she said and began brushing her teeth furiously. She spat out a wad of green foam laced with blood from her bleeding gums. "When was the last time we talked, anyway? Like, the summer before last?"

Serena looked down at her scuffed brown leather boots. "I know. I'm sorry. I suck."

Blair rinsed her toothbrush off and stuck it back in the holder. She stared at her reflection in the bathroom mirror. "Well, you missed a lot," she said, wiping a smudge of mascara from beneath her eye with the tip of her pinky. "I mean, last year was really . . . different." She'd been about to say "hard," but "hard" made her sound like a victim. Like she'd barely survived without Serena around. "Different" was better.

With a sudden sense of power, Blair glanced down at Serena, seated on the toilet. "Nate and I have become really close, you know. We tell each other everything."

Yeah, right.

The two girls eyed each other warily for a moment.

Then Serena inhaled and let it all out in one giant confused breath. Blair needed to know the truth. "Well, you don't have to worry about me and Nate," she began. "I sort of wanted to kill him, but Jeremy got to the pot first and smoked the poison and now he's dead instead of Nate, which I'm glad about, because you love Nate, and I just want everyone to be happy, especially you."

She gazed up at her friend hopefully. Maybe that was all she needed to do to make things right—just spill her guts so they could both move on.

The corners of Blair's mouth curled up in a sneer. So Serena had poisoned Jeremy. She'd even tried to murder Nate—*her* Nate. Blair tugged her sweater down and glanced at her reflection in the mirror. A coldhearted, steely eyed warrior stared back at her.

No way was Serena going to get away with this. Blair was the one who wanted to kill people—all the time. And if Serena could actually go through with it, then so could she. Murder was probably a lot easier than she thought. Jeremy's exploding eyeballs weren't even that bad. The maid had already cleaned up most of it. Serena thought she was such a trendsetter, such a revolutionary. But Blair was the better student, and she wasn't taking AP Physics for nothing. She could come up with something way more impressive than exploding eyeballs. Guillotines, garrotes, rapiers, machetes! She would excel at killing, just as she excelled at everything else.

"We're missing the espresso," she announced, and abruptly left the bathroom.

Damn, Serena thought, staying put. Wasn't Blair even remotely surprised that she, Serena van der Woodsen, was the one responsible for Jeremy's gruesome death? That she had tried to kill Nate? Well, it was no use going after Blair now, while she was obviously in such a crappy mood. Things would be better tomorrow at school. She and Blair would have one of their famous heart-to-hearts in the lunchroom over lemon yogurts and romaine lettuce. It wasn't like they could just stop being friends.

She stood up and examined her eyebrows in the bathroom mirror, using Blair's tweezers to pluck out a few stray hairs. She pulled a tube of Urban Decay *Gash* lip gloss from her pocket and smeared another layer on her lips. When she returned to the table, Blair was eating her second helping of pudding and Nate was drawing a small-scale picture of his kickass sailboat for Cyrus on the back of a matchbook. Across the table, Chuck raised his wine glass and Serena raised hers in return. She had no idea what she was toasting, but she was always up for anything.

Even murder.

Blair reached for her wine glass, gripping the stem in a viselike fist. The glass's delicate base broke and the remaining red wine sloshed onto the table. It seeped through the tablecloth and bled between her fingers.

Someone, someone at that very table, was going to die.

gossipgirl.net

Disclaimer: All the real names of places, people, and events have been altered or abbreviated to protect the innocent. Namely, me.

topics   sightings   your e-mail   post a question

hey people!

S SEEN DANGLING HEAD OUT WINDOW

Is it just me, or is everyone a little jumpy of late? Is it the change of seasons? One day it's hot, one day it's freezing. Is it the harvest moon? Is it that extra shot of espresso Starbucks puts in their venti latte? Is it due to lack of sleep, jet lag, PMS, STDs, S.E.X.?

No?

Yet we can't throw off that haunting, horror movie feeling that something or someone is watching us, waiting for us, just around the corner or behind the next tree.

Can we just make a little pinky swear right now and promise not to wander the streets of the Upper East Side alone, especially after dark?

Jeepers creepers. I've got the willies just thinking about it.

On a lighter note, we're certainly off to a good start. You sent me tons of e-mail, and I had the best time reading it all. Thanks so much. Doesn't it feel good to be bad?

YOUR E-MAIL

q: hey gossip girl,
i heard about a girl up in New Hampshire who

NEW HAMPSHIRE

the police found naked in a field, with a bunch of dead chickens. ew. they thought she was into some kind of voodoo or something. do you think that was S? i mean it sounds like her, right? l8ter.
—catee3

a: Dear catee3,
I don't know, but I wouldn't be surprised. **S** isn't such a big fan of chickens. Once, in the park, I saw her ripping the wings off a whole bucket of fried chicken without taking a single bite. I wouldn't put anything past her.
—GG

q: Dear GG,
My name starts with S and I have blond hair!!! I also just came back from boarding school to my old school in NYC. I was just so sick of all the rules, like no drinking or smoking or boys in your room. : (Anyway, I have my own apartment now and I'm having a party next Saturday—wanna come? :)
—S969

a: Dear S969,
The **S** I'm writing about still lives with her parents like most of us seventeen-year-olds. But that certainly doesn't cramp her style. Check your closets though—she might just use your pad to store her bodies in. Don't say I didn't warn you if it starts to smell.
—GG

q: whassup, gossip girl?
last night some guys I know got a handful of pills from some blond chick on the steps of the metropolitan museum of art. they had the letter *S* stamped all over them. coincidink, or what?
—N00name

a: Dear N00name,
Whoa, is all I have to say. Oh, and if you savor the use of your basic bodily functions and want to keep your eyeballs intact, don't ingest those

pills. They'll take you on a trip with no return ticket, and no one wants to clean up the blood-spattered mess you'll leave behind.

—GG

3 GUYS AND 2 GIRLS

I and *K* are going to have a little trouble fitting into those cute dresses they picked up at **Bendel's** if they keep stopping in at the **3 Guys Coffee Shop** for hot chocolate and French fries every day. I went in there myself to see what the fuss was about, and I guess I could say my waiter was cute, if you like ear fuzz, but the food is worse than at **Jackson Hole** and the average person in there is like, 100 years old. It is safe in there, though. Which is a lot more than I can say for the rest of the neighborhood now that you-know-who is back.

SIGHTINGS

C at **Hermès** picking up yet another pair of those custom-made pigskin loafers he likes. The boy practically *lives* in that store. *B*'s mother holding hands with her new man in **Cartier**. Hmmm, when's the wedding? Also: a girl bearing a striking resemblance to *S*, coming out of one of those warehouses in the meatpacking district that have not been turned into a boutique hotel or fashion boutique and still have walk-in freezers full of carcasses inside them. Booking her own private freezer? *B* in **Hammacher Schlemmer** on Fifty-seventh Street, trying out the darts, the knives, the bowling balls, and the golf clubs, looking fiercely determined, as usual. Wedding gifts for Mom, or is she gearing up for battle? And finally, very late last night, *S* was seen leaning out her bedroom window over **Fifth Avenue**, looking a little lost.

Well, don't jump, sweetie. Things are just starting to get good.

That's all for now. See you in school tomorrow—if we survive the night.

You know you love me,

i know what you did last winter

"Serena? Aren't you up?" Lillian van der Woodsen glided into her daughter's room and swept back the heavy white curtains cloaking the windows. "You're going to school today, remember? They're expecting you."

A streak of morning light fell upon Serena's closed, long-lashed eyelids. *I must look so peaceful and innocent,* she mused as she pretended to be sound asleep.

Her mother ducked under the bed's white eyelet canopy and tugged back the white eyelet quilt. "Serena, honestly. We don't want any trouble on your first day."

As if being late was such a terrible crime. If her mother only knew.

"But Mommy," Serena moaned, yanking her skimpy gray Calvin Klein cashmere slip down over her hips. "It's freezing!"

Ignoring her daughter's protests, Lillian opened the closet door and rifled through the clothes. Something scratchy and heavy landed on Serena's long, bare legs.

"There's your new uniform," her mother instructed. "Hurry up and put it on."

Before leaving for boarding school, Serena had burned all her old school uniforms and flushed them down the toilet. Last week Lillian had purchased two new ones from Constance Billard's online store. One for winter and one for spring.

Serena sat up and fingered the pleated maroon skirt. "Pretty," she yawned with lazy disinterest. She glanced outside. The Metropolitan Museum of Art stared coldly back at her from across Fifth Avenue, its cool limestone steps abandoned and lifeless save for a lone tourist wearing a backpack and a beret. "Wait," she demanded. "Where is everybody?"

Her mother pulled open the top drawer of her dresser, frowning with displeasure at the mess inside. "Where do you think they are? At school already. Tights. Where do you keep your tights?"

Beneath the tangled array of bras, underpants, socks, and tights, tucked inside a black velvet sleeve, was an Italian switchblade with a mother-of-pearl handle, custom-made to fit Serena's hand. She bolted out of bed and shoved her mother out of the way. "Thank you. I've got it. I can dress myself."

Ten minutes later, Serena stood in the penthouse foyer, chewing a morsel of croissant as she waited for the elevator. Her Burberry raincoat was unbuttoned. Her Ralph Lauren boots were untied. Her Wolford tights were old and holey. Her Brooks Brothers boy's shirt was tattered and frayed. And her hair was unbrushed. But at least she was on her way.

The elevator pinged perkily and the doors rolled open. Serena went inside and perched on the tiny red velvet bench in the corner, bending over to tie her boots as the elevator plummeted toward the lobby.

Ping.

The doors rolled open and she stood up, only to be confronted by a short girl with a prim auburn bob and fearful gray eyes. The elevator had not yet reached the lobby. It had stopped on the third floor.

"Oh!" the girl gasped, hesitating between the doors. She wore a new Constance uniform, just like Serena's. "I—"

"Nice skirt," Serena commented with a friendly smile. "Come on, get in. I think we're late."

But the girl just stood there blocking the doors.

"Parlez-vous français?" Serena tried. "Viens, viens. Vite, vite!"

Ping, ping, ping, went the doors as they attempted to close.

"Serena," the girl whispered slowly, her mouth agape. "Serena van der Woodsen."

"That's my name. Don't wear it out," Serena quipped, borrowing a phrase Blair used to repeat over and over again back in third grade. She frowned at the younger girl. "Are you coming or what?"

The girl's cheeks were pale. "I know what you did," she stammered. "Up at Hanover . . . You killed him—my brother Jude. I saw from the window. I was visiting."

Now it was Serena's turn to stare. She'd always thought of those Hanover boys as disposable, without identities or connections. But perhaps Jude wasn't so obscure after all.

"Jude was from Massachusetts."

The girl nodded. "Our parents are divorced. Dad got Jude and took him to Boston." She adjusted her white turtleneck and buttoned the top button of her navy blue J.Crew cardigan, as if to protect her bare neck from harm. "Mom got me."

Serena chewed on her thumbnail, reopening a scab on the cuticle. Blood smeared her bottom lip, staining it red. "Lucky Mom," she said, staring the girl down.

Ping, ping, ping, went the doors. The switchblade hung heavy in the pocket of Serena's plastic Burberry raincoat.

"Get in here." She grabbed the girl's wrist and pulled her inside the elevator. "We're late for school."

As soon as the doors closed and the elevator began to descend, Serena pulled out the red STOP button and the elevator froze, suspended mid-floor.

"You shouldn't even be in school," the girl whimpered. She wiped her nose on her sleeve, leaving a trail of slimy green mucous on the blue cashmere. "You should be in prison. *Murderer.*"

Serena grasped the switchblade and removed it from her pocket. It wasn't as though she enjoyed killing people. All she wanted was for things to go back to normal. But she couldn't very well allow this girl to go blabbing all over Constance about how Serena had shish-kebabbed her brother. She took a deep breath. She was already late for her first day back, and now she had to deal with this. She flicked her wrist and the razor-sharp knife blade sprang to attention with a gratifyingly efficient click.

The joys of fine Italian craftsmanship.

The girl backed against the smooth, mahogany-paneled wall of the elevator. "Don't," she pleaded. "Please, don't."

Serena raised her hand. The girl lunged for the STOP button, hoping to depress it and get to the lobby before it was too late. But when she reached it she found that her right hand was no longer attached to her wrist. Soon her pretty auburn scalp was no longer attached to her head, nor were her piercing gray eyeballs attached to their sockets.

Unfortunately the carpeting in the elevator was fine, camel-colored lambswool, donated to the building by the wife of the Greek shipping magnate in 12A. It would have to be replaced.

Ping. The elevator doors opened onto the lobby and Serena stepped out, her cheeks rosy from all that exercise.

A dapper uniformed doorman swung open the building's heavy glass and cast iron door. "Have a grand day, dear," he greeted her in an Irish accent, tipping his hat. "'Tis a pleasure to have you back."

Just wait until he sees the mess she left in the elevator.

Serena smiled winningly in reply and hurried up Fifth Avenue toward school. Across the street in Central Park the Hamptons-tanned moms were already out jogging around the reservoir while their attentive nannies pushed their charges toward the playground. Autumn leaves rustled on the bridle path as yellow taxis and loud buses roared past. Serena inhaled deeply, the sights and sounds and smells of the city a tonic to her tormented soul. Oh, it was so good to be back!

And with a bit of Irish luck she'd make the ten blocks to Constance without shedding any more blood.

hark the herald angels sing

"Welcome back, girls," Mrs. McLean said, standing behind the podium at the front of the school auditorium. "I hope you all had a terrific long weekend. I spent the weekend in Vermont, and it was absolutely heavenly."

All seven hundred students at the Constance Billard School for Girls, kindergarten through twelfth grade, and its fifty faculty and staff members tittered discreetly. Everyone knew Mrs. McLean had a girlfriend up in Vermont. Her name was Vonda and she drove a tractor. Mrs. McLean had a tattoo on her inner thigh that said "Ride Me, Vonda," with a picture of two naked women with snakes for hair and wolf heads, long riding whips grasped in their talonlike hands, straddling a John Deere.

It's true, swear to God.

Mrs. McLean, or Mrs. M, as the girls called her, was their headmistress. It was her job to put forth the cream of the crop—send the girls off to the best colleges, the best marriages, the best lives, despite their uncontrollable tempers and mental instabilities—and she was very good at what she did. She had no patience for losers, and if she caught one of her girls acting like a loser—persistently calling in sick, doing poorly on the SATs, or trying to cut off one her classmates' fingers—she would call in the shrinks, counselors, and tutors and make sure the girl got the personal attention she needed to get good grades, high scores, no criminal record, and a warm welcome to the college of her choice.

Mrs. M also didn't tolerate meanness. Constance was supposed to be a school free of cliques and prejudices of any sort. Her favorite saying was, "When you assume, you make an *ass* out of *u* and *me*." The slightest slander of one girl by another was punished with a day of isolation in a dark basement chamber and a letter of apology, written in blood. But those punishments were rare. Mrs. M was blissfully ignorant of what really went on in the school. She certainly couldn't hear the whispering going on in the very back of the auditorium, where the seniors sat, dissecting the social dramas of the day.

"I thought you said Serena was coming back today," Rain Hoffstetter whispered to Isabel Coates.

That morning, Blair and Kati and Isabel and Rain had met on their usual stoop around the corner for cigarettes and coffee before school began. They'd been doing the same thing every morning for two years, and they half expected Serena to join them. But school had started ten minutes ago, and Serena still hadn't shown up.

Blair couldn't help feeling annoyed at Serena for creating even more mystery around her return than there already was. Her friends were practically squirming in their seats, eager to catch their first glimpse of Serena, as if she were some kind of celebrity. If Serena wound up killing them, they totally deserved it. Or maybe she'd do it herself.

That'll teach 'em.

"She's probably too drugged up to come to school today," Isabel whispered back. "I swear, she spent like, an hour in the bathroom last night at Blair's house. Who knows what she was doing in there."

"I heard she's selling these pills with the letter *S* stamped on them. She's completely addicted to them," Kati told Rain.

"Wait till you see her," Isabel said. "She's a total mess."

"Yeah," Rain whispered back. "I heard she'd started some kind of voodoo cult up in New Hampshire."

Kati giggled. "I wonder if she'll ask us to join."

"Hello?" said Isabel. "She can dance around naked with chickens all she wants, but I don't want to be there. No way."

"Where can you get live chickens in the city, anyway?" Kati asked.

"I don't know, Brooklyn? Ew," Rain said.

"Now, I'd like to begin by singing a hymn. If you would please rise and open up your hymnals to page forty-three," Mrs. M instructed.

Mrs. Weeds, the frizzy-haired hippie music teacher, began banging out the first few chords of the familiar hymn on the piano in the corner; then all seven hundred girls stood up and began to sing.

Their voices floated down Ninety-third Street, where Serena van der Woodsen was just turning the corner, cursing herself for sleeping late.

Never mind the little hold-up in the elevator.

"Hark the herald angels si-ing!
Glory to the newborn king!

Peace on Earth and mercy mi-ild,
God and sinners reconciled."

Constance ninth grader Jenny Humphrey silently mouthed the words, sharing with her neighbor the hymnal that Jenny herself had been commissioned to pen in her exceptional calligraphy. It had taken all summer, and the hymnals were beautiful. In three years the Pratt Institute of Art and Design would be knocking down her door. Still, Jenny felt sick with embarrassment every time they used the hymnals, which was why she couldn't sing out loud. To sing aloud seemed like an act of bravado, as if she were saying, "Look at me, I made these hymnals. Aren't I cool?"

Bossy and defiant at home with her father and brother, Jenny rarely spoke at all in school. She had only one friend in her class, a pushy, awkwardly overconfident girl named Elise. Mostly Jenny watched the popular and beautiful older girls, like Blair Waldorf, Kati Farkas, Isabel Coates, and Rain Hoffstetter, studying them with hungry intensity, hating them and loving them, mimicking them and dreading them. She wanted desperately to be a part of their special world, but at the same time they terrified her into a sort of rigor mortis. To them she was smaller than a pimple. She was practically invisible. A curly-haired, tiny freshman with boobs so unfortunately gigantic they were her only noticeable feature besides her big brown baby seal eyes. She was like the cartoon character SpongeBob SquarePants, except instead of a sponge with feet and arms she was a walking pair of boobs.

JennyBetty BoobyPants?

"Hark the heavenly host proclaims,
Christ i-is born in Beth-le-hem!"

Jenny stood at the end of a row of folding chairs, next to the big auditorium windows overlooking Ninety-third Street. Suddenly a movement out on the street caught her eye. Blond hair flying. Plastic Burberry coat. Scuffed brown paddock boots. New maroon uniform—odd choice, but she made it work. It looked like . . . it couldn't be . . . could it possibly . . . No! . . . Was it?

Yes. It was.

A moment later Serena van der Woodsen pushed open the heavy wooden door of the auditorium and stood in the doorway, looking for her class. She was out of breath and her hair was windblown. Her cheeks were rosy and her eyes were bright from murdering that poor redhead and running the ten blocks up Fifth Avenue to school. She looked even more perfect than Jenny had remembered. When it came down to sublime beauty and absolute coolness, Serena van der Woodsen blew every last one of the other senior girls away.

Literally. Just watch.

"Oh. My. God," Rain whispered to Kati in the back of the room. "Did she like, pick up her clothes at a homeless shelter on the way here?"

"She didn't even brush her hair," Isabel giggled. "I wonder where she slept last night."

Mrs. Weeds ended the hymn with a crashing chord.

Mrs. M cleared her throat. "And now, a moment of silence for those less fortunate than we are. Especially for the Native Americans who were brutally slaughtered in the founding of this country, of whom we ask no hard feelings for celebrating Columbus Day yesterday," she said.

What about the native Upper East Siders who were slaughtered?

The room fell silent. Well, almost.

"Look, see how Serena's resting her hands on her stomach? She's probably pregnant," Isabel Coates whispered to Rain Hoffstetter. "You only do that when you're pregnant."

"She could have had an abortion this morning. Maybe that's why she's late," Rain whispered back.

"My father gives money to Phoenix House," Kati told Laura Salmon. "I'm going to find out if Serena's been there. I bet that's why she came back halfway through term. She's been in rehab."

"I hear they're doing this thing in boarding school where they mix Comet and cinnamon and instant coffee and snort it. It's like speed, but it makes your skin turn green if you do it too long," Nicki Button piped up from the seat in front of Blair. She tugged on the huge Swarovski crystal icicle pendant she'd brought back from her family trip to Russia this summer. "You go blind, and then you die. That kid Jeremy? He was totally addicted."

Blair kicked the metal legs of Nicki's chair in annoyance. Comet and cinnamon? Try a maniacal blond bitch on a killing spree. Her friends could be so clueless sometimes.

Mrs. M turned to nod at Serena.

"Girls, I'd like you all to welcome back our old friend Serena van der Woodsen. Serena will be rejoining the senior class today." Mrs. M smiled. "Why don't you find a seat, Serena?"

Serena walked lightly down the center aisle of the auditorium and sat in an empty chair next to a chronic nose-picking second grader named Lisa Sykes.

Jenny could hardly contain herself. Serena van der Woodsen! She was there, in the same room, only a few feet away. So real, and so mature-looking now. And what was that on her shirtsleeve and spattered on her cheek? *Blood?*

Well, it certainly isn't ketchup.

Sordid stories about Serena had already trickled down to the ninth grade, along with the tale of Jeremy Scott Tompkinson's messy demise. To a young girl like Jenny, nothing was more alluring than a scandal-ridden older girl who might also very well be a dangerous killer.

She's come back to rescue us from those mean senior girls, Jenny mused. *She's going to kill them and set us all free.*

Still staring at Serena, Jenny uncapped her favorite black calligraphy pen and began to doodle a soaring blond angel in the margin of her hymnal. Blood dripped from the angel's hands and from the knife tucked under her wing.

How cool, Jenny thought. Hands down, Serena van der Woodsen was absolutely the coolest girl in the entire world. Definitely cooler than any of the other seniors. And how cool to come in late, in the middle of the term, looking like that.

Boarding school does have a way of grungifying even the most beautiful souls. Beautifully damaged soul, in this case.

Serena hadn't had a haircut in over a year. Last night she'd pulled her hair back for the Waldorfs' party, but today it was down and looking pretty shaggy. Her blood-spattered white boy's oxford shirt was frayed at the collar and cuffs, and through it, her purple lace bra was visible. On her feet was her favorite pair of brown lace-up boots, and her black stockings had a big hole behind one knee. But her new uniform was what stuck out the most.

The new uniforms were the plague of the sixth grade, which was the year Constance girls graduated from tunics to skirts. The new skirts were made out of polyester and had unnaturally rigid pleats. The material had a terrible, tacky sheen and came in a new color: maroon. It was hideous. And it was this maroon uniform that Serena had chosen to wear on her first day back at

Constance. Plus, hers came all the way down to her knees! All of the other seniors were wearing the same old navy blue wool skirts they'd been wearing since sixth grade. They'd grown so much their skirts were extremely short. The shorter the skirt, the cooler the girl. Blair actually hadn't grown that much, so she'd secretly had hers shortened.

"What the fuck is she wearing, anyway?" Kati Farkas hissed.

"Maybe she thinks the maroon looks like Prada or something," Laura sniggered back.

"I think she's trying to make some kind of statement," Isabel whispered. "Like, 'Look at me, I'm Serena, I'm beautiful, I kill people, and I can wear whatever I want.'"

And she can, Blair thought. That was one of the things that always infuriated her about Serena. She looked good in anything.

But never mind how Serena looked. What Jenny and every other person in the room wanted to know was: *Why is she back?*

They craned their necks to see. Did she look stoned? Did she have a black eye? Did she have all her teeth? Was she pregnant? Had she stabbed anyone recently? Was there anything truly different about her at all?

"Is that a scar on her cheek?" Rain whispered.

Blair glared at her, wondering when everyone was going to stop talking about Serena. So she was back? Big deal. Time to move on, people.

"She was knifed one night dealing drugs," Nicki Button turned around to whisper, her crystal icicle pendant swinging from her neck. "I heard she had plastic surgery in Europe this summer, but they didn't do a very good job. And now she like, kills boys to get revenge. She's totally lost it."

Mrs. McLean was reading out loud now. Serena sat back in her chair, crossed her legs, and closed her eyes, basking in the old familiar feeling of sitting in this room full of girls, listening to Mrs. M's voice. She didn't know why she'd been so nervous that morning before school. She was home now. This was where she belonged.

"Oh my God, I think she's asleep," Kati whispered to Laura.

"Maybe she's just tired," Laura whispered back. "I heard she got kicked out for sleeping with every boy on campus. There were notches in the wall above her bed. Her roommate told on her—that's the only way they found out."

"Plus, all those late-night chicken dances," Isabel added, sending the girls into a giggling frenzy.

"The notches were for all the boys she killed," Nicki insisted. "She was the one who came up with the Comet and cinnamon thing. It was her invention."

Blair bit her lip, fighting back a snarl. Enough was enough. She couldn't stand it any longer. She reached for Nicki's ponytail, pretending to remove a piece of lint from the shiny blond strands. Then, with a sharp yank on the gold chain around Nicki's neck, she crushed the girl's windpipe before ramming the ridiculous crystal icicle pendant through her yellow Ralph Lauren turtleneck and into her jugular.

Tennis does wonders for one's reflexes.

"All rise," Mrs. McLean instructed. "Now go forth and have a wonderful week."

Mrs. Weeds pounded out the notes to "The Battle Hymn of the Republic" and both she and Mrs. McLean began to sing in tone-deaf operatic voices as the girls filed out of the auditorium.

"Glo-ry, glo-ry, hal-lelu-u-u-jah!
Glo-ry, glo-ry, hal-lelu-u-u-jah!"

Nicki slumped in her chair, her red Coach backpack at her feet.

"Come *on,* Nicki," Rain Hoffstetter hissed. "We have Double French."

Blair shoved Rain toward the door. "She's just looking for a tampon. She'll catch up with us later."

But Nicki was still there when Jenny Humphrey's class marched by.

Amazing, Jenny remarked silently, noting Nicki's lifeless form. Serena wasn't wasting any time. She'd only been back at Constance for five minutes and she'd already made her first kill!

Aw, how cute. The killer has a stalker.

s's other fan

The minute Prayers was dismissed, Jenny pushed past her classmates and darted out into the hallway to make a phone call. Her brother, Daniel, was going to totally lose it when she told him.

"Hello." Daniel Humphrey answered his cell phone on the seventh ring in his toneless speaking-from-the-land-of-the-dead voice. He was standing on the corner of Seventy-seventh Street and West End Avenue, outside Riverside Prep, chainsmoking cigarettes. He squinted his dark brown eyes, trying to block out the harsh October sunlight. Dan wasn't into sun. He spent most of his free time in his room, reading existentialist haikus by long-dead Japanese poets. He was paler than a corpse, his hair was shaggy and lifeless, and he was dead rock star thin.

Existentialism has a way of killing your appetite.

"Guess who's back?" Dan heard his little sister squeal excitedly into the phone.

When Jenny needed someone to talk to, she always called Dan. She was the one who had bought them both iPhones. And it was a good thing too, because Dan was more of a loner than she was.

Sometimes he went for days without speaking. He'd even considered cutting out his own tongue, just to see if it would make any difference to anyone, including himself.

"Jenny, can't this wait?" Dan responded hoarsely, sounding annoyed in the way only older brothers can.

"Serena van der Woodsen!" Jenny interrupted him. "Serena is back at Constance. I saw her in Prayers. Can you believe it?"

Dan watched a plastic coffee cup lid skitter down the sidewalk. A red Prius sped down West End Avenue and through a yellow light. His socks felt damp inside his faded brown suede Hush Puppies.

Serena van der Woodsen. He took a long drag on his Camel. His hands were shaking so much he almost missed his mouth.

"Dan?" his sister squeaked into the phone. "Can you hear me? Did you hear what I said? Serena is back. Serena van der Woodsen."

Dan sucked in his breath sharply. "Yeah," he said, feigning disinterest. "So what?"

"So what?" Jenny repeated incredulously. "Oh, right, like you didn't just have a mini heart attack. You're so full of it, Dan."

"Not really," Dan said, pissily. "What do I care?"

Jenny sighed loudly. Dan could be so irritating. Why couldn't he just act happy for once? She was so tired of his pale, miserable, introspective poet act. Half the reason she called him during the school day was to make sure he hadn't thrown himself in front of a bus or locked himself in the furnace room at school. Dan courted death the way most teenage boys court pretty girls. Someone had to make sure he was still alive.

He'd be way more fun if he tried killing other people instead of himself.

"I'm pretty sure she had blood on her sleeve," Jenny continued breathlessly, sure this little tidbit of information would grab Dan's attention. "And everyone's talking about how she got kicked out of boarding school for killing boys. This one guy already died at a party this weekend, and I'm pretty sure she did something to this girl in the senior class just now during Prayers. I have the chills. I mean, it's like she's come back to save us all from something, you know? I mean, I don't really know what I'm talking about, but oh my God, she's like, so cool it's scary!"

Dan wasn't even listening. He was too distracted by his golden memories of Serena: her deep blue eyes, her swinging swath of luxurious blond hair, the way the world always seemed to be perfectly lit in her presence. *Serena.* He closed his eyes dizzily and then opened them again. *Serena.*

"Dan? Hello? Are you alive?"

"Watch it!" a bicycle messenger shouted as Dan stepped blindly off the curb. He was always stepping blindly off curbs, as if willing that moment's sudden intake of breath to be his very last. But now Serena was back in town. He stepped up onto the curb again.

"Never mind," he heard his sister sigh. "Forget it. Eat something. Drink something other than coffee. Get some exercise. I'll talk to you later."

She clicked off and Dan shoved his cell phone back into the pocket of his saggy black corduroys. He lit another cigarette with the burning stub of the one he was already smoking, singeing his thumbnail. He didn't even feel it.

Serena van der Woodsen.

They had first met at a party. No, that wasn't exactly true. He and Jenny had stared at her for hours at a party—his party, the only one he'd ever had at his family's apartment on Ninety-ninth and West End Avenue.

It was April of eighth grade, when Dan was thirteen. The party was ten-year-old Jenny's idea, and their father, Rufus Humphrey, the infamous retired editor of lesser-known beat poets and a party animal himself, was happy to oblige. Rufus had been watching *Criminal Minds* and had realized that Dan had all the makings of a serial killer: abandoned by his mother at a young age; still wet the bed sometimes; loved to set things on fire, including his sister's hair and their large domestic shorthair cat, Marx; engaged in animal torture—see Marx. So far Dan hadn't shown any interest in actually killing anyone but himself, but Rufus thought his son needed to get out more, engage with kids his own age.

Rufus had sent out an e-mail from Dan's account inviting Dan's entire class to the party and asking them to invite as many people as they wanted. More than a hundred kids showed up, and Rufus kept the beer flowing out of a keg in the bathtub, getting many of the kids drunk for the first time. It was the only party Dan had ever been to, but it was also the best. Not because of the booze, but because Serena van der Woodsen had been there. Never mind that she had gotten wasted and wound up playing a stupid Latin drinking game and kissing some guy's stomach with pictures scrawled all over it in permanent marker. Dan couldn't keep his eyes off her. Finally, he'd found a reason to live.

After the party Jenny told him that Serena went to Constance, and from then on Jenny was his little emissary, reporting everything she'd seen Serena do, say, wear, etc. at school, and informing Dan about any upcoming events where he might catch a glimpse of Serena again. Those events were rare. Not because there weren't a lot of them—there were—but because there weren't many Dan had even a chance of going to. Dan didn't inhabit the same world as Serena and Blair and Nate and Chuck. He wasn't anybody—just a depressed and lonely wraith from the Upper West Side.

For two years Dan stalked Serena, yearningly, from a distance. He never spoke to her. When she went away to boarding school, he tried to forget about her, sure that he would be dead by the time she returned to the city.

But now she was back.

Dan walked halfway down the block, then turned around and walked back again. His mind was racing. He could have another party. He could make invitations and get Jenny to slip one into Serena's locker at school. When Serena came to his apartment, Dan would go right up to her and take her mink coat and graciously welcome her back to New York.

I died every day you were gone, he'd say, poetically.

Then they would sneak into his father's library and take each other's clothes off and kiss on the leather couch in front of the fire. And when everyone left the party, they would share a bowl of Red Hots, one of the few foods Dan ate. From then on they would spend every minute together. They would even transfer to a coed high school like Trinity for the rest of senior year because they couldn't stand to be apart. Then they would go to Columbia and live in a cramped, unheated studio apartment on a high floor with a view of the same cold Hudson River that Dan had wanted to jump into on so many bleak nights. Serena's friends would try to lure her back to her old life, but no charity ball, no exclusive black tie dinner, no expensive party favor would tempt her. She wouldn't care if she had to give up her trust fund and her great-grandmother's diamonds. Serena would be willing to live in squalor if it meant she could be with Dan. And when they died, they would die together, holding hands, like Romeo and Juliet, only better.

Brittle bones, hot lips—
Spring, summer, autumn, winter.
Only the worms know.

"Fucking hell, we've only got five minutes until the bell rings," Dan heard someone say in an obnoxious voice.

Dan turned around, and sure enough, it was Chuck Bass, or "Scarf Boy," as Dan liked to call him, since Chuck always wore that ridiculous monogrammed ivory-colored cashmere scarf. Chuck stood only twenty feet away with two of his senior Riverside Prep pals, Roger Paine and Jeffrey Prescott. All three boys wore matching burgundy velvet smoking jackets and fingerless brown leather driving gloves, and Chuck had on his new custom-made pigskin loafers without socks. The three boys—whose hair was cut by Oscar Blandi in overly conditioned cheekbone-length pageboys—didn't speak to Dan or even nod to acknowledge his presence. Why should they? These boys took the Seventy-ninth Street crosstown bus to school through Central Park each morning from the swanky Upper East Side, only venturing to the West Side for school or to attend the odd party. They were in Dan's class at Riverside Prep, but they were certainly not in his class. He was nothing to them. They didn't even notice him.

"Dude," Chuck said to his friends. He lit a cigarette. Chuck smoked his cigarettes like they were joints, holding them between his index finger and thumb and sucking hard on the inhale. Too pathetic for words.

"Guess who I saw last night?" Chuck said, blowing out a stream of gray smoke.

"Amanda Sohotfried or whatever that scary-hot big-eyed blond actress's name is?" Jeffrey said, tucking his hair behind his ears with his ridiculous fingerless-gloved hands.

"Yeah, and you let her scare off your pants and everything else, right?" Roger laughed, brushing cigarette ash off his velvet smoking jacket. "And then she gave you a shoulder ride."

"No, not her. Serena van der Woodsen," Chuck said.

Dan's ears perked up. He was about to head inside for class, but he lit another cigarette and stayed put so he could listen.

"Blair Waldorf's mom had this little party, and Serena was there with her parents," Chuck continued. "And she was *all over* me. She's like, the sluttiest girl I've ever met." Chuck took another toke on his smoke. "Plus, she's totally psychotic. I mean, she's killed people. Lots of people."

"Really?" Jeffrey said. "I'd heard that, but you know, you can't believe everything you hear."

"Oh yes you can," Chuck countered. "First of all, I just found out that she's been doing it with Nate Archibald since tenth grade. And she's definitely gotten an education at boarding school, if you know what I mean. They had to get rid of her, she's so slutty."

"No way," Roger said. "Come on, dude, you don't get kicked out for being a slut."

"You do if you keep a record of all the boys you slept with. If you get them hooked on the same drugs you're doing and then you kill them. Her parents had to go up there and get her. She was like, taking over the school!" Chuck was really worked up. His face was turning red and he was spitting all over his pigskin loafers as he talked.

"I heard she's got diseases too," he added. "Like STDs. Someone saw her going into a clinic in the East Village. She was wearing a wig. And she has this thing for chickens. She kills them and drinks their blood."

Chuck's friends put their index fingers in their mouths and pretended to gag.

"Nasty!" they said, simultaneously.

"You heard about that kid Jeremy, right?" Chuck took a poignant drag on his cigarette as the other two boys nodded eagerly. "That was all Serena. She'd only been at the party for five minutes and *bam*, guy's eyeballs are exploding all over the fucking walls. She's a deadly weapon." He chuckled and stamped out his cigarette. "Fully fucking loaded at all times."

Dan had never heard such crap. Serena was no slut, and she wouldn't kill anyone unless it was in self-defense. Serena was perfect.

Perfectly psychotic.

"So, you guys hear about that bird party?" Roger asked. "You going?"

"What bird party?" Jeffrey said, looking miffed that his best friend knew about something he didn't.

"That benefit for the Central Park birds of prey?" Chuck said. "Blair Waldorf is planning it. At the Frick." He took another drag on his cigarette. "Dude, everybody's going."

Everybody didn't include Dan, of course. But it very definitely included Serena van der Woodsen.

"They're sending out the invitations this week," Roger said. "It has a funny name, I can't remember what it is, something girly."

"*Kiss Me or Die*," Chuck said, stubbing out his cigarette with his obnoxious custom-made shoes. "It's the *Kiss Me or Die* party."

"Oh yeah," Jeffrey said. "And I bet there's going to be a lot more than kissing going on." He sniggered. "Especially if Serena's there."

The boys laughed, congratulating each other on their incredible wit.

Dan had had enough. He tossed his cigarette on the sidewalk only inches from Chuck's shoes and headed for the school doors. As he passed the three boys he turned his head and puckered his lips, making a smooching sound three times as if he were giving each boy a big, fat kiss. Then he turned and went inside, banging the door shut behind him.

Kiss that and die, assholes.

at the heart of every socially alienated cynic is a hopeless romantic

"What I'm going for is tension," Vanessa Abrams explained to Constance's small Advanced Film Studies class. She stood at the front of the room, presenting her idea for the new film she was making, a loose adaptation of *Natural Born Killers*, the gleefully violent and weirdly beautiful Oliver Stone film about a pair of murderous, lovestruck psychopaths. Vanessa's earlier repertoire included a short animated film using Legos and featuring the owls of *Harry Potter* during a rabies epidemic, and an underwater version of *Twilight* starring a cast of catfish and one piranha. Oliver Stone seemed like a logical next step. Besides, fairy tales about wizards and vampires weren't really her thing. Fairy tales about serial killers were.

Vanessa reveled in the idea of an audience of her peers, munching popcorn while they watched the most vile and graphic images of violence she was capable of producing onscreen. They all acted like such goody-goodies. She wanted to show them the gritty underside of the very world they in which lived. Shove their faces in it and force it down their diamond-studded throats. She wanted to lure them in with a love story, and then make them gag.

"First I'm going to shoot the wedding scene, when Mallory and Mickey become Mallory and Mickey Knox, but only she talks. Actually, her voice is my voice, not the actress's voice, in voice-over. And he never has any lines." Vanessa paused dramatically, waiting for one of her classmates to say something. Mr. Beckham, their teacher, was always telling them to keep their scenes alive with dialogue and action, and Vanessa was deliberately doing just the opposite. "And then I'm going to film the mayhem and destruction that happens every day all over the city, as if it's them causing the chaos. And then I'm going to show them dying, violently."

"So just a voice-over for the whole film? There's no actual dialogue?" Mr. Beckham observed from where he was standing in the back of the classroom. He was painfully aware that no one else in the class was listening to a word Vanessa said.

"It's going to be pretty graphic," Vanessa insisted. "I want the images to scream. I don't need much talk."

She reached for the slide projector's remote control and began clicking through slides of the black and white pictures she'd taken to demonstrate the mayhem and destruction she'd already captured. A pigeon pecking at a bloody paper towel. A headless black wig draped on a park bench. A homeless person's pale, dead-looking, dirty-fingernailed hand. A bloody, openmouthed rat smushed flat by a car on the street.

"Ha!" someone exclaimed from the back of the room. It was Blair Waldorf, laughing out loud as she read the note Rain Hoffstetter had just passed to her.

For a good time
call Serena v. d. Woodsen
Get it—VD??

Vanessa glared at Blair. Film was Vanessa's favorite class, the only reason she came to school at all. She took it very seriously, while most of the other girls, like Blair, were only taking Film as a break from Advanced Placement hell—AP Calculus, AP Bio, AP History, AP English Literature, AP French. They were on the straight and narrow path to Yale or Harvard or Brown, where their families had all gone for generations. Vanessa wasn't like them. Her parents hadn't even gone to college. They were artists, and Vanessa wanted only one thing in life: to go to NYU and major in film and make the artiest slasher films ever made.

Actually, there was something else she coveted. Or some*one* else, to be precise, but we'll get to that soon.

Vanessa was an anomaly at Constance, the only girl in the school who had a nearly shaved head, wore black turtlenecks every day, read *The Silence of the Lambs* over and over like it was the Bible, listened to the Smiths, and drank unsweetened black tea. She had no friends at all at Constance and lived in Williamsburg, Brooklyn, with her twenty-two-year-old sister, Ruby. So what was she doing at a tiny, exclusive private girls' school on the Upper East Side with Gucci-Pucci-tutu-wearing competitive princess freaks like Blair Waldorf? It was a question Vanessa asked herself every day.

She also asked herself every day why she didn't kill them all and torch the school.

Vanessa's parents were older, revolutionary artists who lived in Vermont in a rubber house made out of recycled car tires. When she turned fifteen, Vanessa had shaved her head and stopped smiling. She threatened to transform the woodstove into a live bomb and melt the house unless her parents let her move in with her bass guitarist older sister in Brooklyn. Her parents finally gave in, but they wanted to be sure the perpetually unhappy Vanessa got a good, safe high school education. So they made her go to Constance, which she soon found out was the worst form of torture imaginable.

Vanessa loathed Constance and every other girl who went there, but she never said anything to her parents. At least she was in New York, and there were only eight months left until graduation. Eight more months and she could blow this fuckhole sky-high and escape downtown to NYU.

Eight more months of bitchy Blair Waldorf—that is, if Vanessa didn't kill her sooner—and even worse, Serena van der Woodsen, who was back in all her splendor. Blair Waldorf looked like she was absolutely orgasmic over the return of her best friend. In fact, the whole back row of Film Studies was atwitter, passing notes. Fuck them. Vanessa wanted to stuff their notes down their throats and strangle each one of them with the arms of their annoying cashmere sweaters.

But she had a film to make. She lifted her chin and went on with her presentation. She was above their petty bullshit anyway. *Only eight more months.*

Perhaps if Vanessa had seen the note Kati Farkas had just passed to Blair, she might have had a tad more sympathy for Serena.

Dear Blair,
   Can I borrow five million dollars? I have to bail myself out of jail because I've already killed my parents and my grandparents and that nice bail bondsman and now I have no one left.
   Shit, my head itches. I think I have lice.
   Let me know about the money.
Love,
Serena v. d. Woodsen

Blair, Rain, and Kati giggled noisily.

"Shhssh," Mr. Beckham whispered, glancing at Vanessa sympathetically. Blair turned the note over and scrawled a reply.

Sure, Serena. Whatever you need. Text me from jail and I'll wire you the money . . . NOT. I hear the food is excellent in prison. Nate and I will visit you whenever we're free, which might be . . . NEVER.

Sorry about the lice. I hear mayonnaise under a shower cap gets rid of them. That'll go great with your outfit today.
Love,
Blair

Blair handed the note back to Kati, feeling not the tiniest speck of remorse for being so mean. There were so many stories about Serena flying around she honestly didn't know what to believe anymore. Maybe some of it was true. Maybe some of this stuff had really happened. After all, Serena had admitted to accidentally engineering Jeremy's death while intending to kill Nate. Who knew what else she was capable of? Besides, passing notes distracted everyone from Nicki's rather abrupt disappearance this morning.

And passing notes is much more fun than taking them.

"Attention, ladies and faculty," Mrs. McLean's voice sounded over the school-wide sound system. "Due to an earlier incident, the auditorium will be closed for maintenance for the remainder of the day. Drama and dance classes will be relocated to the gymnasium. Thank you."

So Nicki's body had finally been discovered. Blair wondered if Serena had killed anyone yet today. For every person Serena offed, she planned to off someone too.

Vanessa cleared her throat. "I'm going to be writing, directing, and filming. I've already cast my friend Daniel Humphrey from Riverside Prep as Mickey Knox."

Her cheeks heated up when she uttered Dan's name. He didn't talk much and was very morbid, but he'd let her in out of the cold when she was locked out at a party two years ago and she'd been bossing him around ever since. Dan was her only friend in the entire city, although she would kill for them to be more than just friends.

"I still need a Mallory. I'm casting her tomorrow on the middle of the Brooklyn Bridge at dusk." Secretly she wanted to don a wig and play Mallory herself, but then there'd be no one to hold the camera. The original Mickey and Mallory Knox had been played by the hugely muscular bald cowboy Woody Harrelson and the gangly doe-eyed Southern teen bride Juliette Lewis. Dan and Vanessa couldn't have looked more different. But that was the fun of an adaptation—she could use the story and fuck with it.

"Anyone interested?" she asked. The question was a private little joke with herself. Vanessa knew no one in the room was even listening.

Blair's arm shot up. "I'll be the director!" she announced. Obviously she hadn't heard the question, but Blair was so desperate to impress the admissions office at Yale, she was always the first to volunteer for anything.

Vanessa opened her mouth to speak. *Direct this*, she wanted to say, before firing a bazooka and blowing up Blair's perfectly coiffed head.

"Put your hand down, Blair," Mr. Beckham sighed tiredly. "Vanessa just got through telling us *she* is directing and writing and filming. Unless you'd like to try out for the part of Mallory, I suggest you focus on your own project."

Blair glared sourly at him. She hated teachers like Mr. Beckham. He had such a chip on his shoulder because he was from Nebraska and had finally attained his sad dream of living in New York City only to find himself teaching a useless class instead of directing cutting-edge films and becoming famous. One day Mrs. McLean would probably make an announcement over the loudspeaker that Mr. Beckham had crawled into the space-saver oven in his pathetically tiny studio apartment and had never come out.

Or maybe Blair should just kill him herself and put him out of his misery.

"Whatever," Blair said, tucking her dark hair behind her ears. "I guess I really don't have time."

And she didn't.

Blair was chair of the Social Services Board and ran the French Club; she tutored third graders in reading; she worked in a soup kitchen one night a week, had SAT prep on Tuesdays, and on Thursday afternoons she took a fashion design course with Tim Gunn. On weekends she played tennis so she could keep up her national ranking. Besides all that, she was on the planning committee of every social function anyone could be bothered to go to, and the fall/winter calendar was *busy, busy, busy*.

Never mind all the murders she'd have to commit to keep up with Serena.

Vanessa flicked on the lights and walked back to her seat at the front of the room.

"It's okay, Blair, I wanted a taller girl for Mallory anyway." Vanessa smoothed her uniform around her stocky thighs and sat down daintily, in an almost perfect imitation of Blair.

Blair smirked at Vanessa's prickly shaved head and glanced at Mr. Beckham. Would he notice if she pulled Vanessa's ugly black turtleneck over her eyes and pushed her out the school doors in front of a moving Hummer?

Vanessa smirked back at her, wondering if she could get the Mason Pearson boar-bristle hairbrush sticking out of Blair's Miu Miu handbag all the way up Blair's ass before the bell rang.

Mr. Beckham cleared his throat and stood up. "Well, that's it, girls. You can leave a little early today. Vanessa, why don't you put a sign-up sheet out in the hall for your casting tomorrow?"

The girls began to pack up their bags and file out of the room. Vanessa ripped a blank sheet of paper out of her notebook and wrote the necessary details at the top of it. *Natural Born Killers, a modern retelling of the violently romantic Oliver Stone classic. Try out for Mallory. Wednesday, sunset. Brooklyn Bridge.*

She resisted writing a description of the girl she was looking for because she didn't want to scare anyone away.

In the original, Woody Harrelson and Juliette Lewis were an oddly complementary couple. He was big and strong, while she was willowy and baby-faced. He looked like he could take on ten men and was totally smitten with her. She was the more brutal killer and doubted his fidelity. In her remake, Vanessa wanted to reverse the roles. Mickey would be frail, mentally unbalanced, and deadly. Mallory would be a statuesque beauty, confident and strong, and madly in love with Mickey. Like in the original, her Mickey and Mallory Knox would become icons of their own fucked-up world, a serial-killing Bonnie and Clyde. But the more they killed, the more they were doomed. Death hung around their necks like a boa constrictor, choking them. Vanessa wanted her film to be shocking and depressing and graphic and beautiful—like the poetry Dan wrote, only grosser.

The perfect Mallory would be the kind of girl to make Dan glow, even though he never ate and walked around all day chain-smoking and looking half-dead. Mallory would be full of movement and laughter—exactly the opposite of Dan, whose silent, caffeine- and nicotine-fueled energy caused his eyelids to twitch and made his hands shake sometimes.

Vanessa hugged herself. Just thinking about Dan made her feel like she had to pee. Under that shaved head, that pale skin, and that impossible black turtleneck, she was just another neurotic, demonic, boy-crazy girl.

Face it: We're all the same.

a power lunch

"The invitations, the gift bags, and the champagne. That's all we have left." Blair lifted a cucumber slice off her plate and nibbled at it thoughtfully. "Kate Spade is still doing the gift bags, but I don't know—do you think Kate Spade is too boring?"

"I think Kate Spade is perfect," Isabel said, winding her dark hair into a knot on top of her head. "I mean, think how cool it is to have a plain black satin handbag now instead of all those faux animal skins with zippers and chains. It's all such . . . *bad taste*, don't you think?"

Blair nodded. "Completely," she agreed. "Plus, black doesn't stain."

Always a plus when you're out and there's a bloody murder weapon to stash.

"Hey, what about my leopard sealskin coat?" Kati demanded, looking hurt.

"That's *real* seal," Blair argued. "It's different."

The three girls were sitting in the Constance cafeteria, discussing the upcoming *Kiss Me or Die* benefit to raise money for the Central Park birds of prey. Blair was chair of the organizing committee, of course.

"Those poor birds," Blair sighed.

As if she could give two shits about the damned birds.

Isabel withdrew a tube of Chanel *Goldtrotter* lip gloss from her bag and began to smear it over her plump, dry lips.

"Wait, isn't that Nicki's?" Kati asked.

Isabel shrugged her shoulders and tossed the lip gloss back into her bag. "I took it from her locker. It's not like she's going to use it anymore."

The girls had heard through the Constance grapevine that Nicki Button had suffered a brain hemorrhage right after morning assembly and would no longer be attending school, because she was dead.

"I really want this party to be good," Blair insisted, eager to get back to the topic at hand. "You guys are coming to my planning committee meeting tomorrow, right?"

"Of course we're coming," Isabel said. "What about Serena— did you tell her about the party? Is she joining the committee?"

Blair stared blankly back at her.

Kati wrinkled her pert little ski-jump nose and nudged Isabel with her elbow. "I bet Serena is too busy, you know, dealing with everything. All her *problems*. She probably doesn't have time."

Across the cafeteria, Serena herself was just joining the lunch line. She noticed Blair right away and smiled, waving cheerfully as if to say, "I'll be there in a minute!" Blair blinked, pretending she'd forgotten to put in her contacts, even though she didn't wear them.

Serena slid her tray along the metal counter, choosing a lemon yogurt and skipping all the other lunch selections until she came to the water dispenser, where she filled up a cup with boiling water and placed a Lipton tea bag, a slice of lemon, and a packet of sugar on the saucer. Then she carried her tray over to the salad bar, where she filled up a plate with a pile of romaine lettuce and poured a small puddle of blue cheese dressing beside it. She would have preferred a shaved horse meat and arugula sandwich in the Gare du Nord in Paris, eaten in a hurry before leaping onto the Eurostar train to London, but this was almost as good. It was the same lunch she'd eaten at Constance every day since sixth grade. Blair always got the same thing too. They called it the "starvation plate."

Blair watched Serena assemble her lunch with compulsive precision, dreading the moment when the psychotic blonde would sit down next to her in all her glory and start trying to be friends again. Ugh.

"Hey guys." Serena smiled radiantly as she sat down next to Blair. "Just like old times, huh?" She laughed and peeled back the top of her yogurt. The cuffs of her brother's old shirt were frayed and bloodstained. Stray threads dangled in the yogurt's watery whey.

"Hello, Serena," Kati and Isabel responded in unison.

Blair lifted her head and forced the corners of her glossy lips upwards. It was almost a smile.

Serena stirred her yogurt and nodded at Blair's tray, where the remains of her bagel with cream cheese and cucumber were strewn. "I guess you outgrew the starvation plate," she observed.

"I guess," Blair said. She smashed a lump of cream cheese into her paper napkin with her thumb, staring at Serena's sloppy cuffs in bewilderment. It was fine to wear your brother's old clothes in ninth and tenth grade. Then, it was cool. But now, with the cuffs so obviously bloodstained, it just seemed unsanitary.

"So my schedule totally sucks," Serena said, licking her spoon. "I don't have a single class with you guys."

"Um, that's because you're not taking any APs," Kati observed. "I'm surprised you didn't have to repeat your junior year."

Serena frowned. The teachers at Hanover who'd given her Cs had boosted her grades when she'd asked them to. Right before they died.

"My grades were okay."

"You're lucky you're not taking any APs," Isabel sighed at her untouched bagel. "I have so much work to do I can't eat."

Luckily the trend this fall is "fatally thin."

"Well, at least I'll have more time for fun." Serena nudged Blair's elbow. "What's going on this month, anyway? I feel so completely out of it."

Blair sat up straight and picked up her plastic cup, only to find there was no water left in it to drink. She knew she should tell Serena all about the *Kiss Me or Die* party and how Serena could help with the preparations and how fun it was all going to be. But somehow she couldn't bring herself to do it. Serena was out of it, all right. And Blair wanted her to stay that way.

"It's been pretty lame. There really isn't much going on until Christmas," Blair lied, shooting a warning glance at Kati and Isabel.

"Really?" Serena said, disappointed. "Well, what about tonight? You guys want to go out?"

Blair glanced at her friends. She was all for going out, but it was only Tuesday. The most she ever did on a Tuesday night was rent a movie with Nate. Leave it to Serena to make her feel boring.

"I have to study for my AP French test tomorrow." Blair stood up. "Actually, I have a meeting with Madame Rogers right now."

Serena frowned and began to chew on her raw thumbnail, a

new habit she'd picked up at boarding school. "Well, maybe I'll give Nate a call. He'll go out with me."

Blair picked up her tray and resisted hurling it in Serena's face. *Keep your hands off him!* she wanted to scream, jumping onto the table ninja-style. *Hiyeeh-yah!* But she'd already killed one person in plain sight today.

Speaking of which . . .

"Did you hear what happened to Nicki Button?" Blair said, her voice laced with acid.

Serena shook her head. "What about her? I haven't seen—"

"Gone," Blair interrupted her. "For good," she added with a smirk.

Serena stared at her.

That's right, S. You created a monster.

"I'll see you later, guys," Blair told the other two girls, and walked stiffly away.

Serena sighed and flicked a piece of lettuce off her plate. Blair was being such a bitch. When were they going to start having fun? She looked up at Kati and Isabel hopefully, but they were getting ready to leave too.

"I've got a stupid college advisor meeting," Kati said.

"And I have to go up to the art room and put my painting away," Isabel said.

"Before anyone slashes it?" Kati joked.

"Oh, shut up," Isabel said.

They stood up with their trays.

"It's so good to have you back, Serena," Kati said in her fakest voice.

"Yeah," Isabel agreed before they walked away.

Serena twirled her spoon around and around in her yogurt

container, wondering what had happened to everyone. They were all acting like freaks. She plucked at a blood-soaked thread dangling from her shirt cuff and bit it off with her teeth. She needed to get happy. Everyone needed to get happy. And she of all people knew just what to do.

When in doubt, throw a party.

gossipgirl.net

hey people!

TWO PARTIES TO CHOOSE FROM AND IT'S ONLY TUESDAY NIGHT

Looks like **S** didn't come home to lie low. Tonight she's ringing in the fall season with a pajamas-and-papaya-peppertinis soiree at her house, complete with tiki torches, and there is no guest list, so you can bring your little brother and his nose-picking friends and get them drunk for the first time, and her maid will even clean up afterwards. Or, you can go to **B**'s house because now that **S** is having a shindig, she's throwing a bigger and better one with a DJ, full bar, and catering. Not that we mind. These are the sort of choices we live for. Until one of us dies, which is inevitable.

ABOUT THOSE VIOLENT, INEXPLICABLE DEATHS

Is it just me being paranoid, or is this neighborhood getting weirdly and wildly unsafe? I heard that New Jersey arms heiress is having a yard sale. Hopefully all the pretty purse-sized handguns won't sell out before I get there. Although I haven't a clue how to use one. Maybe I'm more the hunting-dagger-in-a-thigh-holster type. Or I could just get a big dog with teeth the size of steak knives. We girls have to protect ourselves—from each other.

WHERE THE BOYS ARE

Thanks for checking in, although most of you had little to say about **S** or **B**. Too scared to talk? You'd much rather talk about boys. Wouldn't we all?

YOUR E-MAIL

q: Dear gg,
D sounds sweet. Whys he so hot for **S**? Shes just a ho.
—Bebe

a: Dear Bebe,
I happen to know that **D** is not that sweet and innocent. Try reading over his shoulder. That's some kinky shit.
—GG

q: dear GG,
what does **N** do at lunchtime?? i go to school near him, and i wonder if i see him all the time without realizing it. Yikes!
—ShyGirl

a: Okay, if you want to know so badly, then I'll tell you.
St. Jude's lets its senior boys out for lunch. So right now **N** is probably headed up to that little pizza joint on the corner of Eightieth and Madison. Vino's? Vinnie's? Whatever. Anyway, they have good slices and one of the delivery guys sells pretty decent pot. **N** is one of his regulars. There's usually a group of girls from L'Ecole standing around outside the pizza place, so **N** will stop and flirt with this one girl who I'll call **Claire**, who acts all shy and pretends she doesn't speak English, but she's actually really bad at French and a huge slut.

N has this cute little gag where he buys two slices and he always offers **Claire** one. She holds on to it the whole time they're talking and finally takes a little weensy bite off the tip of the slice. Then **N** goes, "I can't believe you did that, you're eating my pizza!" and swipes it out of her hands and eats the whole thing in like two bites. This makes **Claire** laugh so hard her boobs nearly pop out of her shirt. The L'Ecole girls all wear really tight clothes and short skirts and high heels. They're like, the ho's of the Upper East Side school system. **N** likes to flirt with them, and so far that's as far as it's gone. But if **B** leads him

A L'ECOLE GIRL

on any longer, he might start giving **Claire** more than just a bite of his pizza. This time, though, **Claire** surprises him by asking if he's heard about **S**. **Claire** claims to have heard that **S** not only got pregnant last year, but that she gave birth in France. Her baby's name is **Jules** and he is alive and well and living in Marseilles.

As for **D**—well, he's sitting in a dark corner of the Riverside Prep courtyard again, reading a book of Sylvia Plath poems and drinking a ninety-nine-cent cup of coffee. I know that sounds extremely sad, but don't worry about **D**. His time is about to come. Stay tuned.

SIGHTINGS

K was seen returning a suede zebra-print Betsey Johnson handbag at **Saks Fifth Avenue**. Personally, I thought the bag was cute. But someone must have changed her mind for her. Heaven forbid she change her *own* mind.

See you at **B**'s party. Bet you're too scared to go to **S**'s.

Aren't we all?

You know you love me,

gossip girl

the naked and the dead

"Hey, Nate. It's Serena. Just calling to see if you're planning to stop by my pajama party tonight. Hope so. There are real torches. Can't wait. Love you. Bye."

Serena hung up. Some party. She'd spread the word around school and posted an open invite online. She'd changed into a pair of gold Chanel short-shorts and a smiley face–embellished pajama tank top she'd had since eighth grade. The cook had filled the bathtubs with ice and pepper-flavored vodka and papayas. The maid had lit tall tiki torches in every corner. Serena's favorite party playlist was on, a slow three-hour build from acoustic guitar to dance music. Now, the acoustic part was almost over, but so far no one had shown up.

Her room was quiet. Even Fifth Avenue was still, except for the occasional passing taxi. From where she sat on her big canopy bed, she could see the silver-framed photograph of her family, taken on a chartered sailboat in Greece when she was twelve. They were all in bathing suits. Her brother, Erik, who was fourteen at the time, was making a big fart kiss on Serena's cheek while their parents looked on, laughing. Serena had gotten her period for the first time on that trip and Erik had swum ashore, stolen a Vespa, and bought her some maxipads. He came back with them in a little plastic bag, tied on top of his head, her hero. Serena had thrown her ruined underwear overboard. They were probably still there, stuck on a reef somewhere along with the remains of some of the boys she'd killed.

Oceans are so convenient like that.

Now Erik was a freshman at Brown, and Serena never got to see him. He'd been in France with her this past summer, but she'd spent the whole time chasing or being chased by boys while Erik chased girls, so they'd never really had time to hang out.

Serena picked up the phone again and pressed the speed-dial button for Erik's off-campus apartment. The phone rang and rang until finally the voicemail system picked up, just as it had every other time she'd tried to call her brother at school. Sometimes she wondered if he was avoiding her.

"If you would like to leave a message for Dillon, press one. If you would like to leave a message for Tim, press two. If you would like to leave a message for Drew, press three. If you would like to leave a message for Erik, press four."

Serena pressed four and then hesitated. ". . . Hey . . . it's Serena. Sorry I haven't called in a while. But you could have called me too, you big jerk. I was stuck up in Ridgefield, bored out of my mind. Now I'm back in the city. It's my first week of school. It's kind of strange. Actually, it sucks. Everyone is . . . everything is . . . I don't know . . . it's weird. . . . Anyway, call me back sometime. I miss your hairy ass. Love you. Bye."

She picked up her MacBook and began to browse through the list of international boarding schools where her parents had offered to send her as an alternative to coming home. One of them was a monastery in Tibet. Another was a "camp" in Uganda. Another was a "tree village" in a rainforest in Borneo. And there was one in the South Pacific called Saint Get Away that sounded strangely like a leper colony.

Perfect.

The downstairs buzzer buzzed. She leapt up to answer it.

The doorman announced the arrival of Mr. Nathaniel Archibald. He was on his way up.

"Oh, Natie. I knew I could count on you!" Serena exclaimed, throwing open the door and twining her arms around his adorable neck.

"Hi," Nate said shyly. Serena's breath smelled of pepperflavored vodka and her turquoise silk La Perla bra was clearly visible beneath her smiley face pajama tank top. "Hi," he said again, chuckling softly as Serena kissed him on the lips.

"I'm so glad you're here," she sighed, leading him into the empty, half-dark penthouse. Music played from a distant bedroom. "I didn't think anyone was coming. Are you hungry? Thirsty?"

Nate held on to her hand. Yes, he was hungry and thirsty. And horny. Christ, why had he come? He never could control himself around Serena.

"Is that Nirvana *Unplugged*?"

She shrugged. "I think so."

"Let's go see," he said, tugging her toward her bedroom. It felt so nice to be at home with her, sort of like it had always felt when they were younger—everything smelling like flowers and smoke, the white canopy bed, the hulking Metropolitan Museum staring at them from across the street, Serena's addictive laughter, her dark blue eyes and sexy mouth, her piles of blond hair, him wanting to touch her—except this time, they were alone. Blair wasn't there.

She sat down on the bed.

"I'm glad you came back," Nate said and sat down next to her.

Serena rested her head on his shoulder. The smoky honey patchouli scent of her shampoo mingled with the lavender linen scent the maid spritzed on the sheets, overtaking his nostrils and making him woozy.

Serena didn't want to have a party anymore. A small tête-à-tête would do. And unlike those of some of the boys she'd gone out with last year at Hanover, Nate's gorgeous head would remain firmly on his shoulders. She couldn't believe she'd spent almost the entire spring term last year at boarding school plotting his death. Nate was the one person on earth she couldn't bear to kill.

How reassuring.

"Me too," she whispered hoarsely into his warm neck. "I'm glad I'm back." Then she lifted her head and kissed his closed eyelids, ever grateful that she hadn't succeeded in exploding his marvelous green eyes.

Nate didn't know why he'd taken so long picking out a shirt. Serena's slender, nimble fingers wasted no time undoing the buttons and throwing the crumpled shirt to the floor. The shirt was followed by her tank top and shorts. Soon they were both naked beneath the covers as Serena's iPod crooned out songs of tortured heartache, raging jealousy, and love sublime.

Kati and Isabel had decided to drop in on Serena's party before reporting back to Blair. The doorman recognized them from parties past and waved them on to the elevator without buzzing up to the van der Woodsen penthouse.

The elevator doors rolled open onto a dark and empty foyer. Tiki torches flickered and smoked in the corners. It looked like the entrance hall to a wealthy Tahitian cannibal's palace.

"Whoa," Kati breathed. "There's like, nobody here."

"I think that's the idea. They're all at Blair's party. She invited everyone we know. Except Serena, of course." Isabel stepped onto the gleaming parquet floor and glanced around. "I think I hear music."

Both girls paused to listen as the crooning heartbreak of Bob Dylan's vintage *Blood on the Tracks* album wafted down the long hall leading to Serena's bedroom.

"Slow songs," Kati observed meaningfully. She pointed at Nate's discarded Abercrombie & Fitch waxed canvas anorak. "Look."

Wordlessly the two girls crept down the torchlit hall, cell phones clutched in their hands.

Serena lazed on her bed with only a white sheet wrapped around her, wondering idly whether to put her shorts back on or if jeans would be better, in case she and Nate decided to venture out. Nate was in the shower. Steam rose from the crack under the door as he ran through fake lacrosse plays in a loud sportscaster's voice.

"*And it's Archibald sprinting in from midfield. He makes an impossible catch! Look at him go! And it's Archibald again! Goal!!!*"

"Hi, Serena," Isabel taunted from the doorway. "I know it's a pajama party, but that doesn't mean you have to spend it in bed."

Serena bolted upright. Nate's jubilant shouts from the

shower were impossible to conceal. And everything—the clothes on the floor, the steamy air, the rumpled sheets—spelled one thing: S-E-X.

"What are you guys doing?" she demanded. "Spying on me?"

Kati crossed her arms over her chest. "You invited us, remember? You invited everyone. You're supposed to be having a party. Although Blair's having one too now, and hers sounds way more fun."

Something about the way Kati's brown eyebrows were waxed so very thin, the way her beige face powder stood out in little dots on her nose in the humid air, the way she crossed her legs one over the other like she had to pee or was trying to look taller and thinner, made Serena decide that both she and Isabel would have to die.

"Hey." Serena pointed at the delicate garnet heart earrings dangling from Isabel's ears. "Weren't those Nicki Button's earrings?"

Isabel touched the earrings with her fingertips. "So?" she rolled her eyes. "I'm the one who bought them for her. And it's not like she's going to wear them again."

Neither will you, Serena thought.

It wasn't just Kati's face or Isabel's sarcasm. The real problem was them knowing about her and Nate. If she didn't kill them now, Kati and Isabel would tell Blair, and then Blair would absolutely and finally never be friends with Serena again.

The two girls were carrying cell phones. She had to act fast.

"Uh-oh. Nate and I made such a mess." Serena rolled off the far side of the bed and pulled Nate's big white button-down shirt on over her head, covering all the necessary naked parts. She began to yank the Frette sheets and comforter into a big pile on top of the mattress. "Could you guys help me get these sheets into the incinerator? There's like, chocolate sauce and champagne all over them. I don't want the maid telling my mom. Mom hates it when I stain the linens."

"*I'm bringing sexy back. . . . Yeah,*" Nate sang embarrassingly from the shower.

Kati and Isabel nudged each other with their bony elbows.

"The garbage chute is right outside the back door," Serena said, gathering a handful of bedding in her arms. "You guys grab the comforter and I'll get the sheets and pillows."

Excited by the prospect of having even more dirt to spill to Blair, the two girls were happy to oblige. The white Swedish down duvet was heavy and awkward. Kati and Isabel followed behind the barefoot Serena, dragging the duvet between them as she padded through the enormous white kitchen.

"The maid's out shopping, thank God." She unlocked the back door and held it open for them. "Go ahead. Chute's on the left." The girls dragged the duvet into the dusty back hallway of the building, where only the super and the help were meant to go.

"It smells weird back here," Kati observed.

Isabel glanced around nervously. "Quick, open the chute."

Kati pulled open the heavy metal door and they began to stuff the duvet into the chute. Just then, Serena appeared with a bottle of Absolut Pepper vodka and a flaming tiki torch in her hands. She doused their hair and faces with the pepper-flavored vodka. Blinded, Kati and Isabel fell on their hands and knees, moaning. Serena tossed in the torch and the two girls became a giant, flaming flambé. Their eyelashes and hair crackled and shriveled. Their skin blistered and smoked. Their clothes seemed to swell and then pucker and shrink as they burned.

"*Owee*, it stings!" Kati screeched as Serena removed Kati's iPhone from her flaming back pocket.

"You insane bitch!" Isabel shrieked, crawling around in a circle like a blind Labradoodle on fire. "What did you do to me?"

The flames began to die out. Serena snatched up Isabel's cell phone from off the floor, grasped Isabel's skinny-jeaned ankles, and dragged her toward the garbage chute. Yanking the duvet out of the way, she stuffed her writhing classmate down the chute leading to the building's high-efficiency, industrial-grade incinerator. A blinded, toasted, and whimpering Kati slid down easily afterwards. The door to the chute slammed closed with a metallic bang, sealing off the pungent, carcinogenic scent of burning denim, torched hair, and melted Jimmy Choos.

Serena wadded up the duvet and the sheets and carried them into the kitchen, leaving them in a pile on the floor next to the washing machine for the maid to launder.

The iPod was now in full dance party mode. Nate shimmied around her bedroom wearing only a towel. His chest muscles bulged and his normally tousled hair was slicked back and wet.

"*A-a-a-ahhhh, freak out! Le freak, c'est Chic . . .*" he sang goofily into Serena's hairbrush along to the old disco song.

He is definitely not le freak.

"Hey. What happened to the covers?" He looked up at Serena. "You're wearing my shirt."

His oblivious puppy dog hotness never failed to slay her. Eager for a distraction from the demise of her classmates and energized by the effort of stuffing them down the incinerator chute, Serena tackled Nate and pulled him down on the bare mattress. It occurred to her that maybe they should crash Blair's party—together—just to shock everyone. But first she had to show Nate just how freaking special he was—for coming to her party, and for being the only person she wanted to keep alive.

That *is* special.

only the good die young

"They looked like maraschino cherries, they were so bloodshot. No—more like golf balls dipped in ketchup."

If Blair had to watch Chuck Bass reenact Jeremy Scott Tompkinson's exploding eyeballs incident one more time, she was going to personally strangle every single one of the eighty-seven partygoers in her living room and then explode her own eyeballs. What was the point of having a party when you hated everyone there? The music on her iPod was old and played out, her mother and Cyrus Rose had drunk all the good champagne and scotch, Kati and Isabel had completely disappeared, Nate still hadn't shown up, the hired bartender had decided to feature Cosmo-flavored slushies and pickled onions, both of which made her gag, and she was bored, bored, bored.

She watched the hot gay man behind the bar stab at a frozen block of ice cubes with a metal ice pick before dropping the cubes into a blender full of gelatinous pink Cosmo mix. He blended the icy gunk, poured it into a pink plastic Cosmo glass, skewered a pickled onion with a blue plastic cocktail sword, and slung it into the slush.

Bloody eyeball, anyone?

"I'm getting *so drunk*," squealed a girl Blair had never seen before. The girl seemed to be no older than twelve and she was flirting with the bartender, even though he was so obviously gay. She wore a hideously '80s blue suede jacket and ugly ruched leggings with zippers on the ankles, and her blond chin-length hair looked like a wig made out of dirty straw. Blair had spent the last hour waiting for Nate to show up so she could kick everyone out of the party and finally have sex, but it occurred to her now that she could just kick everyone out anyway and have a nice mug of hot chocolate in bed with one of her box sets of Stephen King DVDs—*Cujo*, *The Stand*, *Firestarter*, *Thinner*. After all, it was a school night, and this twelve-year-old really ought to have been home in bed.

"Did you hear about the vultures in Central Park?" Chuck Bass intoned from behind her. "Freaking vultures are *breeding*. They're not endangered. They're eating the goddamned squirrels and pigeons right out of the fucking trees."

The bartender worked at another lump of ice with his pick. Blair regarded him enviously. Oh, what she could do to Chuck's face with that pick.

"My friend better get here quick before I drink too much and embarrass myself," the twelve-year-old told the bartender. Then she looked up and covered her mouth in surprise. "Whoa. Oh my God. Blair Waldorf is *so not* happy right now."

Blair followed the annoying girl's gaze to see what it was she was supposed to be so upset about. Nate and Serena stood in the foyer, cheeks aglow beneath the Waldorfs' ancient brass chandelier, smiling like assholes. Serena unbuttoned her coat and Nate helped her out of it like the gentleman he was.

Or used to be.

Surely it was only an accident that they had arrived together. But what was Serena doing here in the first place? She was supposed to be having her own lame party.

Serena grinned at Blair and waved. In her hand were Kati's and Isabel's cell phones, Kati's in its tacky red patent leather Coach case and Isabel's in its Tiffany blue leather sleeve. Blair had always secretly coveted that sleeve.

A warning chill ran up Blair's spine.

"*I whip my hair back and forth, I whip my hair back and forth, I whip my hair . . . !*"

All of a sudden that ridiculous Willow Smith song came on and Serena and a bunch of other girls put their hands on their knees and began to whip their hair back and forth, over and over and over again, with embarrassing zeal.

Blair crossed her arms over her chest. Fucking idiots.

Nate walked over to the bar and ordered a Sam Adams and a Cosmo slushie, presumably for Serena.

Hello? Was she invisible? Blair lit a Parliament and blew smoke in his direction, knowing she would pay for it later when her mother grilled her on which of her so-called friends would dare smoke in the house.

The twelve-year-old girl was whipping her straw hair back and forth right next to Nate's elbow. She stopped and grinned shyly up at him. "So, are you and Serena like, together now?" she asked loudly enough for Blair to hear. The bartender stabbed at another chunk of ice with his ice pick and then dropped the ice into the blender. Across the expansive living room, Serena was still whipping her gorgeous blond hair all over the place, like Lady Godiva at an orgy.

Blair took a deep breath and approached the bar. "Hello,

Nate," she hissed, snatching the ice pick out of the ice tray. She turned to the twelve-year-old. "Hello, little blond girl I've never seen before. Can you help me with something?"

The girl's blue eyes lit up. "Really?"

Clutching the ice pick, Blair led her into the kitchen. "I was just thinking," she said, slowing down to wrap one arm around the girl's shoulders, "how much I'd love to watch you"—she turned and rammed the ice pick into the girl's chest, spattering the white tile of the kitchen island with droplets of red blood—"die."

The girl slumped to the ground, her blue eyes wide and surprised-looking. Blair wasn't exactly sure what to do next. The body was too big for the trash can, which was Swiss chrome and tubular, and if she dragged it all the way to the big trash can outside the back door, she'd smear blood all over the clean white floor tiles. Besides, the building's superintendent would see the body and say something to her mom. Behind Blair loomed the wide, farm-style kitchen sink. And on the wall behind the faucet, the switch for the garbage disposal.

All of a sudden the girl groaned and threw up a vomitous mix of Cosmo slushie and blood. It oozed over the toes of Blair's new black Ferragamo flats.

"Ew. I thought you were dead. Come on, let's go." Blair grabbed the girl angrily by the hair and yanked her to her feet.

She forced the girl's blond head down the drain and flicked on the disposal. Its blades began to grind, sending up sparks as they met bone. Chunks of flesh and bits of hair spattered the white kitchen ceiling.

Just as Blair was feeding the girl's ankles and feet down the drain, Myrtle, the cook, came in the back door to spy on the party for her employer.

"Blair, what a mess!" Myrtle exclaimed in her singsong Trinidadian accent. She retrieved the mop from the pantry. "Next time you want Bloody Marys, ask me to fix them for you."

Downstairs in the lobby Dan and Jenny Humphrey were still alive and well, but a little down on their luck.

What else is new?

"Elise promised me she'd get us in," Jenny insisted as she dialed her Constance Billard classmate once more. Earlier that day she and Elise had hatched a plan to get into Blair's party, where everyone who was anyone was going to be. Elise would wear her mom's blue suede jacket and pretend to be an actress. Jenny would wear a V-neck and pretend to be Dan's date, or, better yet, she'd bump into some cute St. Jude's boy in the elevator who would refuse to go to the party without her enormous cleavage by his side. Both girls had sworn that whoever got into the party first would help the other girl get in.

Dan was only going because his father would probably send him out later to pick up Jenny anyway. Plus he had nowhere else to be. Plus Serena might be there, even though Jenny had mentioned something about Serena maybe having her own party, although she had a feeling no one was going because oddly the senior girls at Constance were all being sort of mean about Serena coming back and— And that was when Dan had tuned Jenny out.

Dan had never been inside the lobby of such a fancy apartment building. The ceiling was twenty feet high, with elaborate gold moldings and a glittering crystal chandelier. One wall sported an enormous gilded mirror and the other a mural of a stag being chased by a mounted hunt. On a marble-topped table in front of the mirror stood a giant gold and cream china urn decorated with black pug dog faces and filled with at least one hundred fresh white roses. The floors were a creamy marble that sounded beneath Jenny's Nine West boots and squeaked under Dan's Converse sneakers. A doorman wearing white gloves and a gold waistcoat with his hunter green doorman uniform stood by the building's glass and cast iron front door, while another white-gloved doorman manned the intercom system behind an imposing dark wood and green leather-paneled station.

"I think my friend is up there," Jenny squeaked timidly at this second doorman. He was seven feet tall, buck-toothed and shriveled, and totally terrifying. "She just called me. She's like, *waiting* for me."

"As I said before, you're too late," the doorman insisted. "I just received instructions from Miss Waldorf herself. No more guests. The mother will be home soon and Miss Waldorf is going to bed."

"But it's only ten o'clock!" Jenny protested. It had taken all her courage to come to the party and she wasn't giving up easily.

"It is a school night," Dan mumbled at the floor. He'd been working on a new haiku about his murderous feelings toward Chuck Bass, compounded with his murderous feelings toward himself, compounded with his sister's taste for raw meat, and illuminated by his love of cigarettes.

> *Meat is murder.*
> *I love smoking—which*
>   *one of us is better off dead?*

Dan still wasn't sure about the first line. He'd be happy to go home and ponder it some more.

"Oh, be quiet," Jenny snapped, as if reading his mind. She stabbed at the buttons on her cell phone. Stupid Elise. Jenny should have guessed she was lying. Elise was probably already tucked in bed with her teddy bears, like the immature baby that she was, dead to the world.

Oh, she's dead all right.

The doorman glanced at his watch, which was gold and looked like it had been keeping perfect time for all of the four thousand years he'd been a doorman.

"It would probably be best for you to take it outside," he told Dan politely but firmly.

"It"? Dan wanted to protest for Jenny's sake, but feared the insults would only get worse. "Let's just go," he whispered, leading his sister toward the door. Chances were Serena wasn't even at the party anyway, and she was the only reason he'd come.

If only they'd lingered in the lobby a moment longer.

After killing Elise, Blair asked Myrtle to remove the food and tell the bartender to stop serving. Then Blair called down to the doorman requesting that no additional guests be allowed up. Serena was still dancing, the center of a hub of gyrating boys and girls, while Nate watched from the bar. She was acutely aware that if she stopped dancing every boy in the room might stop looking at her. In addition, she might have to talk to Blair, who might be sort of mad at her for killing Kati and Isabel, Blair's loyal followers.

She might.

Blair stepped in front of Nate, blocking his view. "Remember the last time you were over? When we were on my bed?" she asked. She stole a sip of Nate's beer even though beer tasted like moldy socks. All that activity in the kitchen had given her quite a thirst.

Nate nodded. He remembered.

"Didn't we start something and sort of not finish it?" Blair elaborated.

Nate frowned and then shrugged his shoulders. He was so used to Blair almost having sex with him but never actually having it that he didn't believe she ever intended to do it. "Maybe," he said.

Blair stepped forward and put her hands on his chest. "Well, I want to do it now." She frowned. "Actually, not now—my mom will be home in a minute and I really need to clean up and take a bath. This Friday. I want to do it on Friday." She lifted her chin and gazed up into Nate's pretty green eyes. Every time she got this close to him she could not stop smiling. "It's going to be Friday the thirteenth," she added kinkily.

Nate smiled back and kissed her smiling red mouth. He could never resist when Blair was being all coy and sweet and suggestive and smiley. It made him want to be all coy and sweet and suggestive and smiley right back. "Okay," he agreed. "Sounds like fun."

Across the living room Serena saw them kissing and stopped dancing. She stepped into the hall to retrieve her coat. Guests milled around, wondering whether to stay or go now that the bar had run dry. Serena buttoned her coat. The elevator was crowded. The lobby was bright. Sadness stabbed at her broken heart as she walked up the quiet, leaf-strewn sidewalks of Fifth Avenue toward home, alone.

life is fragile and absurd

"You're so full of it, Dan," Jenny told her brother. They were sitting at the kitchen table in their large and crumbling tenth-floor, four-bedroom West End Avenue apartment. It was a beautiful old place with twelve-foot ceilings, lots of sunny windows, big walk-in closets, and huge bathtubs with feet, but it hadn't been renovated since the 1940s. The walls were water-stained and cracked, and the wood floors were scratched and dull. Ancient, mammoth dust bunnies had gathered in the corners and along the baseboards like moss. Once in a while Jenny and Dan's father, Rufus, hired a cleaning service to scrub the place down, and their enormous cat, Marx, kept the cockroaches in order, but most of the time their home felt like a meandering, neglected attic. It was the kind of place where you'd expect to find lost treasures—ancient photographs, vintage shoes, or the skeleton of that chemistry teacher who took a sudden early retirement after giving you a D-minus on the final last year.

Jenny was eating raw hamburger meat with a grapefruit spoon and drinking a cup of cinnamon tea. Ever since she'd gotten her period last spring, she'd had the weirdest cravings. And everything she ate went straight to her boobs. Dan was on his fourth cup of Folgers instant coffee made with lukewarm tap water and eight teaspoons of sugar. He worried about his little sister's eating habits, but he never ate anything at all, so what did he know?

Vanessa Abrams's short film script, the film he was supposed to star in, lay on the table in front of him. He wouldn't actually have to speak in the movie—thank goodness—because Vanessa was narrating the whole thing herself, but she'd asked him to read it anyway. Over and over the same lines popped out at him: *"Life is fragile and absurd. Murdering someone's not so hard."*

"Tell me you don't care about Serena van der Woodsen being back," Jenny challenged. She put a spoonful of meat in her mouth and sucked on it. Then she stuck her fingers in her mouth, pulled out a white piece of fat gristle, and wiped it on her plate. "You should see her," she went on. "She looks so completely cool. It's like she has this whole new look. I don't mean her clothes. It's her face. She looks older, but it's not like wrinkles or anything. It's like she's Kate Moss or some model who's like, died and come back to life. Like she's totally *experienced*."

Jenny waited for her brother to respond, but he just stared into his coffee cup.

"Don't you even want to see her?" Jenny asked. "It's too bad we didn't try to get into her party instead of Blair's."

Dan remembered what he'd heard Chuck Bass say about Serena. That she was the sluttiest, druggiest, most venereally diseased girl in New York. That she'd maybe even murdered someone. And Jenny had just said she looked experienced. But Dan didn't believe a word of it. It was all just a bunch of terrible lies and bullshit rumors. And the more he thought about it, the more he wanted to kill Chuck Bass for spreading them.

Life is fragile and absurd. Murdering someone's not so hard.

Dan pointed at the little pile of gristle on Jenny's plate and wrinkled his nose in disgust.

"What's wrong with it?" Jenny said. "I don't like the fat, I just like the meat."

Dan pushed his coffee away, careful not to slop any onto his script.

"Oh, be quiet, Mr. Anorexic," Jenny sighed. "Anyway, you didn't answer my question."

Dan shrugged his scrawny shoulders.

Jenny put her elbows on the table and leaned forward. "About Serena," she said. "I know you want to see her."

Dan scowled into his lap. "Whatever," he mumbled.

"Yeah, whatever." Jenny rolled her eyes. "Look, I know last night didn't work out, but there's this party a week from Friday—*Kiss Me or Die?* It's like, a benefit to save the birds of prey that live in Central Park. Did you know there were vultures in Central Park? I didn't. Anyway, Blair Waldorf is organizing it, and you know she and Serena are still sort of best friends, so of course Serena will be there."

And most likely, if Serena was there, she would kill at least one person, or maybe even lots of people. And Jenny wanted to watch.

Dan kept reading his script, completely ignoring his sister. And Jenny went on, ignoring the fact that Dan was ignoring her. She was used to it, since Dan rarely said anything anyway.

"All we have to do is find a way to get into that party," Jenny continued. She grabbed a paper napkin off the table, scrunched it into a ball, and threw it at her brother's head. "Dan, please.

We'll have more time to plan than we did last night. Come on. We have to go!"

Dan tossed the script aside and looked at his sister, his brown eyes serious and sad.

"Jenny," he said, his voice hoarse from lack of use, "do you really want to get kicked out by another doorman? I don't want to go to that party. Next Friday I'm supposed to hang out with Vanessa and watch her sister's band. You can come if you want."

Jenny kicked at the legs of her chair like a little girl, pouting her bloody, meat-stained lips. "But why, Dan? Why won't you go to the party?"

Dan shook his head and refused to say anything else.

"Oh, shut up. You're such a wimp! You drive me crazy," Jenny huffed, rolling her eyes. She stood up and dumped her dishes in the sink, scrubbing at them furiously with a Brillo pad. Then she whirled around and put her hands on her hips. She wore a pink flannel nightshirt and her curly brown hair was sticking out all over because she had gone to sleep with it wet. She looked like a mini disgruntled housewife with boobs that were ten times too big for her body.

"I don't care what you say. I'm going to that party!" she insisted.

"What party?" their father asked, appearing in the kitchen doorway.

If there were an award for the most embarrassing dad on the planet, Rufus Humphrey would have won it. He wore a sweat-stained white wifebeater and red checked boxer shorts, and was scratching his hairy belly. He hadn't shaved in a few days, and his gray beard seemed to be growing at different intervals. Some of it was thick and long, but in between were bald areas and patches of five o'clock shadow. His curly gray hair was matted and his brown eyes bleary. There was a cigarette tucked behind each of his ears.

Jenny and Dan looked at their father for a moment in silence. Then Jenny sighed and turned back to the dishes. "Never mind."

Dan smirked and leaned back in his chair. Their father hated the Upper East Side and all its pretensions. He only sent Jenny to Constance because it was a very good school and because he used to date one of the English teachers there. But he hated the idea that Jenny might be influenced by her classmates, or "those spoiled debutantes," as he called them.

Dan knew their dad was going to love this. He tapped his foot on the floor expectantly.

"Dan won't take me to this benefit I want to go to next week," Jenny explained, still at the sink.

Mr. Humphrey pulled one of the cigarettes from behind his ear and stuck it in his mouth, playing with it between his lips. "A benefit for what?" he demanded.

Dan rocked his chair back and forth, a smug look on his face.

Jenny turned off the faucet and spun around to glare at him. "It's a party to raise money for those poor vultures that live in Central Park."

Dan snickered.

"Oh, shut up," Jenny snapped, furious. "You think you know everything. It's just a stupid party. I never said it was a great cause."

"You call that a *cause*?" her father bellowed. "Shame on you. Those people only want those birds around because it makes them feel like they're in the pretty *countryside*, like they're at their houses in *Connecticut* or *Maine*. They're probably going to build birdhouse mansions for them or something. Like there aren't thousands of homeless people that could use the money. Leave it to the leisure class to come up with some charity that does absolutely *no one* any good at all!"

Jenny leaned back against the kitchen counter, crossed her arms over her chest, and tuned her father out. She'd heard this tirade before. It didn't change anything. She still wanted to go to that party. She was tired of always hearing about all the cool things the cool girls did the next day. She wanted to be part of the coolness. If blood was going to be spilled at the *Kiss Me or Die* party, she wanted to see it spill, live and in person.

"I just want to have some fun," she retorted. "Why does it have to be such a big deal?"

"It's a big deal because you're going to get used to this silly debutante nonsense, and you're going to wind up a big fake like your mother, who hangs around rich people all the time because she's too scared to think for herself," her father shouted, his unshaven face turning dark red. "Dammit, Jenny. You remind me more and more of your mother every day."

Dan suddenly felt bad. Their mother had run off to Prague with a count or prince, and she was basically a kept woman, letting the count or prince or whatever he was dress her and put her up in castles all over Europe. All she did all day was shop, eat, drink, and go hunting with the prince. She wrote them letters a few times a year, paid for their schooling, and sent them the odd present. Last Christmas she'd sent them the taxidermied head of some pig-deer type rodent she'd shot and killed in Bavaria. It hung from a towel hook on the bathroom wall.

It wasn't a nice thing for their father to say that Jenny reminded him of their mother. It wasn't nice at all.

Jenny looked like she was about to cry.

"It's okay, Dad," Dan spoke up. "We weren't invited anyway."

"See what I mean!" Mr. Humphrey said triumphantly. "Why would you want to hang out with those snobs anyway? Besides, every time I look at the paper there's a new murder, and they're all on the Upper East Side. I don't want you over there after dark. It's too dangerous. You're staying home."

Jenny stared glassy-eyed at the dirty kitchen floor. She could see how Serena might find it easy to kill people. She herself could think of two people she would very much like to kill right now.

Dan stood up. "Get dressed, Jenny," he said quietly. "I'll walk you to your bus stop."

partially naked lunch

To: narchibald@stjudes.edu
From: blairw@constancebillard.edu

I'm at my mom's hair place. Lunch is over in 38 minutes and they're making me wait. Missed you when you left last night. Mom and Cyrus are going away Friday. You can sleep over. This time it's really going to happen.
I love you. Call me. xo B
PS: I'm not cutting my hair short, just waxing my bikini ;)

Every Wednesday, Nate and Blair had grown accustomed to e-mailing each other a quick love note (okay, it was Blair's idea), to help them get over the hump of the boring school week. Only two more days until the weekend, when they could spend as much time together as they wanted. Nate scanned the note without really reading it. Which hairs Blair chose to cut or wax didn't concern him. In fact, he'd really rather not know. He liked to think she looked pretty without really trying. But that would be a different girl.

He scrolled through the other junk in his inbox and was thrilled to discover an e-mail from that girl.

To: narchibald@stjudes.edu
From: serenavdw@constancebillard.edu
Re: Friday

Hey. I didn't even see you leave last night. Sorry. Let's all get together Friday night. OK? Love, S

"Hey, Archibald! Quit fucking with your phone!"

It was a sunny October day in Central Park. Out in Sheep Meadow lots of kids were cutting class, just lying in the grass, smoking, or playing Frisbee. The trees surrounding the meadow were a blaze of yellows, oranges, and reds, and beyond the trees loomed the beautiful old apartment buildings on Central Park West. A guy was selling weed, and Anthony Avuldsen had bought some to add to what Nate had picked up at the pizza parlor the day before at lunch.

Nate shot Serena back a quick "OK" and joined his friends. He and Anthony and Charlie Dern passed an enormous joint between them as they dribbled a soccer ball around on the grass, pretending not to miss their goofy friend Jeremy.

Charlie puffed on the joint and passed it to Anthony. Nate shot Charlie the ball and Charlie tripped over it. He was six feet tall and his head was too big for his body. People called him Frankenstein. Ever the athletic one, even when he was stoned, Anthony dove for the ball, kicked it up in the air, and headed it back to Nate, catching him in the chest. Nate let the ball roll to the ground and dribbled it between his feet.

"Shit, this stuff is strong," Anthony said, hitching up his grass-stained St. Jude's sweatpants.

"Yeah, it is," Nate agreed, passing him the ball. "I'm already all fucked up." His feet were itchy. It felt like the grass was growing through the rubber soles of his sneakers. If Jeremy had been there he would have had something funny to say to distract him. Without Jeremy there, Nate could feel himself starting to freak out.

Tufts of park grass sprouted in the damp, warm spaces between his toes. Bugs scurried across the arches of his feet. He rubbed the bones of his ankles together. Soon the ants and weevils and creepy-crawlies would scurry up his legs and torso and neck, into his ears and nose, and lay their eggs in his brain. When he opened his mouth all that would come out were bugs. He couldn't move his legs. He was being eaten alive by the grass, swallowed whole in Central Park. He couldn't breathe. He was dying.

Anthony stopped dribbling the ball. "Hey, Nate. You've seen Serena van der Woodsen, right?" he asked. "I keep hearing all this crazy shit about her."

Nate could feel the other two boys staring at him. He bent down and poked at the tops of his feet. Damn. They were numb. "Yeah, I saw her last night," he said, trying to keep his voice casual even though his tongue was a mass of spiders and he was being devoured by the earth.

Charlie cleared his throat and spat in the grass. "Well?" he asked. "Is she totally psycho now? That's what I heard. I heard she had sex with this whole group of guys in her room and then killed them all. Her roommate ratted her out." He snorted. "Oops! Like, maybe Serena should have killed her too?"

Anthony laughed and sucked on the roach. "I heard she has a kid. I'm serious. She had it in France and left it there. Her parents are paying to have it raised in some French nunnery where the nuns whack you with thistles if you speak out of turn and there's nothing to eat but wormy old bread and like, you have to whiz in a chamber pot. It's like a book by whatthefuck'shisname—the dude we had to read for English—Thomas Hardy. No, it's a fucking horror movie adaptation of a Thomas Hardy book."

Serena of the Doobievilles?

"Can you imagine Serena with all these guys in her dorm room? Like, '*Ooh, baby. Harder, harder!*' And then, '*Hasta la vista, baby!*'" Anthony fell down on the grass, rubbing his toned belly and cackling hysterically. "Oh, man!"

Nate couldn't believe what he was hearing. When his friends were stoned they got so outrageous. He dropped down in the grass and began to remove his shoes and socks. He didn't speak out in Serena's defense. He just sat there, watching the veins pulse in his feet, wondering if they were going to explode like Jeremy's eyeballs.

Meanwhile Blair was getting impatient. On her back in a treatment room, naked from the waist down save for a paper "waxing skirt," she'd been waiting for her aesthetician for nearly a quarter of an hour. She'd wanted to get a Brazilian bikini wax before Friday night, leaving enough time for the little rash she sometimes got afterwards to go away, and had chosen her mother's salon to do the job because it was close to school and there was an open lunchtime appointment. The meatpacking district salon where she usually went for haircuts and waxing was huge and busy and modern, with cool music, fresh cappuccinos, and a separate floor for spa treatments. This salon was intimate—meaning cramped—with powder blue carpeting, gilt mirrors, and classical music, and was full of Park Avenue matrons with their dogs in their laps having their roots done by obnoxiously talkative stylists. The door to her treatment room was open just a hair, and she could hear one of the stylists talking to his client.

"Hair is like a muscle," he was saying. "It has like, a memory. And it has to be worked out, otherwise it just falls all blah, you know? It's like a child. It needs exercise. It needs to be fed. And it needs to go to school. Or else it won't get into a good college." The stylist chuckled. "Not *your* children, babe. Yours are all geniuses, clearly."

Blair had never heard anything more asinine in her life. Hair was nothing like a muscle. Hair was dead. Dead, dead, dead. Just like that idiot hairdresser should have been for saying something so stupid. She checked her e-mail on her phone for the twelfth time. Nate still hadn't replied to her message. Where was he? Flirting with those slutty L'Ecole girls outside that pizzeria he always went to? Cutting class with his pals? Or worse, sharing a bottle of chardonnay and a baguette in the park with Serena?

Stop it, she told herself. *You're acting crazy.* But she was tired of lying there, partially exposed, with the door practically wide open and no one paying her any attention.

"Is someone going to come in here and do my wax?" she called, hating that she sounded like a fifty-year-old high-maintenance housewife from New Jersey. "I have to get back to class."

The chatty hairstylist stuck his head in the door. He wore a short bleached blond goatee and a slicked back blond ponytail. On every finger of both hands were sparkling gold David Yurman rings. His skinny black jeans were complemented by a pair of red suspenders and a black oxford shirt unbuttoned to reveal a tanned, muscular chest. Rounding off the look was a pair of black Prada biker boots. His over-fifty clients probably thought he was sexy. Blair could barely stand to look at him.

She crossed her legs one over the other beneath the paper skirt. "I'm waiting for Mina," she snapped.

The stylist tried to wrinkle his Botox-injected forehead into a frown. "Sorry, babe. Mina had to go pick up her son. Strep throat. Just give me a sec to finish this blowout. I'll do your wax."

He closed the door, leaving Blair feeling more exposed than ever. She was about to put her clothes back on when the guy returned.

"So. How do you want it?" he asked, donning a pair of latex gloves and pulling them carefully over his tacky rings. He cocked his index fingers at Blair like two latex-covered pistols. "Project Runway, the Bermuda Triangle, or Completely Spank-Me Bare?"

He'd chosen the wrong girl to fire at. Blair sat up. No way was she letting this jerk anywhere near her bikini line. "No, thank you. I'll reschedule," she told him briskly.

The hairstylist glanced at the pot of boiling hot melted wax on the countertop and then eyeballed her bare knees. He grinned, his bleached blond goatee punctuating a set of hideously crooked yellow teeth. "Babe, trust me. I've seen it all."

Ew. Blair had had enough of this hairdryer-wielding idiot. Never again would she return to this salon. She jumped to her feet, buttoned on her Constance uniform, stamped back into her gold and black Chanel flats, snatched her dove gray cashmere Calvin Klein blazer off the hook, and slung her wine-colored Mulberry school bag over her arm.

"Try waxing off your ugly face," she spat, grabbing the guy's ponytail with her serving hand. Then, with the strength of a nationally ranked tennis player, she dunked his entire head into the pot of bubbling hot wax.

He'd look so much better bald. Like a boiled potato in suspenders and boots. Mr. Frédéric Fuckkai Potatohead.

If he survived, that is.

The atmosphere in the Constance Billard cafeteria was substantially subdued now that Kati, Isabel, and Nicki were dead and no longer attending school. Blair had run off somewhere, and Laura Salmon and Rain Hoffstetter sat by themselves at the senior girls' regular table, sharing a pumpernickel bagel. Serena started toward them, hushed stares stabbing at her back. When they spied her, Laura and Rain dropped their bagel halves and glared at her so menacingly that Serena altered her course and pretended to examine the salad bar.

Even the olives and cherry tomatoes stared back at her, appalled and accusing. Serena abandoned her tray, backing out of the cafeteria and fleeing to one of her old school haunts, the private bathroom next to the nurse's office.

The bathroom seemed to have escaped the renovations the school had undergone in 1973, 1992, and 2002. The floor was old-fashioned black and white mosaic tile. The walls were white subway tile, graying and marked with girlish graffiti in some places. There was an old claw-foot bathtub, used by no one. The girls used to whisper that after hours Mrs. McLean invited her girlfriend Vonda over to the school for a bubble bath, but even that hadn't happened in a while, since the tub was lined with a powdery film of white dust.

Serena checked the wall to the left of the paper towel dispenser and there it was. s + b forever, scrawled inside a skinny heart. Blair had written it with a turquoise-colored Sharpie in fifth grade while she and Serena took turns shaving their legs for the first time with Blair's dad's razor. How many times had Serena and Blair escaped to this bathroom together to discuss their hair, share their period woes, and apply lip gloss? How many times had Serena stood outside that very bathroom door while Blair pretended to have a stomach virus, quickly flushing down the remains of her regurgitated lunch?

Blair was barely speaking to her now.

Serena washed her hands, even though they were already clean.

What, no blood?

Her reflection in the mirror was tense and her skin looked dull. She kept the cold tap running and began to splash icy water on her face, over and over, willing all the badness and loneliness and meanness to go away.

Behind her the bathroom door swung open.

"Oh my gosh!" exclaimed a short girl with curly dark hair and a chest that was way too big for her tiny frame.

"I should've locked it," Serena said, reaching for a wad of paper towels. She patted them against her dripping face as the girl stared at her with enormous dark brown eyes. "What're you staring at?" Serena demanded more harshly than she'd intended.

The girl blinked. "I just can't believe I'm talking to you. I'm Jenny. You're Serena. I—" The girl bit her tiny red button lips. "I know everything about you. You're amazing. You're like, famous."

The girl, Jenny, was almost a foot shorter than Serena, with soft brown eyes like those adorable baby seals' eyes in the World Wildlife Fund board members' updates Serena's mother received in the mail twice a year.

Serena took a step toward her. "Like what? What do you know about me?"

"Not all those silly rumors," the girl said, quivering from head to toe. "But I know you killed Nicki Button. And Kati Farkas. And Isabel Coates. You're like a superhero. You're like Robin Hood. You're killing all the meanest girls so girls like me can have a chance."

This thought had never occurred to Serena. And, although she liked the sound of it, Jenny had her facts completely wrong. Who knew what she'd say next, and to whom? For all Serena knew, Jenny had been sent there by Blair, like some sort of suicide bomber, just to rile Serena up.

Jenny might be cute, but unfortunately the little curly-haired, button-lipped, seal-eyed imposter would have to die.

"Go on," Serena coaxed, buying time as she glanced around the bathroom, looking for some useful appliance with which to kill the little minx. There was the toilet plunger, but who knew where that had been. The china soap dish looked too brittle. The metal towel rack might work. She could get it off the wall, stab Jenny through the heart, and then drown her in the bathtub.

"I won't tell anyone," Jenny promised, turning to go. "And don't worry, I can use the bathroom upstairs. I just wanted you to know how cool I think you are."

Sure, you won't tell anyone, Serena thought bitterly. No one on this goddamned island could ever keep their mouth shut.

"Wait!" Serena called sharply. She gripped the towel rack, bracing herself to yank it out of the wall.

Jenny turned around and blinked her big brown baby seal eyes up at her idol.

Serena hesitated. She could kill this little Jenny, easy. But then what? She'd go back out to the cafeteria and the first person to talk to her would say the wrong thing and she'd kill them too?

When was this going to end? How many more people were going to die before she and Blair became friends again? Wasn't that why she'd come back? Wasn't that why she'd tried to kill Nate? Why she'd killed Jeremy, and that girl in the elevator, and Kati and Isabel—to protect her friendship with Blair? But it wasn't happening. Things were different now, irreparably different. She and Blair would never be friends again.

She let go of the towel rack. "Never mind," she said dismissively. "I was going to ask to borrow a hairbrush, but I just remembered I have mine." She tried to smile. "Nice meeting you, Jenny."

The younger girl's face flushed with Serena's utterance of her name. "You too!" she squealed before closing the bathroom door behind her.

Pulling another paper towel from the dispenser, Serena rubbed at her cheeks, trying to bring some color back into them. She spied the turquoise heart again, reflected in the mirror. S + B FOREVER.

She'd come back to the city and to Constance hoping everything would go back to the way it had been. But then she'd slipped up. She'd slept with Nate again. And whether Blair knew about their trysts yet or not, Serena could never be the friend Blair wanted her to be. Because Serena loved Nate and wanted him for herself. And Blair would always hate her for that.

Last fall at Hanover, Serena had studied the reign of the

Tudors in England, featuring Henry VIII, the famous king who'd beheaded two of his six wives and hundreds of his loyal servants. She and Blair were sort of like King Henry VIII and Thomas Cromwell, the king's chief officer. Their bond was so strong it eventually became toxic, because both men wanted the same thing—power.

Still looking in the mirror, Serena lifted her chin and narrowed her eyes into a regal glare. When their friendship had finally played itself out, King Henry VIII had had Thomas Cromwell beheaded for treason. And so it went with her and Blair. They couldn't just keep killing other people and fighting over Nate. Of course Serena would kill whomever she must to protect herself. But if she really wanted to take back her old station and hold on to Nate, the one person she would have to kill, whether she liked it or not, was Blair herself.

Serena glanced at her watch. Only three more classes left in the day. She was late for Double Latin, and after that she had an appointment with Constance's college admissions advisor. Blair would probably be busy after school with one of her many activities. Serena wasn't exactly sure when she'd have the chance to get Blair alone with the right weapon and the blind resolve to do away with her best friend since birth. But when she did, Blair was going down.

Cutting yet another class, the three boys lay on their backs in the grass, far too stoned now to kick the ball. Anthony, whose grandfather was an Oscar-winning film director, took this moment to show off his extensive knowledge of film.

"How come so many famous old movies, you know, like *The Big Chill*—movies that our parents watch—show people getting high? If it's such a cool, acceptable thing, then why is it illegal?"

"Because people become assholes after college," Charlie explained. "They start policing themselves. But it's all a bunch of bullshit. Pot is good for you."

"Word," Anthony agreed. "Unless you're like Jeremy and you smoke some bad weed and your fucking eyeballs explode."

All three boys tapped on their eyelids with cautious fingertips.

"Man, why'd you have to bring that up?" Charlie moaned. "Now I'm all paranoid."

Nate was already paranoid. His feet no longer bothered him. The paranoia was of a different sort.

It was only Wednesday. Was it possible that Blair could remain ignorant about him and Serena—doing it not once, but twice—until Friday, even though she was in school with Serena every day and they were still sort of best friends and probably still told each other everything? Chances were, no. And what about Chuck Bass? He wasn't exactly good at keeping secrets. The entire Upper East Side probably knew by now.

Nate rubbed his pretty green eyes viciously. It didn't matter how Blair found out. Any way he looked at it, he was fucked. He tried to come up with a plan, but the only plan his stoned mind could think of was to wait and see what happened when he saw Blair on Friday night. He could tell her then himself. Make a complete confession. After they had sex. Or before.

Good plan.

"Wonder if Serena even knows who the daddy is," Charlie mused, wandering back into Serena territory. He turned his head to look at Nate. "You and her had a thing, didn't you, Archibald?"

"Where'd you hear that?" Nate shot back.

Charlie shook his head and smiled. "I don't know, man. Around. What's the problem? She's hot."

"Yeah, well, I've had hotter," Nate said, and immediately regretted it. What was he talking about?

"Yeah, Blair's pretty hot too, I guess," Charlie said, digging the heels of his green and white Stan Smith tennis sneakers into the grass. "I bet she gets pretty crazy in bed."

"Dude's tired just thinking about it!" Anthony said, rolling toward Nate and poking him in the ribs.

Annoyed, Nate rolled away, lay back in the grass, and stared at the empty blue sky. If he tilted his head all the way back, he could just see the limestone rooftops of the penthouses along Fifth Avenue jutting out above the treetops, Serena's and Blair's included. He tucked his chin down so all he could see was blue sky again. He was too baked to deal with any of this. He tuned his friends out and tried to clear his mind completely, his head as empty and blank as the sky. Images of Serena and Blair, naked, rose before him and crowded out the blankness.

"*You know you love me*," they teased in unison, making him smile.

gossipgirl.net

Disclaimer: All the real names of places, people, and events have been altered or abbreviated to protect the innocent. Namely, me.

topics   sightings   your e-mail   post a question

hey people!

I can't resist writing more about **N**, my new favorite topic. He is so stunningly beautiful, after all. Even if he is kind of lacking in the get-up-and-go (aka balls) department.

STONED IN CENTRAL PARK

Actually, my new favorite topic is the Waspoid—the elite version of the waste-oid, or stoner boy. Unlike the average stoner wasteoid, the Waspoid isn't into metal or online dungeon games or skateboarding or eating raw food. He gets cute haircuts and has good skin. He smells nice, he wears the cashmere sweaters his girlfriend buys for him, he gets decent grades, and he's sweet

A WASPOID

to his mom. He sails and plays soccer and lacrosse. He knows how to tie a necktie. He knows how to dance. He's sexy! And he would never kill anyone. Too messy. Too final. In fact, the Waspoid never fully invests himself in anything or anyone. He isn't a go-getter and he never says what's on his mind. He doesn't take risks, which is what makes him so risky to fall in love with.

You might have noticed that I'm just the opposite. Not that I'm into murdering people, but I never know when to shut up! And I seriously believe that opposites attract. I have to confess, I'm becoming a Waspoid groupie.

Apparently I'm not the only one.

YOUR E-MAIL

q: dear gossip girl,
i hooked up majorly with **N** on a blanket in central park. at least, i think it's the same **N**. he's all freckly, right? does he smell like suntan lotion and weed?
—blanketbaby

a: Dear blanketbaby,
Mmmm. I bet he does.
—GG

SIGHTINGS

B buying condoms at **Zitomer Pharmacy**. Lifestyles Extra-Long Super-Ribbed! What I want to know is how she knew what size to get. I guess they've done everything but. Afterward, **B** made a beeline (no pun intended!) to a cheesy nail salon on Lexington for a Brazilian bikini wax. Ouch. That's not something you want to skimp on. Also spotted, **S** at the post office, either receiving or mailing a big package. **Barneys** baby clothes for her little French tot, maybe? Caught **R** and **L** in the **3 Guys Coffee Shop**, eating fries and slurping hot cocoa again. They might have to return those cute little dresses they bought at **Bendel's** the other day. Too bad *Kiss Me or Die* is not a muumuu party. And finally, **D** and **V** in the Hunting and Fishing department of **Paragon Sports**—either suiting up to film her movie or getting ready for a wild night of . . . hunting and fishing.

VOCAB

Since so many of you have been asking, I'm going to answer the big question that's been baffling you since you found out about the *Kiss Me or Die* party.

A VULTURE

Here we go. According to my handy *Webster's* unabridged dictionary:

> **bird of prey, n. any number of flesh-eating birds, as the eagle, hawk, owl, vulture, etc.**

I'm sure I had you on the edge of your seat over that one. Just trying to keep you in the know. That's my job. Besides, the birds aren't the only ones stalking their prey these days.

See you in the park!

You know you love me,

gossip girl

a boy's guide to hunting and fishing

Paragon Sports, the only sporting goods superstore in all of Manhattan, located on Broadway near Union Square, carried a large selection of impressive-looking hunting knives. Vanessa and Dan had arranged to meet there during his PE class and her free study period after lunch in order to equip Dan with a suitable costume to wear as deranged killer Mickey Knox in her remake of *Natural Born Killers*.

Right now Dan was wearing a tight white O'Neill kids' sleeveless rash guard tucked into a pair of men's size extra-small slim-fit green camouflage cargo pants by The North Face, a shiny black faux-leather Patagonia women's size extra-small belt, black Red Wing men's work boots, and some sort of black polyester webbing over-the-shoulder harness that was supposed to carry a yoga mat, but which Vanessa was sure they could make good use of as Mickey Knox's multi-weapon holster.

"I look like one of the Village People," Dan mumbled, regarding himself in the full-length mirror beside the upstairs hunting knife display. The white rash guard emphasized his bony rib cage and skinny arms. Vanessa hadn't told him he'd have to dress like a tool before he'd agreed to be in her movie.

Vanessa ignored him as she studied the knives. Mickey Knox was an ace knife-thrower. Of course he carried guns too, but for those she'd have to go to Toys R Us. Even a toy gun was risky on the Brooklyn Bridge though. Unless it was neon orange or electric green, someone might mistake it for a real gun and call the police. Knives were safer.

And way cooler. She'd never appreciated how pretty knives could be, with their variously carved handles and curved, finely pointed blades. And then there was the Leatherman, which included a knife, a pair of scissors, two screwdrivers, an Allen wrench, and a saw, and came in a neat little leather sleeve.

"May I ask what you need a hunting knife for?" said the sporty-looking geek behind the display. He wore thick, black-framed glasses and had long sideburns and probably went to NYU, Vanessa thought enviously. She bet he rock-climbed in the Palisades in New Jersey on the weekends and lived in a grubby, loud studio apartment on the Lower East Side on some dismally cool street over a bar, where people like Blair Waldorf would never dream of setting foot.

"It's a prop. For a movie I'm making." Vanessa grinned and pointed at Dan. "He's going to slice open a lot of innocent people with it."

Dan glanced down at his stupid cargo pants with the tags dangling from the belt loops. He wished he could change.

"It has to look impressive," Vanessa told the sales guy. She pointed to a fourteen-inch textured steel bowie knife in the display. "That one's nice."

Dan peered over her shoulder. The knife was huge and beautiful, with a gold and white pearl inlaid titanium handle and a wide blue steel blade that only tapered at the very end, like a mini-machete.

The salesman sucked in his breath and pulled his purple plaid flannel shirt away from his chest in a gesture that suggested the room was heating up. "Yup. That is a nice one. For a total of $4,500."

Vanessa frowned. Maybe she should have gone to a cooking store. A nice sharp carving knife probably only cost around thirty bucks.

The salesman picked up the knife and set it down on top of the glass display case. "Comes with a hand-stitched leather sheath and its own sharpener." He ran his thumb over the blade. "Feel that," he said, holding the knife up for Dan and Vanessa to touch.

Dan pressed his entire hand against the sharpest part of the blade, pulling it away again before the salesman could see he'd drawn blood. "Cool."

Vanessa didn't want to touch it. What was the point? She was already spending a small fortune on Dan's outfit. "Do you have anything in the thirty- to fifty-dollar range?"

The salesman put the knife down and leaned toward her. His breath smelled like Altoids. "I'll tell you what. I'll let you have this one on loan if you bring it back safe and sound. No one's going to buy it anyway. Hunting's not real big in Manhattan."

Is that so?

"You would do that?" Vanessa asked incredulously. Every time she ventured below Twenty-third Street the people just got nicer and nicer.

Dan sucked on his bleeding hand.

"You can return the clothes too," the sales guy said, lowering his voice. He jerked his chin at Dan. "As long as he doesn't soil them," he added, implying that Dan was mentally challenged and might have trouble keeping his pants clean. "Keep the tags on, hold on to the receipt, and bring them back within thirty days. My girlfriend works as an assistant props stylist for commercials. They do it all the time."

Vanessa wanted to hug him, but that wouldn't be cool. Besides, he had a girlfriend, and she was supposed to be in love with Dan. "Thank you. Thank you so, so much."

She glanced at Dan. He was staring at the knife, still sucking on his hand.

"Go get changed so we can pay," Vanessa told him. Sometimes she wondered if Dan *was* a little slow. Maybe he just needed to eat something.

Dan wandered back to the dressing room where he'd left his school clothes, marveling at how good his own blood tasted. Maybe Jenny was on to something. Maybe if he tried it, he'd enjoy the taste of raw meat.

As he changed back into his regular clothes, Mickey Knox's lines from Vanessa's script reverberated in his head. *"Life is fragile and absurd. Murdering someone's not so hard."*

Dan bent down to tie his Converse sneakers, tugging violently at the laces and knotting them tight. A true poet, he could see the words from the script in his head, each letter distinct, with glistening edges. He moved a letter here, added one there, deleted a few, until they aligned to form a new haiku:

> *Rage, hate, pretty knife—*
> *October moon, tight white shirt.*
> *This blade cuts through bone.*

s tries to improve herself

"Well, it's wonderful to have you back, dear," Ms. Glos, the Constance Billard School's elderly college advisor, told Serena. She picked her glasses up from where they were hanging around her neck on a gold chain and slid them onto her nose so she could examine Serena's schedule, which was lying on her desk. "Let's see, now. Mmmm," she muttered, reading over the schedule.

Serena sat in front of Ms. Glos with her legs crossed, waiting patiently. There were no diplomas on Ms. Glos's wall, no evidence of any accreditations at all, just pictures of her grandchildren. Serena wondered if Ms. Glos had even gone to college. You would have thought if she were going to dish out advice on the subject she could have at least tried it.

Ms. Glos cleared her throat. "Yes, well, your schedule is perfectly acceptable. Not stellar, mind you, but adequate. I imagine you're making up for it with extracurriculars, yes?"

Serena shrugged her shoulders and allowed herself a small, embarrassed grin. *If you can call drinking Pernod and dancing naked on a beach in Cannes an extracurricular.*

What about setting people on fire, or scalping them? Or how about having sex with your best friend's boyfriend—*twice*?

"Not really," she said. "I mean, I'm not actually signed up for any extracurricular activities at the moment."

Ms. Glos let her glasses drop. Her nostrils were turning very red and Serena wondered if she was about to have a bloody nose. Of course, Serena was used to blood, but she didn't know if she could handle one of Ms. Glos's famous bloody noses. The college advisor's hair was thin and white and her skin was very pale, with a yellowish tinge. All the girls thought she had some terrible, ancient contagious disease like bubonic plague or leprosy.

"No extracurriculars? But what are you doing to improve yourself?"

Serena gave Ms. Glos a polite, blank look. Who said she needed improving?

"I see. Well, we'll have to get you involved in *something*, won't we?" Ms. Glos said. "I'm afraid the colleges aren't going to even look at you without any extracurriculars." She bent over and pulled a big loose-leaf binder out of a drawer in her desk and began flipping through pages and pages of flyers printed on colored paper. "Here's something that starts this week. 'Feng Shui Flowers, the Art of Floral Design.'"

She looked up at Serena, who was frowning doubtfully. "No, you're right. That's not going to get you into Harvard, is it?" She pushed up the sleeves of her blouse and flipped briskly through the binder's pages. She wasn't about to give up after only one try. She was very good at her job.

Serena gnawed on her thumbnail. She hadn't thought about this. That colleges would actually need her to be anything more than she already was. And she definitely wanted to go to college.

A good one. Her parents certainly expected her to go to one of the best schools. Not that they put any pressure on her—but it went without saying. And the more Serena thought about it, the more she realized she really didn't have anything going for her. She'd been kicked out of boarding school, her grades had fallen, she had no idea what was going on in any of her classes, and she had no legal hobbies or cool after-school activities except browsing exotic weaponry websites, giving herself Dead Sea mud facials, taking catnaps, and hooking up with Nate. Her SAT scores sucked because her mind always wandered during those stupid fill-in-the-bubble tests, and when she took them again, they would probably suck even worse. Basically, she was screwed.

What about her death toll? Surely that would stand out on an application.

"What about drama? Your English grades are quite good; you'd like drama," Ms. Glos suggested. "They've only been rehearsing this one for a little over a week. It's the Interschool Drama Club doing a modern version of *Sweeney Todd*." She looked up again. "How 'bout it?"

Serena jiggled her foot up and down and chewed on her pinky nail. She tried to imagine herself onstage, singing in a musical. She would have to dance too, wear a corset and a hoopskirt. Maybe even a wig. She'd seen *Sweeney Todd*. It was all about a barber who cut his customers' throats and then pulled a lever in the barber's chair, dumping the poor customer into the basement where his accomplice, Mrs. Lovett, would dispose of them by making them into mince pies, which she sold at her bakery next door. The drama club at Hanover had staged the musical last winter, providing Serena with much inspiration.

She took the flyer from Ms. Glos's hand, careful not to touch the paper where the diseased woman had touched it. "Maybe," she said doubtfully.

Ms. Glos closed the binder. "Your friend Blair Waldorf might be able to help," she suggested. "Blair has always participated in so many marvelous extracurricular activities. Sometimes I wonder how she does it." She smiled fondly. "Blair's applying early admission to Yale, you know."

Blair. Serena's heart rate quickened. Her hackles rose. *Blair.*

Blair was so smart, so perfect, so Ivy League–bound. Blair had Nate. Blair had friends and a sweet little brother who still lived at home. Blair had a pretty pedigreed cat and an amazing selection of Christian Louboutin shoes. Blair was going to Yale, and she was going nowhere.

Hot white anger coursed into Serena's blood, energizing her body like sugar. She ground her molars together. "Good for Blair," she said bitterly.

Ms. Glos squeezed her red-tinged nostrils between her thumb and forefinger. "Oh dear, I think I might be having one of my spells."

Serena tossed aside the perky drama flyer and rose to her feet.

"Here, have a tissue," she offered and plunged her hand inside the Kleenex box on Ms. Glos's desk. She yanked out the entire wad of tissues. Folders and papers slid to the floor as she lunged across the desk and began to shove the tissues up the surprised college admissions advisor's nostrils, into her open mouth, and down her throat. One by one, Serena balled up the tissues and stuffed them in, finishing off with the crumpled *Sweeney Todd* flyer and suffocating the white-haired, jaundiced woman completely.

Winded, Serena clambered off the desk, straightened her skirt, and pulled up her knee socks, feeling slightly aghast at her own behavior. Killing a teacher for suggesting that she try out for a musical was so rash, something Blair would do, not her.

Alas, S. Peer pressure preys on even the best of us.

The final classes of the day were just letting out. The *Sweeney Todd* rehearsal was in the auditorium but didn't start until six, so that girls who participated in after-school sports could also be in the play. Serena walked up Constance's wide central stairwell to the fourth floor to retrieve her coat from her locker and see if anyone wanted to hang out. All around her, girls were flying past, a blur of end of the day energy, rushing to their next meeting, practice, rehearsal, or club. Out of habit, the younger girls paused for half a second to say hello to Serena, because ever since they could remember, to be seen talking to Serena van der Woodsen was to be *seen*.

"Hey, Serena," Elizabeth Young, a junior, sang out before diving down the stairs for Glee Club in the basement music room. *Please don't follow me*, she prayed silently, crossing her fingers as she went.

"Later, Serena," muttered Anna Quintana, the sophomore sports prodigy, speed-walking by in her gym shorts and cleats. *Why didn't I take kickboxing instead of soccer?* she scolded herself. *Then I could take you on.*

"See you tomorrow, Serena," Lily Reed, a freshman, chirped softly, blushing down at her riding breeches. *Sometimes I have dreams that I'm a knight on horseback and I gallop up to you on my horse and loan you my lance.*

"Bye," snarled tough Carmen Fortier, one of the few scholarship girls in the junior class. Carmen was headed to the Art of Floral Design Club, although she told her friends in her Bronx neighborhood that she took karate. *Wow. Her hair is so not extensions. It's totally real.*

Suddenly the hallway was empty. Serena opened her locker, pulled her plastic Burberry raincoat off the hook, and put it on. Then she slammed her locker shut and trotted downstairs and out the school doors, turning left down Ninety-third Street toward Central Park.

There was a box of orange Tic Tacs in her pocket with only one Tic Tac left. Serena fished the Tic Tac out and put it on her tongue, but Ms. Glos had made her feel so anxious about her future that she could barely taste it.

She crossed Fifth Avenue, walking along the sidewalk that bordered the park. Fallen leaves scattered the pavement. Down the block, two little Sacred Heart girls in their cute red and white–checked pinafores were walking an enormous black rottweiler.

Guard dogs seem to be getting more and more popular these days.

A cluster of vultures flapped up from the treetops and soared over Fifth Avenue toward Constance Billard. Serena thought about entering the park at Eighty-ninth Street and sitting down for a while to kill time before doing her homework.

Better to kill time than people.

But alone? What would she do, bird-watch? Instead, she went home.

Nine ninety-four Fifth Avenue was a stark, white-glove building next to the Stanhope Hotel and directly across the street from the Metropolitan Museum of Art. The van der Woodsens owned half of the top floor. Their apartment had fourteen rooms, including five bedrooms with private bathrooms, a maid's apartment, a ballroom-sized living room, and two seriously cool lounges with wet bars and huge entertainment systems.

When Serena got home the enormous apartment was empty. Her parents were rarely home. Her father ran the same Dutch shipping firm his great-great-grandfather had founded in the 1700s, and both her parents were on the boards of all the big charities and arts organizations in the city. They were out all day and every night, attending meetings and lunches, art openings and cocktail parties, fundraising auctions and dinner dances. Right now Deidre the housekeeper was out shopping, but the place was spotless, and there were vases of fresh cut flowers in every room, including the bathrooms.

An enormous butcher block table stood in the center of the kitchen—oh, what she could do to Blair's straight-A, extracurricular activity–toned body on that table. First she'd cleave the meat from the bone and then she'd tenderize it into pan-sized fat free filets. The Yale-bound brain she'd pound into a supersized mincemeat pie and deliver to Constance Billard's headmistress in a pretty blue and white china pie dish. . . .

On the butcher block table was today's pile of mail. Serena sifted through it. Mostly there were benefit invitations for her parents—white square envelopes printed with old-fashioned typefaces. Then there were the art openings—postcards with a picture of the artist's work on one side and the details of the opening on the back. One of these caught Serena's attention. It had obviously been lost in the mail for a little while, because it looked beaten up, and the opening it announced was beginning at 5 P.M. on Wednesday, which was . . . *right now.*

Serena flipped the card over and looked at the picture of the artist's work. It looked like a close-up black and white photograph of an eye, tinted pink. The title of the work was *Stefani*, and the name of the show was "Behind the Scene." Serena squinted at the picture. There was something innocent and beautiful about it, and at the same time it was a little gross, like the bloody hole a ski pole made when she used it to stab someone. Maybe it wasn't an eye. She wasn't sure what it was, but it was definitely cool. No question about it, Serena knew what she was doing for the next couple of hours.

Within minutes she was stepping out of a taxi in front of the Whitehot Gallery downtown in Chelsea. The gallery was full of twenty-something hipsters in cool clothes, drinking free martinis and admiring the photographs hanging on the walls. Each picture was similar to the one on the postcard, that same close-up black and white eye, blown up, all in different shapes and sizes and tinted with different colors. Under each one was a label, and on every label was the first name of its subject: Mary-Kate, Justin, Arizona, Taylor, Miranda, James, Emma, Lindsay, Stefani, Ed, Kristen.

French pop music bubbled out of invisible speakers. The photo-artists themselves, the Remi brothers, identical twin sons of a French model and an English duke, were being interviewed and photographed for *Artforum*, *Vogue*, *W*, *New York*, and the *New York Times*.

Serena studied each photograph carefully. They weren't eyes, she decided, now that she was looking at them blown up. But what were they? Belly buttons?

Suddenly Serena felt an arm around her waist.

"Hello, ma chèrie. Beautiful girl. What is your name?"

It was one of the Remi brothers. He was twenty-six years old and five foot nine, the same height as Serena. He had curly black hair and brilliant blue eyes. He spoke with a French and British accent. He was dressed head to toe in navy blue, and his lips were dark red and curved foxily up at the corners. He was absolutely gorgeous, and so was his twin brother.

Lucky girl.

She was still wearing her Constance uniform but Serena didn't resist when he pulled her into a photograph with him and his brother for the *New York Times'* Sunday Styles section. One brother stood behind Serena and kissed her neck while the other knelt in front of her and hugged her knees. Around them, people watched greedily, eager to catch a glimpse of the new "it" girl.

Everyone in New York wants to be famous. Or at least see someone who is so they can brag about it later.

The *New York Times* society reporter recognized Serena from parties a year or so back, but he had to be sure it was her. "Serena van der Woodsen, right?" he said, looking up from his notepad.

Serena blushed and nodded. She was used to being recognized. "You *must* model for us," one of the Remi brothers gasped, kissing Serena's hand.

"You must," the other one agreed, feeding her an olive.

Serena laughed. "Sure. Why not?" Although she had no idea what she was agreeing to.

One of the Remi brothers pointed to a door marked PRIVATE across the gallery. "We'll meet you in there," he said. "Don't be nervous. We're both gay."

Serena giggled and took a big gulp of her drink. Were they kidding? *They* should have been nervous. She had her switchblade with her.

The other brother patted her on the bottom. "It's all right, darling. You're absolutely stunning, so you've got nothing to worry about. Go on. We'll be there in a minute."

Serena hesitated, but only for a second. She could keep up with the likes of Lady Gaga and Emma Watson, no problem. Chin up, she headed for the door marked PRIVATE.

Just then, a guy from the Public Arts League and a woman from the New York Transit Authority came over to talk to the Remi brothers about a new avant-garde public art program. They wanted to put a Remi brothers photograph on the sides of buses, in subways, and in the advertising boxes on top of taxis all over town.

"Yes, of course," the Remis agreed. "If you can wait a moment, we'll have a brand new one. We can give it to you exclusively!"

"What's this one called?" the Transit Authority woman asked eagerly.

"*Serena*," the Remi boys said in unison.

social awareness is next to godliness

"I found a printer who will do it by tomorrow afternoon and hand-deliver each of the invitations so they get there by Friday morning," Laura said, looking pleased with herself for being so efficient.

"But look how expensive it is. If we use them, then we're going to have to cut costs on other things," Blair pointed out. "See how much Alaric is charging us for the flowers?"

As soon as they were finished with their Wednesday after-school activities, the remaining members of the *Kiss Me or Die* organizing committee had convened over french fries and hot chocolate in a booth at the 3 Guys Coffee Shop to deal with the last-minute preparations for the party. Blair Waldorf, Laura Salmon, Rain Hoffstetter, and Tina Ford, from the Seaton Arms School, were all present. Nicki Button, Kati Farkas, and Isabel Coates were not, because they were dead.

The crisis at hand was the fact that the party was only nine days away, and no one had received an invitation yet. The invitations had been ordered weeks ago, but due to a mix-up, the location of the party had to be changed from Pier 60 in Chelsea to the Frick, an old mansion on Fifth Avenue, rendering the invitations useless. The girls were in a tight spot. They had to get a new set of invitations out, and fast, or there wasn't going to be a party at all.

"But Alaric is the *only* place to get flower centerpieces for the tables. I know it's expensive but it's so worth it. Oh, come on, Blair, think how cool they'll be," Tina whined.

"There are plenty of other places to get flowers," Blair insisted.

"Or maybe we can ask the birds of prey people to pitch in," Rain suggested. She reached for a french fry, dunked it in ketchup, and popped it into her mouth. "They've barely done anything."

Blair rolled her eyes and blew into her hot chocolate. "That's the whole point. *We're* raising money for *them*. It's a *cause*."

Rain wound a lock of her gleaming dark hair around her finger. "What is a bird of prey anyway?" she said. "Is it like a woodpecker?"

"No, they're like eagles and vultures," Tina said. "And they eat other animals, like rabbits and mice and squirrels and stuff. Even if they're already dead."

"Gross," Rain said.

"I just read a definition," Laura mused. "I can't remember where I saw it."

On the Internet, perhaps?

"They're almost extinct," Blair added. "Which is sort of the whole point." She thumbed through the list of people they were inviting. Three hundred and sixteen. All young people—no parents, thank God.

Blair's eyes were automatically drawn to a name toward the bottom of the list: Serena van der Woodsen. The address given was her dorm room at Hanover Academy, in New Hampshire. Blair put the list back down on the table without correcting it.

"We're going to have to spend the extra money on the printer and cut corners where we can," she said quickly. "I can tell Alaric to use lilies instead of orchids and forget about the peacock feathers around the rims of the vases."

"I can do the invitations," a small, young-sounding voice spoke up from behind them. "For free."

The four girls turned around to see who it was.

Oh look, it's that little Ginny girl, Blair thought. *The ninth grader who did the calligraphy and creepy dead angel drawings in our school hymnals.*

"I can do them all by hand tonight. The materials are the only cost, but I know where to get good quality paper cheap," Jenny Humphrey said.

"She did all our hymnals at school," Laura whispered to Tina. "They look really good."

"Yeah," Rain agreed. "They're pretty cool."

Jenny blushed and stared at the shiny linoleum floor of the coffee shop, waiting for Blair to make up her mind. She knew Blair was the one who mattered.

"And you'll do it all for free?" Blair demanded suspiciously.

Jenny lifted her gaze. "I was kind of hoping that if I did the invites, maybe I could come to the party?"

Blair weighed the pros and cons in her mind. Pros: The invitations would be unique and, best of all, free, so they wouldn't have to skimp on the flowers. Cons: There really weren't any, except that the little freshman's boobs were going to take up a lot of space at the party.

Blair looked the Ginny girl up and down. Their cute little

ninth-grade helper with the huge chest. She was a total glutton for punishment, and she'd be totally out of place at the party. But who cared?

"Sure, you can make yourself an invitation. Make one for one of your girlfriends, too," Blair said, handing the guest list over to Jenny.

How generous. Too bad she already disposed of Jenny's only girlfriend.

Blair gave Jenny all the necessary information and Jenny dashed out of the coffee shop breathlessly. The stores would be closing soon, and she didn't have much time. The guest list was longer than she'd anticipated, and she'd have to stay up all night working on the invitations, but she was going to the party; that was all that mattered.

Just wait until she told Dan. He was going to *freak*. And she was going to make him come with her to the party, whether he liked it or not—especially since Elise seemed to have moved away without telling her and totally didn't respond to her texts.

She hailed a cab, and told the cabbie to take her to Michaels, the huge crafts store on upper Broadway. The cab's window was halfway down and the crisp late afternoon air had the distinct scent of New York in autumn—a mixture of smoking fireplaces, dried leaves, decomposing bodies, dog pee, and bus exhaust—a scent that to Jenny seemed full of promise. She hugged herself. It was happening: She was going to *Kiss Me or Die*. She'd buy a cool new dress and wear the highest heels she could get away with. She'd straighten her hair—or at least try to—and curl her eyelashes. And at the party she was going to get kissed.

Or die?

natural born killers

Two martinis and three rolls of Remi brothers' film later, Serena jumped out of a cab in front of Constance and ran up the stairs to the auditorium, where the interschool play rehearsal had already begun. After having her photograph taken from every possible angle, she'd had a crisis of conscience, realizing that this sort of extracurricular activity wasn't going to get her into college either. As always, she was half an hour late.

Jaunty piano music drifted down the hallway. Serena pushed open the auditorium door to find an old preschool acquaintance, Ralph Bottoms III, onstage singing "The Ballad of Sweeney Todd" with passion. He was dressed as an old-fashioned barber, complete with fake mustache, open white shirt, suspenders, shiny black boots, and a bloody straight razor. Ralph had gained weight in the last few years, and his face was ruddy, as if he'd been eating too much rare steak. He held hands with a stocky girl with straight black hair and a heart-shaped face, wearing a red velvet nineteenth-century prostitute dress. She was singing too, belting out the words in a thick Korean accent.

"He shaved the faces of gentlemen who never thereafter were heard of again."

Serena leaned against the wall to watch with a mixture of horror and fascination. The scene at the art gallery hadn't fazed her, but this—this was scary. Even the opportunity to wield the bloody straight razor couldn't tempt her.

The drama teacher, a sweaty, enthusiastic Englishwoman in clogs, finished the song with a prolonged piano chord. The rest of the Interschool Drama Club whistled and cheered. Then the drama teacher began to direct the next scene.

"Put your hands on your hips," she instructed. "Show me, show me. That's it. Imagine you're the Justin Bieber of Fleet Street!"

Serena turned to gaze out the window and saw three girls get out of a cab together on the corner of Ninety-third and Madison. She squinted, recognizing Blair, Laura, and Rain. Serena hugged herself, warding off the strange feeling that had been stalking her since she'd come back to the city. For the first time in her entire life, she felt left out.

Without a word to anyone in the drama club—*Hello? Goodbye!*—Serena slipped out of the auditorium and into the hallway outside. The wall was littered with flyers and notices and she stopped to read them. One of the flyers advertised the tryout for Vanessa Abrams's film: *Natural Born Killers, a modern retelling of the violently romantic Oliver Stone classic. Try out for Mallory. Wednesday, sunset. Brooklyn Bridge.*

Knowing what little she did about Vanessa, the film was going to be very serious and obscure, but it was better than shouting goofy songs and doing the Hokey-Pokey with fat, red-faced Ralph Bottoms III. It was still light out. Hopefully the tryout wasn't over. Once again, Serena found herself running for a cab, headed downtown.

"This is how I want you to do it," Vanessa told Marjorie Jaffe, a sophomore at Constance and the only girl who had shown up to try out for the role of Mallory Knox, the murderous teen bride in Vanessa's film. Marjorie was short and stocky, with curly auburn hair, freckles, and a little pug nose. She chewed gum while she talked, had flabby arms that jiggled when she moved them, and was completely, nightmarishly wrong for the part.

The sun was setting and the Brooklyn Bridge pedestrian footpath basked in a pretty pink glow. Ferries, container ships, barges, cruise ships, tugboats, yachts, small motor craft, and sailboats traversed the busy harbor. Cars zoomed back and forth over the bridge and helicopters policed the sky—all under the blandly imperious watch of the Statue of Liberty. The gusty sea air was fresh and cool, but tainted with the scent of New Jersey and the landfill on Staten Island. As always, the footpath was crawling with camera-toting tourists, eager to capture themselves in front of the most famous backdrop in the world.

Dan hung over the side of the bridge, waiting for the enormous orange Staten Island ferry to go off course and crash into Governor's Island. A favorite haiku by Bashō came to mind:

> *A fishy smell—*
> *perch guts*
> > *in the water weeds.*

Dan was dressed in his Mickey Knox costume, with the Paragon Sports price tags tucked in so they wouldn't show, and armed with the bowie knife, a crowbar, and a baseball bat, all hanging from the black yoga mat harness strapped over his shoulders and across his chest. Dan's hollow cheeks and sunken eyes looked almost grotesque in the pinkish-gray twilight, and his ribs stuck out impossibly through the tight white sleeveless rash guard. In him Vanessa thought she had created a very believable psychopath.

"Watch," Vanessa told Marjorie. She yanked the bowie knife out of the hand-stitched leather sheath tied to the harness strapped to Dan's chest, and pretended to cut open her own hand.

"Is that a real knife?" Marjorie whined, chomping on her gum. "What if I cut myself for real?"

Vanessa put her video camera down on the ground.

"Why don't I run through the scene with Dan while you watch?" she said. "We're going to say our lines this time. When you do it you don't need to say them, you just need to think them. Got it?"

She slipped the bowie knife back into its sheath and smiled up at Dan. God, he looked hot. In a starving, miserable sort of way.

"Okay. Let's go. Action!"

Dan swung from the bridge's cables and gaped at the water with a crazed smile. "Life is fragile and absurd. Murdering someone's not so hard." It was the most he'd spoken all day.

Vanessa put her arms around him and yanked the knife from out of its sheath, praying the tourists on the bridge would be too busy taking photographs to pay them any mind. She mimed cutting her hand open, baring her teeth at the pain.

"Mickey Knox, will you marry me?" she asked, wondering if in real life she would ever get to utter those words to Dan. *Will you marry me?*

Dan reached for the knife and cut his own hand open for real. Man, he loved that sharp, sharp knife. "I will," he said. "I will."

It was just a shallow cut, like a paper cut, but still. Vanessa was pissed that he'd gotten the knife dirty. They reached out and clasped each other's hands in a bloody handshake.

"We're Mickey and Mallory Knox now," she proclaimed. "And we'll stay together until we die and die and die again!"

"I love you, Mallory," Dan said quietly, swinging in for a kiss.

Whoa. Vanessa's face flushed red. She'd imagined them kissing hundreds of times, but not like this, in front of an audience, playing other people—playing psychopaths! Before their lips met, she braced her hands against his bony chest and pushed him away. Dan wiped the blood on his hand onto his new white shirt.

So much for returning it.

Vanessa collected her wits. "Now your turn," she told Marjorie.

"'Kay," Marjorie said, chewing her gum with her mouth open. She pulled the purple metallic scrunchy out of her wiry red hair and fluffed it up with her hand. "I'm still kinda scared of that knife though." She held up her script. "'Kay," she said again, bravely. "Let's do it."

Dan slipped the knife back into place and swung his arms around in circles a few times. The crowbar was digging into his back and the baseball bat was giving him splinters.

Vanessa picked up her camera. "Action!"

Dan swung from the cables and said his line, thinking of how much he hated that asshole Chuck Bass and sounding even more convincing this time.

"Mickey Fox, will you marry me?" Marjorie said, batting her eyes flirtatiously and cracking her gum.

Dan closed his eyes. He could get through this without laughing if he kept his eyes closed. "I will. I will."

Marjorie fumbled for the knife. Her gum fell out of her mouth and onto Dan's new Red Wing boots. "Ew!" she shrieked. "The knife—it's got blood on it!"

"Cut!" Vanessa yelled, grateful that they hadn't made it to the kiss. "Marjorie, it's Knox, not Fox. And you're not supposed to be chewing gum or even talking. You're just supposed to be acting."

Someone nudged Vanessa's arm and whispered into her ear. "Can I try?"

Vanessa turned around to find the glorious Serena van der Woodsen standing behind her, windblown and breathless from running halfway across the bridge. Her cheeks were flushed, her golden hair was wild, and her blue eyes gleamed like the darkening sky. Serena was the girl to play Mallory Knox, if ever there was one.

Dan stared at Serena. A Paragon Sports tag sprang out of the waistband of his cargo pants. He wiped the bloody knife on the white rash guard and sheathed the knife, wishing he didn't look like a walking circus act. Instantly a new haiku sprang into his head.

Beautiful stranger,
why are you here? Breathing—
on this bridge tonight?

"Marjorie, I think that's a wrap," Vanessa called over. "Would you mind loaning Serena your script?"

"'Kay."

Serena and Marjorie traded places. Dan had his eyes open

now. He didn't dare blink. Vanessa decided not to give Serena any direction and just see what happened.

"Action!"

They began to read.

"Life is fragile and absurd," Dan felt like shouting, he was so excited. "Murdering someone's not so hard." He'd murder a hundred people if it meant he could be with Serena.

Serena withdrew the knife from its sheath with expert precision. Dan's chest trembled at her almost-touch.

She drew the knife blade against her palm and raised it up to show Dan the cut. Her blood was redder than any he'd ever seen. He wanted to lick it. He wanted to eat her whole hand. Or at least suck on it for a while.

> *Is that juice your blood?*
> *Seasonless fruit—pink, ripe, red.*
> *I thought I was dead.*

"Mickey Knox, will you marry me?" Serena asked with the perfect blend of excitement, expectation, and girlish embarrassment.

Dan took the knife eagerly and hacked at his hand. "I will," he said, meaning every word. Blood dripped on his new pants. "I *will*."

Serena clasped her bleeding hand around his. Dan gasped. He could actually feel their blood mingling and exchanging cells. He felt faint. In fact, he thought he might faint.

> *Like a loose tooth, my*
> *heart dangles. Take it. Keep it—*
> *under your pillow.*

"We're Mickey and Mallory Knox now," Serena was saying. God she was good. "And we'll stay together until we die and die and die again."

Time for the kiss. Dan lurched toward her, stumbling over the laces of his new boots and losing his balance as the crowbar and baseball bat swung from his back in the opposite direction.

"I love you, Mallory," he gasped, falling.

Maybe he should have eaten a muffin or something before play practice.

"Whoa," Serena giggled, catching him.

Dan lay in her arms feeling like he'd died an exquisite death and was now in heaven. Serena was enjoying herself too. Dan was cute and the script was a hoot.

I could get into this. She had never really thought about what she wanted to do with her life, but maybe acting was her thing.

"Cut!" Vanessa shouted. And not too soon either. The chemistry between Dan and Serena was totally nauseating. If there weren't so many people around she would have grabbed that bowie knife and cut Serena's perfect face and body in two and thrown each half off of opposite sides of the bridge.

Boys are so predictable, she thought, angrily snapping the lens protector back onto her camera.

"Thanks, guys." She pretended to scribble comments in a little notebook. "I'll let you know tomorrow, Serena. Okay?" *Fuck off and die,* she scrawled jealously.

"That was fun!" Serena said, taking the knife as she helped the trembling Dan to his feet.

Still hungover from the moment, Dan removed the cumbersome harness and wiped his bloody hands in his hair. It stuck up pinkly, like some kind of messed-up punk do. "You were great," he told Serena earnestly, finding his voice. "Really great."

Vanessa scowled and fiddled with her camera. "Marjorie, I'll let you know tomorrow, too. Okay?" she told the redhead.

"'Kay," Marjorie said, still chomping. "Thanks."

Dan just stood there, swaying weakly in the breeze, his cut hand oozing blood, his hair sticking up, and a goofy smile plastered on his face.

"Thanks so much for letting me try out," Serena told Vanessa sweetly, still holding the knife. She turned to go.

"See you later," Dan said, feeling drugged.

"I live in Brooklyn Heights. So I'm gonna walk home now. Bye," Marjorie called, waving as she continued on across the bridge.

Vanessa looked up from her camera. "Put the harness back on," she told Dan. "We're not done yet. I want to try shooting your monologue."

Dan bent down and put his arms through the straps of the weapon-laden harness once more. The hand-stitched leather sheath dangled emptily from its strap. He whirled around and searched the ground.

"Hey," he said. "Where's the knife?"

But the knife was already headed uptown in a taxi with a certain blonde so used to carrying expensive knives she'd thought nothing of taking it.

vive la france—or maybe not

"Iz dat peppers-oni?"

Nate looked up from his pizza slice. He and his friends had spent the entire afternoon in the park, skipping school, ignoring their cell phones, and basically wasting away the day because it was Wednesday, and Wednesdays sucked.

Nate was supposed to be eating dinner with his parents but had been so overcome by his craving for pizza that he'd made a detour on his way home.

A gorgeous dark-haired L'Ecole girl wearing a minuscule gray flannel uniform skirt and black knee-high high-heeled boots was standing directly in front of him on the sidewalk.

"Iz good?" she asked.

"Uh-huh," he said as the ground lurched beneath him.

Too much sunshine, Sunshine?

"I's been seeing you at diz pizzeria all zee time," the girl said, opening her big, mascaraed, olive green eyes wide. "I's been watching for you!"

Nate chuckled. L'Ecole girls were famous for pretending to barely speak English while, more often than not, they and their

parents were born and raised in the U.S. of A. Their parents thought it would make their daughters more desirable if they were bilingual. The girls thought boys would like them better if they forgot English altogether and just spoke bedroom Franglish. L'Ecole was the only school in the city that allowed their female students to wear high heels, red lipstick, push-up bras, and barely buttoned shirts, which they started to do in sixth grade. By the time they were seniors they were seasoned adulterers. Almost every boy in Nate's St. Jude's class who had lost his virginity had done it with a girl from L'Ecole.

"Pizza is my favorite food," Nate explained, chewing.

It was sort of a relief, talking to a girl who didn't make him work very hard. Blair needed so much attention. And Serena was so . . . dangerous, and demanding in her own way. It was nice to just talk to an easy girl for once.

He held out his slice. "You want a bite?"

Down boy. Down.

Only a few blocks away, Blair marched down Madison toward home, knocking over small children, bumping into parking meters, and nearly besmirching her Chanel flats with German shepherd poo as she checked and rechecked the voicemails, e-mails, and text messages on her phone. She'd sent Nate an e-mail and two texts, and left three voicemails today, and he still hadn't responded to any of them. Not that she needed to see him right now. That would be too distracting. In ten minutes she had to meet her SAT prep tutor at home. Then there was the AP French test to study for, followed by a late dinner with her mom and that nitwit boyfriend of hers. Then she had about three hundred pages of AP English reading to do. Then sleep, followed by tennis early tomorrow morning before school. She just wanted to confirm that Nate was on for Friday night. They were going to have sex and he would spend the night. She liked to know the plan. She hated surprises or deviations of any kind. And they always talked on Wednesdays. So, where the fuck was he?

So close, yet so far away.

Nate took another bite of his pizza. The L'Ecole girl pulled the rubber band holding up her ponytail out of her hair and swung her head from side to side. Her long, nearly black hair cascaded over her shoulders and skimmed her pushed-up breasts.

"What's your name?" he asked.

"Nadège," she said, pursing her full, red-lipsticked lips. "Maman et Papa calls me Nadège after ma grandmére. She was supercool supermodel en France in zee sixties." She arched her thick dark eyebrows sexily and waggled her shoulders so that her milky-white cleavage seemed to be personally introducing itself to Nate. "Nadège meanz 'Hope' en français."

Nate took another bite of pizza, trying to suppress a giggling fit. He *hoped* Nadège might take her clothes off for him, right there on the sidewalk.

"Want another a bite of my pizza, Nadège?" he offered, pointing the slice in the direction of her full red lips.

Blair tucked her phone back into the pocket of her gray cashmere blazer. Nate was with Serena, she was sure of it. There was no other logical explanation. Of course he was with her. Whenever Nate disappeared it was always because of Serena. Blair gritted her teeth. Nate had no idea who he was dealing with. Serena was insane. And she had no feelings for Nate. All she wanted was to take away what was rightfully Blair's—her friends, her boy-friends, her seat at Fashion Week, her spot at Yale, the last pair of size eight silver snakeskin demi boots at Christian Louboutin.

Blair hoped with all her heart that Nate was still alive. After all, she loved him—even if he was a jerk for not calling her back. But whether Serena was kissing him right now or torturing him before she stabbed him to death with a curling iron, Blair was going to rip Serena's head off, boil it in salt water, and serve it with fries the next chance she got.

The sign said DON'T WALK. Blair made a run for it and a cab-bie had to slam on his brakes to avoid her. She glanced across the avenue, at a pizzeria where students from various schools in the neighborhood always gathered. Sure enough, there was Nate, flirting with the sluttiest looking L'Ecole girl Blair had ever seen.

Nate was actually feeding the girl pizza, as if she couldn't feed herself. Knowing the girls from that school, she probably couldn't speak English either. She spoke only the language of slut, with a French accent.

Blair should have been relieved. Nate wasn't with Serena after all. He was alive and eating pizza. But thoughts of Serena had ignited her rage, and somehow seeing Nate with a dark and beau-tiful French girl only served to fuel it.

Crossing Madison on the far corner, Blair darted inside the pizzeria behind Nate's back. She ordered a slice with everything on it, and while the pizza guy was busy with his bins of anchovies, onions, and olives, she snatched his circular pizza knife off the counter and stuffed it into her purse with the deft "you never saw that" motion of an experienced assassin.

Out on the street again with her steaming hot slice of over-decorated pizza, Blair discovered the L'Ecole girl hugging and kissing Nate's face all over as he attempted to peel himself away and say goodbye. Blair slipped around the side of the building to wait.

The French girl had a big appetite. She'd eaten half his slice, and now Nate was still hungry. He headed back inside to order more while Nadège turned down the side street, presumably toward the brothel where she lived.

Blair was waiting for her when she rounded the corner.

"How dare you?" she seethed. The girl's short gray skirt barely covered her underwear.

"Excusez-moi?" The girl paused and gave Blair a quizzical look. "Sorry, my Engleesh not verry—"

"Bullshit," Blair spat. "I know you can understand me. Your parents are probably from Long Island. They probably don't even speak French."

The girl just stood there, staring at Blair. "New Jersey," she admitted, her accent gone. "I was born in Mahwah. My real name is Nancy."

"Shut up!" Blair cried. She dangled the greasy pizza slice in front of the girl's face. "I got you some pizza," she taunted. "You looked like you were pretty hungry, eating *my boyfriend's* pizza." She grabbed the girl by the back of the head and rammed the entire slice into her lipsticked mouth. "Here, have a bite."

The girl gagged and stumbled backwards, but not before Blair slit her throat with the round metal pizza slicer.

Zing!

Blood gushed from her neck, red and thick as tomato sauce.

Ooh la la!

For good measure Blair cut a big slash through the girl's slutty gray uniform skirt, too.

Zing!

The girl teetered on her heels and fell backward into a pile of broken pizza boxes that had been put out to be recycled.

Nate stood in the window of the pizzeria, facing the side street while his second slice with extra cheese was in the oven heating up. The window was lined with shiny chrome, and in the reflection cast by the streetlights he thought he saw his girlfriend Blair use a metal pizza cutter to slit sexy French Nadège's throat from one earlobe to the other. Then she slashed her skirt. Blood was everywhere, and Blair looked like she enjoyed it.

"Dude." Nate pressed his fingertips to his eyes. They felt okay, but surely there was something wrong with the pot in the last joint he'd smoked.

"Dude!" he screamed again, as Nadège fell down dead on the sidewalk. Blair sprinted away, tossing the pizza cutter into the trash can on the corner.

"I'm fucking hallucinating! It's this fucking pot!"

Nate staggered outside, waving his arms wildly. A cab pulled over and he got in.

"Hurry!" he shouted after giving his address. Maybe he was just anxious about Blair discovering that he'd cheated. Maybe he was worried about their hookup this Friday night. Or maybe his eyeballs were really about to explode all over the taxi before he even made it home.

Poor thing. He needs a hot bath and a cup of chamomile tea. And a hug, or two, or three.

a nice slice

Vanessa was in the back of a pedicab, filming background shots for her fucked-up remake of *Natural Born Killers*. She'd instructed the heavy, bearded driver to pedal slowly along the gutter, so as not to shake the camera. Up Madison they went, past Ralph Lauren and E.A.T. and Agnès B. and Crewcuts and Williams-Sonoma. Vanessa wanted to get footage of the ritzy sort of places Mickey and Mallory Knox's victims shopped in before they died.

As the cab cycled past the pizzeria she zoomed in on a body sprawled on top of a pile of bloody pizza boxes. Perfect. A pair of adolescent male vultures swooped in and perched on the body's bare knees. The vultures squawked and strutted and fought for the best feasting spot, flapping their black and brown feathered wings, undulating their raw, pink, white-ruffed necks, and blinking their black, glass bead eyes. Their sharp, hooked, yellowish-gray beaks were punctuated by little pink nostril dents, giving them an almost human appearance.

"Hold it," Vanessa told the pedicab driver. "I have to get this."

She got out of the pedicab and approached the murder scene. The vultures were pecking at the ground now, tossing their heads back as they swallowed the larger morsels. And it wasn't pizza they were eating.

gossipgirl.net

Disclaimer: All the real names of places, people, and events have been altered or abbreviated to protect the innocent. Namely, me.

| topics | sightings | your e-mail | post a question |

hey people!

AN ICEBERG

I was in an interschool play once. I had one great line: "Iceberg!" Guess which play I was in and what I was dressed as? The one hundredth person to get it right will win a Remi brothers original print.

But enough about me.

S'S MODELING DEBUT!

Be on the lookout this weekend for the cool new poster decorating the sides of buses, the insides of subways, the tops of taxis, and available online through yours truly. It's a great big picture of *S*—not her face, but it has her name on it so you'll know it's her. A particular part of her, anyway. Congratulations to *S* on her modeling debut!

SIGHTINGS

B, *L*, and *R* all in **3 Guys** eating fries and hot chocolates with big fat **Bendel's** bags under the table. Don't those girls have anywhere else to go? And we thought they were always out boozing it up and partying down. So disappointing. I did see *B* slip a few splashes of brandy into her hot chocolate, though. Naughty girl, that's more like it. Also saw that same wigged girl going into the STD clinic downtown. If that is **S**, she's definitely got a bad case of the nasties. Oh, and in case you're wondering why I frequent the neighborhood of the STD clinic—I get my hair trimmed at a very trendy salon across the street.

YOUR E-MAIL

q: dear gossip girl,
are u really even a girl? u seem like the type 2 pretend to be a girl when u'r really a 50-yrs-old bored journalist with nothing better 2 do than to harsh on kids like me. loser.
—jdwack

a: Dearest jdwack,
I'm the girliest girl you'd ever want to meet. And I'm pre-college, pre-voting age, too. How do I know you're not some bitter fifty-year-old geometry teacher with boils on her face taking her inner angst out on innocent girls like me—with a really sharp and scary protractor? Well, my ovoids are bigger than your ovoids. So there.
—GG

q: Dear GG,
I loooove your column so much I showed it to my dad, and he was like, Wow. Everyone wants to know what's going on at the private schools because of all the murders and disappearances. And you have the inside story! Anyway, he has friends who work at the *Observer* and the *New Yorker*. Don't be surprised if your column gets much, much bigger!! I hope you don't mind!!! Love always!!!
—JNYHY

a: *Mind*? No way. I'm all about being big. I'm going to be *huge*. No more crappy one-line parts in interschool plays for me. You might even see me on the side of a bus sometime soon.

If I can stay intact. It's time to start watching our backs, people, and our heads. You've seen the vultures hovering.

I've got your back if you've got mine.

You know you love me,

gossip girl

dissed at recess

"Yum!" Serena crowed, eyeing the cookies laid out on a table in the Constance lunchroom on Thursday. Peanut butter cream, chocolate chip, oatmeal. Next to the cookies were plastic cups full of orange juice or milk. An angry-looking, mustachioed lunch lady doled out the cookies two at a time, rapping students' knuckles with a pair of plastic serving tongs if they tried to take more. This was recess, the daily twenty-minute break Constance gave its girls after second period, no matter what grade they were in.

When the lunch lady's head was turned, Serena grabbed a fistful of peanut butter creams and glided away to stuff her face. It wasn't exactly a healthy breakfast, but it would have to do. She'd stayed up most of the night watching the original *Natural Born Killers* so she'd be better prepared for Vanessa's film, and had woken up five minutes before school began.

Not even enough time to knock someone off on the way.

Vanessa stood on the other side of the cafeteria, blowing into a cup of hot black tea, wearing her usual black turtleneck and bored, angry expression. Serena waved a cookie at her and strode over to say hello.

"Hi," Serena greeted her cheerfully. "Oh my God. I totally took your knife yesterday. I'm such a dope with stuff like that. I steal pens, lip gloss, knives. I'm an idiot." She shook her blond mane to indicate how scatterbrained she was. "I'll get it back to you eventually. Anyway, I watched the original movie last night. Insane—loved it! Yours is going to be even better though. When do we start shooting?"

God, she was cocky. Vanessa waited a moment before answering, allowing the steam from her tea to open up the pores on her chin. She'd tossed and turned all night trying to decide between Serena and Marjorie. Obviously Serena was perfect—too perfect. Vanessa would never forget the moony, dazed, lovestruck expression on Dan's face when he read with Serena. She never wanted to see that again, and she certainly didn't want to capture it on film, unless it involved sawing Serena's pretty head off with a chainsaw on film too.

But that would be a different movie.

Vanessa sipped her tea. "Actually," she responded in a measured voice, "I haven't told Marjorie yet, but I'm giving her the part."

Serena dropped the cookie she was eating on the floor. "Oh."

"Yeah." Vanessa scrambled for a decent reason why she was using Marjorie when Serena was obviously perfect for the part. "Marjorie's really rough and innocent. That's what I'm looking for. Dan and I thought your performance was just a bit too . . . um . . . polished."

"Oh," Serena repeated. She could hardly believe it. Even Dan had vetoed her? But he was so *sweet*. She could feel the consternation bubbling up inside her. No part meant no extra-curricular, which meant no college, which meant doom. If only she hadn't left the knife at home in the old violin case where she'd begun to store all her weapons, she could have used it on Vanessa right now.

Stop it, she told herself. *It's Blair you want to kill now, remember?* Blair was the one trumping everyone with a million extra-curriculars. Blair was the one applying early to Yale, the one harboring Nate, the one acting like such a jerk. Blair was the one who was ruining her life.

"Sorry." Vanessa felt sort of bad for bringing Dan into it. He didn't even know what she'd decided. But it sounded more professional this way; like it wasn't anything personal, it was strictly business. "You have talent," she added. "And I'm going to be filming lots of background stuff. Maybe you can do a cameo, you know, if I happen to catch you in the middle of something really wild."

"Okay," Serena replied through tightly clenched teeth. If Vanessa really wanted something wild, she could give it to her *now*—her own entrails smeared on the cafeteria mirror, maybe, with the lunch ladies' heads all lined up in a row on the floor beneath.

"Don't be discouraged," Vanessa went on. "And don't forget about the knife. I need that fucker back."

At sound of the word *knife*, Serena's muscles tensed. Her anger reared and bucked and fought for its head. No halfway decent college was going to want her now. Her parents would be so disappointed. Damn, she needed to stab someone. It was all she could think about. *Stab, stab, stab.* She bit into a cookie and chewed it up, hard. *Damn, damn, damn.*

Vanessa turned away to call Marjorie and tell her the good news. At least Marjorie lived in Brooklyn. Vanessa could warn her to stay home when she finally got the nerve and enough ammo to blow up Constance with all the pompous knife-stealing bitches like Serena still locked up inside.

She was going to have to change the entire film now that Marjorie her star. It would have to be a comedy. Or maybe she'd wind up using more background stuff and less acting altogether. She already had that great scene from the pizzeria. At least she'd saved herself from making *Endless Love at First Sight on the Bridge After Dark*, starring the gorgeous Serena van der Woodsen and the stupid Daniel Humphrey. Blech.

Serena stood in the corner of the cafeteria, crumbling the remaining cookies in her hand as she tried to calm down. *Sweeney Todd* was a cheesefest and she was too polished for *Natural Born Killers*. What else could she do? She chewed on her thumbnail, deep in thought. Killing Vanessa and Dan wouldn't get her anywhere. She could kill Marjorie, but that seemed sort of unsportsmanlike. She would just have to let it go.

And maybe she could make a movie of her own. When they were younger, Blair and Serena had always talked about making movies. Blair was always going to be the star, wearing cool miniskirts and screaming her head off like Mia Farrow in *Rosemary's Baby* or Janet Leigh in *Psycho*. And Serena always wanted to direct. She would wear floppy linen pants and shout through a bullhorn and sit in a chair with the letter *S* on it.

Maybe she had it all wrong. Maybe Blair didn't have to die after all. What was that expression—something about turning lemons into lemon juice? Maybe this was their chance to do something together and become friends again. She was Serena van der Woodsen, and lemon juice went great with ice and gin.

"Blair!" Serena shouted when she saw Blair by the milk

table. She rushed over excitedly. "I need your help," she gushed, squeezing Blair's arm.

Blair kept her body stiff until Serena let go.

"Sorry." Serena let her hand drop. "But I have the best, best, best idea! I want to make a movie, but I have no idea how to work the cameras and stuff and you do, because you take Film. Remember how we always wanted to make movies together? Well, here's our chance! I'll be the director, and you can be the star!"

Blair glanced at Rain and Laura, quietly sipping their milk. She smiled grimly and shook her head. "Sorry, I can't. I've got activities every single day after school. I don't have time."

"Oh please, Blair," Serena begged, grabbing her old friend's hand. "Remember, you can be Janet Leigh. And I'll be . . . Oliver Stone!"

Blair dragged her hand away and folded her arms across her chest so Serena couldn't touch her anymore.

"I'll do all the work," Serena added desperately. "All you have to do is show me how to use the camera and the lighting and stuff. And we can go shopping and pick out the coolest costumes. We can go to Chanel—"

"I can't," Blair interrupted her. "Sorry."

Serena couldn't have been more hurt if Blair had drawn a serrated knife across her cheek and then stabbed her in the liver. She mashed her lips together to keep them from trembling. Her eyes seemed to be growing larger and larger, and her face was turning splotchy.

Blair had seen this transformation in Serena many times as they grew up together. Serena was about to have a tantrum. Once, when they were both eight, they had walked the three miles from Serena's country house into the town of Ridgefield to buy ice cream cones. Serena stepped out of the ice cream shop with her triple strawberry cone with chocolate sprinkles and bent down to pet a puppy tied up outside. All three scoops fell splat into the dirt. Serena's eyes had grown huge and her face looked like she had the measles. Serena was collecting rocks to throw at the puppy and at the shop window when the nice ice cream man came out with a fresh cone and made it all better.

Seeing Serena on the verge of a tantrum once more touched something deep inside of Blair, like an involuntary reflex. Perhaps she wanted to protect herself. Perhaps she wanted to protect her friends—the few who were still living. Perhaps she wanted to protect the school, where she had gone every day since she was five.

"Want to meet up on Friday?" she asked Serena in a neutral tone. "Drinks around eight at the Tribeca Star?"

Serena took a deep breath and swallowed her rage. "Just like old times?" she asked, her voice quavering.

"Right," Blair assured her. "Exactly."

She made a note in her mental Google calendar to tell Nate not to meet her until later now that Serena was coming out. The new plan was to knock back a few calming, highly alcoholic drinks with Serena at the Tribeca Star, leave early, go home, fill her room with candles, take a bath, and wait for Nate to arrive. Then they'd have sex all night long while listening to the weird Hawaiian music she'd loaded on to her iPod late last night. She wanted Friday night to feel special and different. Like she and Nate were on the beach in Kauai with nothing but the waves and their warm naked bodies, thousands of miles away from any slutty French girls or boyfriend-stealing freakshows.

"Cool," Serena agreed. She sniffed and wiped her nose on the sleeve of the camel-colored Max Mara cardigan she'd stolen from her mom. "Can't wait 'til Friday."

The bell rang and the girls went their separate ways to class; Blair and Rain to their AP Academic Achievers afternoon, and Serena to her plain old Kraft American slices classes.

On her way, Serena popped her head into the photography lab to see if there was any equipment she could steal to make the film she had absolutely no idea how to make, especially not without Blair's help. God, Blair was mean. Serena still didn't feel one hundred percent calmed down. In fact, she was still sort of shaking.

It was dark in the lab. Anna Quintana swished some undeveloped film around in a washtub full of clear, potent fixer, using a pair of black plastic tongs. Her short blond bob was tucked into a navy blue Constance Billard softball cap and her muscular legs rippled in a pair of silver Lycra jogging pants. She whipped her head around and glared at Serena.

"Just so you know," Anna growled, "Isabel texted me. Right before she and Kati disappeared?" She waved the tongs around in the air. "We'd been talking because she needed to add a sport and she wanted to try out for soccer. She said she'd just seen you, and you and Nate had hooked up. He was like, in the shower, which is so gross."

She swished the picture around in the fixer.

"I mean my first thought was, I wonder what Blair would think. And I bet you threatened Kati and Is. I bet you like, murdered them, like, seconds after she texted me."

Anna lifted the picture out of the fixer and clothespinned it to a line overhead to dry. She leveled her green eyes at Serena and added accusingly, "You're like . . . not a good person."

Serena gave Anna her famously luminous smile. She'd wanted to kill someone at recess. Now was her chance.

"I'm in kind of a bad mood," she warned. "Maybe you should be a little nicer to me."

Anna's blond eyebrows shot up in alarm. "Is that a threat?"

Serena shrugged her shoulders. "Not really." She strode calmly across the darkroom, knocked off Anna's softball cap, and seized the blunt blond strands of the girl's hair. "This is more of a threat."

Anna tried to stomp on Serena's foot with her soccer cleats. "Ow. Ow. Ow. Help! Stop it. Ow! Help! Ow!!"

Serena dunked Anna's head in the tub of fixer. "If you haven't got anything nice to say, don't say anything at all."

Anna thrashed her feet. Chocolate chip cookie vomit spewed out of her mouth as she drowned. The air was filled with the fixer's formaldehyde scent mixed with the stench of burnt sugar and rotting chocolate.

Anna's cleated feet kept thrashing until, at last, she was dead.

Serena washed her hands carefully in the darkroom sink and examined the video cameras clustered on a shelf. The cameras were complicated and intimidating. Even if she stole one she wouldn't know how to use it. Besides, she and Blair were going out for drinks tomorrow night with Nate and the rest of the gang. Maybe after a few drinks she'd be able to talk Blair into making the movie with her. And if Blair *still* didn't want to, she might let loose with that tantrum after all. She wouldn't give up so easily.

Her picture wasn't on the side of a bus for nothing.

westsider's romantic dream up in smoke

Vanessa spent the first five minutes of Calculus in the darkroom, filming Anna Quintana's drowned, fixer- and vomit-soaked body before someone cleaned it up. She'd gone in there for a new lens cap and was pleasantly surprised to discover even more great background footage for her film.

Satisfied, she stepped outside school and tried to call Dan. She knew he had Study Hall fourth period on Thursdays. He was probably hanging out outside, writing suicidal haikus while he asphyxiated himself with nicotine. She paced up and down Ninety-third Street, waiting for him to venture out of his manic-depressive vow of silence and answer his fucking phone.

The lower school boys were using the Riverside Prep court-yard for a game of dodgeball, so Dan had exiled himself to a park bench in the traffic island in the middle of Broadway. He'd just cracked open a new collection of haikus by Bashō, Buson, and Issa, which he was reading in the original Japanese, just to torture himself. Dan didn't even take Japanese. He had to use a pocket Japanese dictionary to decipher every line. It was impossible, but he felt pretty hardcore. People hurried past in a busy blur, while he, Dan, just sat there on the bench in the median, poisoning his body with caffeine and nicotine, slowly dying, with a book of indecipherable symbols. There was a certain calm about him today. A certain beauty.

> *People visiting all day—*
> *in between*
> *the quiet of the peony.*

No one paid him any mind. They didn't even realize that he was different today. They didn't notice that the circles under his eyes were more pronounced than usual. That his pale cheeks were more hollow. They didn't know that Dan was *in love*.

He'd lain awake all night, thinking of Serena. They were starring in a movie together. They were even going to kiss. It was too good to be true.

Poor dude, he has that right.

Dan noticed his cell phone ringing.

"Konnichiwa," he answered in Japanese, with uncharacteristic cheer.

"About fucking time," Vanessa snapped. "I thought maybe you were dead."

"Not yet," Dan joked. It was fun to make a joke.

"Listen, I'm supposed to be in Math, so I have to make this quick. I just wanted you to know that I told Marjorie she has the part."

"You mean Serena," Dan said, flicking his ash and taking another drag on his cigarette.

"No, I mean Marjorie."

Dan exhaled and pressed the phone tight against his ear.

"Wait. What are you talking about? Marjorie, with the red hair and the gum?"

"Yes, that's right. I haven't got their names mixed up," Vanessa said patiently.

"But Marjorie stank, you can't use her!"

"Yeah, well, I kind of like that she stank. She's sort of rough around the edges. I think it will make it feel edgier, you know? Like, not what you'd expect."

"Yeah, definitely not," Dan sneered. "Look, you're making a huge mistake. Serena . . . I don't know why you wouldn't want her. She's awesome. This isn't about the knife, is it? I'm sure she'll bring it back."

"She didn't bring it to school today," Vanessa snapped. "Anyway, it's my movie, so it's my choice, and I choose Marjorie." Vanessa really didn't want to hear about how awesome Serena was. "Besides, I keep hearing all these stories about Serena. I don't think she's all that reliable."

Vanessa was pretty sure that everything she'd heard was completely bogus, but it couldn't hurt to mention it to Dan.

"What do you mean?" Dan said. "What stories?"

"Like she manufactures her own drug called S, and she has some pretty bad STDs," Vanessa said. "And she possibly might have murdered some kid up at boarding school. I really don't want to deal with that."

"Where'd you hear that?" Dan demanded.

"I have my sources," Vanessa insisted vaguely.

A bus roared up Madison on its way to the Cloisters. On the side of it was a massive photograph of a belly button. Or was it a gunshot wound? Scrawled in blue girly writing on the side of the poster was the name "Serena."

Vanessa stared after the bus. Was she losing her mind? Or was Serena really and truly everywhere? Every last bit of her?

"I just don't think she's right for us," Vanessa insisted, hoping Dan would come around if she used the word *us*. It was *their* movie, not just hers. "Besides," Vanessa said, remembering her footage of that L'Ecole girl, splayed on the pizza boxes, and of the body she'd just discovered in the darkroom. "I've been getting all this amazing background stuff for the movie. I'm beginning to think I don't need actors. It'll be like, a documentary almost."

"Fine," Dan responded coldly. The words from the angry, life-is-shit Bashō haiku he'd just translated came into his head:

> *Fleas, lice,*
> *a horse peeing*
> *near my pillow.*

"So, want to come out with me and Ruby in Brooklyn tomorrow night?" Vanessa asked, eager to change the subject.

"Nah." Dan clicked off and tossed the phone angrily into his black courier bag.

That morning Jenny had stumbled into his room, eyes all bloodshot, hands covered in red ink, and dropped an invitation to that stupid birds of prey party on the floor beside his bed. He'd actually dared to think that since he was going to be Serena's costar, he might take her to the goddamned party as his date. Now, that little dream was all shot to hell.

Dan couldn't believe it. His one chance to get to know Serena was gone because Vanessa wanted to exercise her artistic license to make the worst film ever made. It was unbelievable. More unbelievable still was that Vanessa, queen of the alterna-rebel scene, had stooped to spreading rumors about a girl she barely knew. Maybe Constance was finally rubbing off on her.

Oh, don't be a spoilsport. Gossip is sexy. Gossip is good. Not everybody does it, but everybody should!

Dan headed back across Broadway toward school. Chuck Bass was standing outside the school doors with Jeffrey Prescott and Roger Paine, smoking Marlboros.

"Just wait 'til I get her up in my suite," Chuck was saying. "She can slice me and dice me as many ways as she wants to."

Dan paused to eavesdrop, pretending to check the messages on his phone.

"You think Serena could really off someone?" Jeffrey said. "Like, with her bare hands?"

"Bare hands. Bare everything!" Chuck crowed.

"Shit." Roger shook his head. "You think she's the one making all those Constance babes disappear?"

Chuck shrugged his shoulders. "Only chicks gone are the ugly ones, so it's not like I'm heartbroken."

"Survival of the fittest!" Jeffrey shouted, slapping palms with Chuck.

Dan lit another cigarette and then tossed it aside without smoking it. He felt a little sick. Not because he believed what Chuck and his friends were saying, but because for the first time in his life he truly felt angry enough to kill someone other than himself. Angry enough that he could taste Chuck's rich, coppery blood as it streamed out of the stumps left by his severed tongue and amputated pigskin loafer–wearing feet.

Or maybe it was just instant coffee residue, all gunked up on his molars.

A bus stopped at a light right in front of the school. First Dan noticed Serena's name. It was scrawled in blue, in messy girl's handwriting on a giant black and white poster of what looked like a rosebud. It was beautiful.

He turned his attention back to Chuck.

Oh roses so red—
my blood is not blue.
You fuck with me, and I'll kill you.

little j, little j, run for your life

Jenny felt like a zombie on Thursday from missing a whole night's sleep, but she was actually still alive, which was something to be proud of these days. She'd gotten all the *Kiss Me or Die* invitations done—calligraphied by hand, with a perfect little heart-shaped blood red ink spatter on each one—and now she and Dan each had an invitation of their very own. The rest of the invitations were all wrapped up in a plastic Gristedes bag in her backpack, ready to be hand delivered to Blair Waldorf the moment Jenny saw her.

It was already lunchtime and Jenny was ravenous. Last night, in a rare eating frenzy, her pig of a brother had devoured all her raw ground beef. The only meat left was a can of Marx's vile-smelling Fancy Feast, but Marx had gobbled it right up the minute Jenny spooned it into a bowl.

Bypassing the grilled cheese sandwiches and Dannon yogurt, Jenny wrangled two raw hot dogs and three raw tuna sushi rolls out of the Constance lunch ladies, then stopped off at the salad bar to stock up on boiled eggs. She carried her feast to the far corner of the cafeteria, looking for a quiet table where she could make up the homework she'd skipped last night.

With only her backpack for company, she began pulling raw tuna strips out of their seaweed and cold rice casing, wrapping them around pieces of raw hot dog before stuffing the whole lot into her mouth. As she chewed she began to notice how eerily quiet the cafeteria was.

Every day it seemed to grow quieter and quieter. Some of the loudest girls were dead or missing. Some girls' parents were keeping them home from school, just to be safe. In less than a week the noise inside the cafeteria had gone from loud hysterics to hushed information-infused whispers to a completely dead and stony silence.

It was totally creepy. But at least it meant Jenny could get a good table.

She whacked a boiled egg against her tray and began to peel it, scattering broken white eggshells all over her navy blue uniform and onto her plate. The egg was not quite hard-boiled, and she quickly sucked out the yellow yolk, reveling in the almost-raw taste of the soft, sulfuric gunk.

A cold draft ran through the cafeteria. Goosebumps stood out on her arms and legs. Did someone open a window?

Jenny shivered and glanced behind her, choking when she saw Serena van der Woodsen coming out of the lunch line and making a beeline for her table. Was Serena actually going to sit with her, live and in person?

More to the point: Would she live to tell the tale?

Jenny put down her mangled egg and tried to compose her face into a semi-cool expression. Deep breath in, deep breath out.

"Hi!" Serena beamed at Jenny and set down her tray. "You're the girl from the bathroom." *You're lucky to be alive,* she almost added, but she didn't want to be mean.

God, Serena was beautiful. Her hair was the pale gold color some of the other Constance girls tried to achieve by spending four hours at the hair salon. But hers was natural. Or maybe she was some kind of albino.

"Hungry?" Serena asked, pointing at Jenny's messy tray.

Jenny nodded, speechless in the presence of such greatness.

"I can't eat again 'til dinner," Serena sighed, resting her beautiful head on her arms. "I ate six cookies this morning. I'm such a pig."

Jenny poked at her hot dogs. She couldn't believe she'd gotten two. Serena probably thought she was some sort of glutton. And she couldn't believe they were talking. Like friends. Just hanging out.

"Oh!" Jenny exclaimed, remembering the invitations. She reached into her backpack and pulled out the Gristedes bag. "I just finished the invitations for that big party next week that everyone's going to," she gushed, eager to impress.

Serena lifted her head. "What party?"

Jenny opened the Gristedes bag and sorted through the stack of thick, cream-colored envelopes. "You know, the one Blair Waldorf's running?" She came to an envelope with Serena's name printed on it in ornate gold calligraphy. The red ink spatter heart on this one was particularly well executed. She handed the envelope to Serena. "The guest list Blair gave me still had your boarding school address. I was going to slip it into your locker or something," she said, blushing. "But now that you're here . . ."

Serena frowned down at the envelope in her hand. "Thanks."

You sound like a stalker, Jenny scolded herself. *Slip it into her locker? You didn't have to say that!*

Serena ripped open the envelope and read the invitation inside, her eyes dark, her forehead creased.

Oh, God. She thinks it's ugly! Jenny panicked, all the while taking mental notes on how to act as mysterious, poised, and cool as Serena was acting at that very moment.

If only she could have heard the livid thoughts in Serena's head, railing against Blair. *She didn't want me to come to the party. She didn't even tell me there was a party. How selfish. How mean. She totally deserves to die.*

"Ginny? What are you doing?"

Both Jenny and Serena turned to look. Blair stood just a few feet away, her foxlike face flushed and angry-looking.

"Ginny, can I talk to you for a moment in private?" Blair called. "We can go in the darkroom."

Serena grabbed Jenny's arm protectively. "Don't go anywhere with her," she whispered. "You stay right here."

"Ginny?" Blair intoned angrily. "I'm speaking to you."

It was terrifying to disobey Blair Waldorf, but Jenny listened to Serena and stayed frozen in her spot. She held up the Gristedes bag. "I have the invitations," she told Blair. "See? They're all done." She pointed at Serena's. "I think they turned out great."

Blair came over and snatched away the flimsy Gristedes bag. "I hope you're not handing them out to just anyone," she snapped.

Jenny's face flushed. The cafeteria was even quieter than it had been before.

Serena wondered what would happen if she grabbed Jenny's fork and stabbed Blair in the neck. It probably wouldn't kill her. She could throw her through a window afterwards, but that might not kill her either.

"Serena was on the list," Jenny said defensively.

Blair smirked. It was all she could do to restrain herself from wrapping the dinky plastic Gristedes bag around Ginny's perky little face and suffocating her, but then the party invitations would get creased and that would never do.

"Jenny corrected my address," Serena said coldly.

"I can see that," Blair replied.

"It sounds like a great party," Serena enthused fakely.

"It's a really good cause," Blair answered fakely back. She glared down at little Ginny, who seemed so thrilled to be caught in the middle of their conversation. *If only I had a pole*, Blair thought. *A long, sharp pole. I could ram it right through Ginny's rib cage and then right through Serena's too. Right into the wall, where I'd let them hang, like warning flags: Don't mess with Blair Waldorf, or you'll wind up stuck on a pole, hanging from the wall.*

"Guess I better get a new dress," Serena observed, rising to her feet. She was taller than Blair, and she was wearing her boots. She could probably stomp Blair to death if she stomped for long enough.

"Me too!" Jenny clapped her hands together. Life was full of miracles. As long as she could stay alive, it would only get better and better. She grinned giddily up at Serena. "Blair let me make an invitation for myself."

"You're lucky," Serena said, reaching for Jenny's fork.

"Really lucky," Blair agreed, stuffing the invitations into her red Longchamp tote. She'd wanted to strangle little Ginny in the darkroom to pay her back for intervening, but the invitations had to be stamped and mailed, and she was running out of time. She raised a perfectly plucked eyebrow at Serena and attempted a smile.

"See you tomorrow night?"

Serena stabbed the fork into one of Jenny's hot dogs and attempted to smile back. "I can hardly wait."

Tension like this might call for something sharper than a fork.

gossipgirl.net

Disclaimer: All the real names of places, people, and events have been altered or abbreviated to protect the innocent. Namely, me.

topics   sightings   your e-mail   post a question

hey people!

S AND *B* HEAT UP THE HOT TUB!

This just in from an anonymous source: Apparently, back when they were still inseparable, *S* and *B* used to spend a lot of time together in the hot tub. I'm not talking about the wooden barrel hot tub Olga and Jurgen have out back behind the cottage in Sweden. I'm talking about the notoriously big and swanky marble hot tub in *C*'s suite at the Tribeca Star. Between soakings, *S* and *B* were known to beat each other's naked bodies raw with green willow sticks. Two silly drunk girls practicing a sacred Eastern European spa treatment, or an expression of their true feelings? Maybe they've hated each other all along!

HOT TUB

LADY GAGA, *S*, AND ME

In case you haven't seen the poster plastered on all the buses, taxis, and subways all over town, the original photo of *S* can still be seen at the Whitehot Gallery in Chelsea, amidst portraits of other notorious scenesters, myself included. Bet your bottom, darling! The Remi brothers know a good one when they see it. And now you can see it too. Wink, wink. An icon knows a good icon when she sees it, and I can tell you, like Warhol before them, the Remis are icons-in-the-making. All they have to do now is die young, which isn't such a challenge these days.

YOUR E-MAIL

q: Dear Gossip Girl,
I won't tell you who I am, but I'm in the Remi brothers show too. I really love their work, and I love the picture they took of me, but no way would I let them put it on the side of a bus. If you ask me, *S* is asking for it.
—Anonomy

a: Dear Anonomy,
It's cool to be modest, but personally, if you wanted to put any bit of me on the side of a bus, I'd be willing. Nobody knows you if nobody knows you.
—GG

SIGHTINGS

Little *J* buying twelve pounds of ground chuck at **Gristedes**. Fueling up for a big night, *J*? *N* hanging out with *C* at a bar over on First Avenue. Guess *N* wants to keep his eye on *C* so *C* doesn't spill the beans, huh? *V* filming rats in the subway. No comment. And *B*, buying candles and body paint at **Ricky's** on Seventy-eighth and Lex for her big night with *N*. Body paint? No comment.

That's all for now. See you at brunch with the parents on Sunday.

You know you love me,

gossip girl

friday the thirteenth: the showdown

The Star Lounge in the Tribeca Star Hotel was big and swanky, filled with comfy black velvet armchairs and ottomans and circular black velvet banquettes, so that the guests could feel like they were having their own private party at each table. The walls were painted dark purple with the ash from that big Icelandic volcano thrown at them, giving the place an eerie, celestial air. Panda bear rugs were tossed willy-nilly across the floor. Black candles flickered on low black-lacquered tables. A famous DJ wearing a hockey mask played the soundtracks to old movies like *Rocky Horror Picture Show* and *The Exorcist*, layering in sitar music and chill dance beats. It was only eight o'clock, but the Star Lounge was the bar of the moment, and it was already jammed with people, all dressed in the hottest fashions and sipping the newest cocktail concoctions.

Blair didn't care what time it was or what she was wearing or what she drank—she just needed a drink.

The stupid bitch of a cocktail waitress was ignoring her because she was wearing faded Hudson jeans and a boring black sweater. Pretty soon, though, she'd be naked, greeting Nate at the door, her body covered in paint.

Sex was a big deal, and Blair had decided to decorate herself with body paint for the occasion, with colorful, suggestive arrows and street signs leading to all the right places, sort of like a Keith Haring painting. Nate was going to love it. Her face grew hot just thinking about it! She looked around the room self-consciously. She felt like a loser sitting all by herself without even a drink. Where was Serena, anyway? She didn't have all goddamned night. She still had to straighten her hair and pick the right glasses for the wine.

If Serena doesn't show up within five minutes, I'm going to shove that burning black candle up that rude cocktail waitress's left nostril, and then get the fuck out of here, she told herself sulkily.

"Ooh. Look at *her*," Blair heard a woman whisper to her friend. "Isn't she something?"

Blair turned to look. And of course it was Serena.

She wore blue suede knee-high boots and a real Pucci-print minidress with swirls of neon blue, traffic cone orange, and lime green. The dress was long-sleeved with a mock turtleneck and a beaded crystal belt. In an ode to Vidal Sassoon, Serena had pulled her hair into a high, tight ponytail on top of her head, with the ponytail part swooping down toward her perfect chin in an angular blond Nike swoosh. Pale blue eye shadow brought out the lake blue of her eyes, and her smiling lips wore a creamy shade of light pink. She waved at Blair from across the room and wove her way through the crowd. Blair watched the heads turn as she passed, and her stomach churned. Just wait 'til she choked them all with the belt of Serena's tacky Pucci dress.

"Hi!" Serena plunked herself down on the black velvet ottoman beside Blair's chair.

Immediately, the cocktail waitress appeared.

"Missy," Serena greeted her with a warm kiss.

"Hey!" Missy exclaimed, delighted that Serena remembered her name. "My sister said she saw you a few days back at a party she was working down in Chelsea. Said that's you in the picture on all those buses. That true?"

Blair rolled her eyes in disgust. All she wanted was a fucking drink.

"That's me. Pretty crazy, huh?"

"You are so rad!" Missy squealed. She glanced at Blair, who was glaring at her. "What can I get you girls?"

"Black Russian," Blair told her, looking her straight in the eye, daring her to card them.

But Missy would rather slit her own wrists than hassle Serena van der Woodsen for being underage.

Hotels are havens for heathens. Which is why we love them so.

"And for you, sweetie?" Missy asked Serena.

"Oh, I'll have a Dark and Stormy," Serena said. "With extra lemons."

Missy hurried away to fetch the drinks, eager to tell the bartender that the girl in the Remi brothers' photo that was all over town was sitting in their bar, and they were pals!

"Sorry I'm late," Serena told Blair, looking around. "I thought everyone else would be here with you."

Blair shrugged her shoulders. "I thought we could hang out by ourselves for a while. No one really comes out until later, anyway."

"Okay," Serena said. Talking alone was a good start. She smoothed out her dress and dug around in her little red purse for a pack of cigarettes. Gauloises, from France. She tapped one out and stuck it in her mouth. "Want one?" she offered Blair.

Blair shook her head no. "You can't smoke in restaurants in this country, remember?" She rolled her eyes. Serena was worse than the girls from L'Ecole.

"Oh, I don't care." Serena laughed. She was about to light up with a match when the bartender swooped in with a lighter.

"Thanks," Serena said, taking a puff. The bartender winked and swiftly stepped back behind the bar. Blair wanted to grab his lighter, pour vodka on the floor, and set the whole place on fire, but before she could move Missy brought them their drinks.

"To old times," Serena said, clinking her glass against Blair's and taking a long sip. She sat back on her stool and sighed with pleasure. "Don't you just love hotels?" she said. "They're so full of secrets."

Blair raised her eyebrows at Serena in silent response, sure that Serena was about to tell her all the wild and crazy things that had happened to her in hotels while she was in Europe last summer. All the boys she'd had sex with and then decapitated or scalped. Whatever. As if Blair cared.

"I mean, don't you always think about what everyone's doing upstairs in their rooms? Like, they could be watching pornos and eating cheese puffs, or they could be stabbing each other in the shower. Or maybe they're ODing on baby aspirin."

Sounds like she's speaking from experience.

"Uh-huh," Blair murmured, gulping her drink. She would have to get pretty drunk if she was going to make it through the night, especially the body paint part. "So what's this about your picture being all over buses and stuff?" she said. "I haven't seen it."

Serena giggled and leaned toward Blair confidentially. "Even if you saw it, you probably wouldn't recognize me. It has my name on it, but it's not a picture of my face."

Blair frowned. "I don't get it," she said.

"It's art," Serena said mysteriously, and giggled again. She took a sip of her drink.

The two girls' faces were only inches apart, and Blair could smell the musky essential oil mixture Serena had started wearing. It smelled like the stuff the exterminator sprayed into the corners of her penthouse.

"I still don't get it. Is it something dirty?" Blair demanded, annoyed.

"Not really," Serena answered with a sly smile. "Lots of people have had theirs done too. You know—celebrities."

"Like who?" Blair said.

"Like Lady Gaga and Justin Timberlake."

"Oh," Blair said, sounding unimpressed.

Serena's eyes narrowed. "What's that supposed to mean?" she demanded.

Blair lifted her chin and tucked her straight brown hair behind her ears. "I don't know, it's like you're willing to do anything just to shock people. Don't you have any pride?"

"Um, last time I checked it wasn't illegal to have your picture taken," Serena replied. "Besides, I've done worse. And I'm pretty sure you have too." A sick, gory, fast-motion film of every person she'd ever murdered flashed before Serena's eyes. It happened when she drank sometimes. It was sort of disturbing.

"Did you ever think about the fact that these are like, the most important years of our lives? Like, for getting into college and everything?" Blair said. "You can't just go around doing what you want when you want. You have to think about the future."

Missy brought them another round. This time Serena only nodded her thanks. She looked down at the floor, her jagged, bloody pinky nail between her teeth. "Yeah, I'm just realizing that now," she admitted. "I hadn't thought about it before—how I should have been joining teams and clubs. You know, getting really into the school thing. But that's why I want you to help me make a movie. Just think how great a team we'd be. . . ." Serena's voice trailed off. Like the bitch that she was, Blair was shaking her head.

"I feel sorry for your parents," Blair said quietly. "You don't know how lucky you are to have parents who are still together. Who still read the paper together on Sunday morning and tuck you in at night. Look at you." She shook her head again. Even the way Serena was biting her nails disgusted her. "You don't deserve them."

Serena's eyes grew big, and her lip began to tremble, but she was determined not to have a tantrum—at least, not yet. Maybe Blair was just getting her period. That always turned her into a monster.

Serena took a huge gulp of her drink and wiped her mouth with her cocktail napkin. "So, I never heard what you and Nate did all last summer. Did you go up to Maine? See that boat he built?"

Blair shook her head. The topic of Nate was completely off limits. "I had tennis camp. I hated it."

They drank their drinks in awkward silence.

"And what about this party next week," Serena demanded, her irritation mounting. "The one you didn't invite me to. What's it for again?"

Blair knew the cause sounded lame and unsexy. That's why she'd named the party *Kiss Me or Die*. To give it an edge.

"It's for those birds of prey that live in Central Park. They're endangered, and everyone's worried that they're going to die or starve or the squirrels will raid their nests or whatever. So they set up a foundation for them," she explained. "Shut up. I know it's stupid."

Serena blew out a puff of smoke. "I didn't say anything. But it's not like there aren't *people* that need saving. I mean, what about the . . . I don't know . . . orphans?"

Or the paraplegic, scalpless survivors of her infamous temper tantrums?

"Well, it's as good a cause as any. We wanted something that wasn't too heavy to start off the season," Blair huffed, annoyed. It was fine for *her* to laugh at the cause she'd chosen for the party, but Serena had no right.

"So is the party like, just for us, or is it for parents, too?" Serena asked.

Blair hesitated. "Just . . . us," she said finally. She downed the rest of her drink and looked at her watch. "Um, I kind of have to take off." She slid the handle of her Mulberry bag over her arm.

Serena frowned. She had taken her time getting dressed, psyching herself up for a wild night out with her friends. She'd expected a big group—Blair and the remaining girls, Nate and his gang, Chuck and his boys—all the people they always used to hang out with. What was left of them anyway. And once Blair got drunk enough, Serena would just blurt it all out, confess to sleeping with Nate that one time—oops, those two times—and then they could start over as best friends and make a movie together. Serena might even start taking an SAT prep course so they could take practice SAT tests together. It would be fun.

That was the story she kept trying to tell herself. Deep down she knew she was just toying with Blair, like a cat toys with a rodent, until she grew tired of the game and was finally ready for Blair to die.

"Where are you going, anyway?" she asked suspiciously.

"I have a tennis match in the morning," Blair said, feeling extremely superior, even though she was lying her ass off. "I need to sleep."

"Oh." Serena crossed her arms and sat back on her stool. "I was hoping we'd all wind up partying in the Basses' suite upstairs. They still have it, don't they?"

Back in tenth grade, Serena and Blair used to drink themselves silly in Chuck's hot tub and do all sorts of crazy, masochistic things.

Like beat each other with sticks?

When their bodies had turned into prunes they'd climb out of the tub and pass out on the king-sized bed, sleeping there until their heads cleared and the wounds had healed, or the maids kicked them out to sterilize the room.

"The Basses still have the suite," Blair said, standing up. "But they really don't appreciate people using it. This isn't tenth grade anymore," she added coldly.

"Okay," Serena said. She couldn't say anything right, could she? At least, not to Blair. She ought to kill her now, just to shut her up, but she'd come to the bar unarmed.

Not that that ever stopped her.

She surveyed the table, taking an inventory of everything she could use to do it. The candle holder. Their drinks glasses. The panda bear rug. The heels of her boots. She could whack Blair in the head, suffocate her with a rug, and gouge her eyes out with the boots.

Serena's lower lip was trembling. Red spots appeared on her eyelids beneath the powdery blue eye shadow. "I really have to go," Blair said, eager to get the fuck out of there before Serena went ballistic.

"Wait!" Serena cried, her blue eyes huge and crazed-looking. Blood from her bitten cuticles was smeared on her teeth.

Blair looked at her watch and sighed impatiently. "What now?" she demanded, tapping her foot.

Serena downed the last dregs of her second Dark and Stormy. Again, a bloody fast-motion film of every one of her kills streaked through her mind's eye.

"Don't you get it?" she demanded, her voice quavering. "Jude and Milos and Soren and Jeremy. Kati and Is and Ms. Glos and Anna." She squeezed her eyes shut in an attempt to stop the film and then opened them again. "I did it all for you, Blair," she said in a monotone. "It's always been for you."

Blair stood over her, hands on her hips, shaking her head. She was about to have sex. She didn't have time for another pathetic, corny speech about how much Serena missed her.

"Save it," she snapped, but then she faltered as Serena rose to her feet, her empty glass clutched in her white-knuckled hand, her fine nostrils quivering. She was nearly six feet tall, and the look in her cobalt blue eyes as she stared Blair down was one of pure rage.

Blair swallowed, her throat dry. She was fine with Serena killing *other* people; it had never occurred to her that Serena might try to kill *her*.

"Well, have a great weekend," she said with a final stiff smile. Sex with Nate was so much more important than any of this bullshit. She dropped a hundred dollars on the table for their drinks. "Excuse me?" she asked the three tall boys who were blocking her path. "Do you mind getting the fuck out of my way?"

Shaking, Serena collapsed onto the black velvet ottoman and swallowed an ice cube, whole, as she watched Blair leave. It burned her throat and tasted like lemons.

Blair kept pushing her way through the crowd and out the door to the street. Gasping for air, she walked over to Sixth Avenue to catch a cab uptown. It started to rain and her hair frizzed. A bus roared by with Serena's picture on the side of it. Was it her belly button? It looked like the dark pit at the center of a peach. Blair turned her back on it and waved her hand in the air to flag down the next taxi. She couldn't get away fast enough. But the first taxi that stopped for her had the same poster in the lighted advertising box on its roof. Blair got in and slammed the door. She could never get completely away—Serena was fucking everywhere.

And she wanted her dead.

friday the thirteenth: the nutcracker suite

Serena reached for another cigarette and stuck it in her mouth with trembling fingers. Suddenly a pinky-ringed hand proffered a Zippo and lit the cigarette for her. The lighter was gold, with the monogram *C.B.* So was the ring.

"Hey Serena. You look seriously hot," Chuck Bass said. "What are you doing sitting here all by yourself?"

Serena inhaled deeply, licked the blood from her cuticles off of her teeth, and smiled. "Hey Chuck. I'm glad you're here. Blair ditched me and now I'm all alone. Anyone else coming?"

Chuck clicked his lighter shut and put it in his pocket. He glanced around the room. "Who knows?" he said casually. "They could come, or they could not come."

He sat down in the armchair where Blair had been sitting.

"You really do look hot," he said again, staring at Serena's legs like he wanted to eat them, with a side of garlicky fava beans and a nice glass of Chianti.

"Thanks," Serena said and laughed. It was kind of a relief to know that Chuck was still exactly the same, even if everyone else was acting like freaks. She had to love him for that.

Before she ripped his head off.

"Hey Missy," Chuck called to the waitress. "Bring us two rounds of my special shots. And put everything on my tab." He handed Serena the hundred-dollar bill Blair had left on the table. "You keep that," he said.

"But it's Blair's." Serena took the bill and examined it. The bland, ugly face of Benjamin Franklin stared back at her, challenging her to a duel. She stuffed the bill into her red velvet handbag.

Missy brought over four brimming-over shot glasses full of nondescript clear liquid.

Chuck pushed two of them toward Serena. "I call this Sunday Bloody Sunday, because you drink it and the next thing you know it's Sunday and there's blood all over your shoes and you can't remember how it got there." He clinked glasses with Serena. "Bottoms up!"

The shot tasted like pickle juice. It was delicious. Serena reached for the second one and tipsily poured it half into her mouth and half down her front.

"Oops," she said, as the shot sloshed all over her. "Damn."

Chuck dove for the spill and sucked it right off her chest. "There. Got it," he said, licking his lips. "You can't even tell."

Serena giggled and pushed him away. "Thanks, Chuck. You should come out with me more often. I'm always making messes." Again the bloody film flashed before her eyes. She shook her long blond ponytail, trying to make the images go away.

Chuck leered at her and grunted before downing his second shot. "I bet you are." He signaled to Missy to bring another round.

Serena closed her eyes and opened them again, giggling drunkenly to herself. Chuck's pageboy haircut swam before her, looking even more ridiculous now that she was drunk.

"Why don't we take this next round up to my suite?" he offered smoothly, his face all teeth.

Serena hesitated, thinking about what Blair had said about the Basses not liking people in their suite anymore. "Are you sure it's okay with your parents?" she asked.

Chuck snorted and held out his hand. "Them?" he said disparagingly. "They're in Caracas. Come on. It's Friday the thirteenth, I'm sure the TV's got good movies to watch. The hot tub's nice and hot. We can order room service. I'll put on your underwear, you can put on mine. Anything you want."

Even though it was raining out and he was freezing his ass off, Nate was in no hurry to get to Blair's house. It was pretty ironic, really. Here he was, a seventeen-year-old guy, about to have sex with his girlfriend for the first time (hers, anyway). He should have been *running*.

She must know by now, he kept telling himself, over and over and over. How could she not? The whole city had to know by now that he'd had sex with Serena. But if Blair knew, then why hadn't she said anything?

Thinking about it was driving Nate insane, literally. First the freakout at the pizzeria. And then last night he saw a paunchy black and white–feathered, pink-beaked vulture standing in his open window, staring at him and looking . . . *hungry*.

He ducked into a liquor store on Madison Avenue and bought a half pint of Jack Daniel's. He'd already smoked a little joint at home, but he'd need a few shots of courage before he saw Blair. His hands were shaking so badly he wasn't sure he could even take her clothes off.

That's okay. She won't be wearing any. And she comes with instructions.

Nate walked the rest of the way as slowly as he could, taking surreptitious sips from the bottle. He turned down Seventy-second Street only yards from Blair's building. A young vulture flapped down to the sidewalk. It waddled along beside Nate, glancing up at him with its beady eyes as if it wanted to make friends.

Nate hurled his bottle at it and broke into a run. The bottle smashed and the vulture squawked. It hopped away, beat its heavy wings once, twice. Then, airborne, it flew away into the night.

Staggering, Serena followed Chuck into the elevator and up to the Basses' ninth-floor suite. It looked exactly the same as it always had: living room with entertainment center and bar; huge bedroom with king-sized bed and another entertainment center, as if they needed two; huge marble bathroom with a sunken round hot tub and two fluffy white terrycloth bathrobes hanging on horseshoe-shaped chrome hooks. That was another thing Serena loved about hotels—the bathrobes. Nothing felt better after a particularly brutal bloodbath than a steaming hot shower and a clean white bathrobe.

Doesn't everyone agree?

On the coffee table in the living room was a pile of old photographs. Serena recognized Nate's face in the top one. She picked them up and shuffled through them.

Chuck glanced at the pictures over her shoulder. "Last year," he said, shaking his head. "We were pretty wild."

Blair, Nate, Chuck, Isabel, Kati, Rain—everyone was in them, naked in the hot tub, their bodies red from the heat, dancing and drinking champagne on the big bed, ghoulish makeup streaking down their sweaty faces. They were all party shots from last year—the date was in the corner of each one—and they were all taken in the suite.

So Blair had lied. Everyone did still party in the Basses' suite, same as always. And Blair wasn't the little goody-goody she pretended to be either, with her mock SAT and her prim black cardigan. In one picture Blair was wearing only a black thong and a red clown wig, jumping up and down on the bed with a bottle of firestarter in her hand.

Serena gulped down her third shot and collapsed on the couch. Chuck sat down beside her and pulled her feet into his lap.

"Chuck," Serena warned woozily. "I'm really drunk."

"Let's take your boots off then," Chuck said helpfully. "I know reflexology."

"Sure you do." Serena lay back on the couch and allowed Chuck to remove her boots and ply her tired feet with his greedy hands. She reached for the remote and clicked on the television. *Jason Goes to Hell: The Final Friday* was on—the scene where the autopsy doctor eats Jason's heart.

Oh, goody.

Serena loved this part. Eyes fixed on the screen, she put down the remote. Chuck began to suck on her toes. He bit her big toe and kissed her ankle.

"Chuck." Serena giggled, wriggling her legs. The room tilted and the TV screen went fuzzy. She never could hold her liquor.

Chuck worked his hands up her legs. His fingers massaged the insides of her knees.

"Chuck," Serena slurred again, sitting up in annoyance. "Do

you mind? I'm pretty drunk, okay? Let's just hang out on the couch and watch *Freaky Friday* or whatever this movie's called. You know, like girls."

Chuck crawled toward Serena on his hands and knees until he was looming over her and she was pinned beneath him. "But I'm not a girl," he growled hungrily. He lowered his face to hers and began to kiss her. His tongue tasted like a big dill pickle.

"Shit!" Blair shrieked when she heard the doorman buzz from downstairs. Nate was early. She was still wearing her clothes, and she had just spilled red candle wax all over her rug.

She switched off her bedroom light and ran to answer the buzzer in the kitchen.

"Yes, send him up," she told the doorman. She unbuttoned her jeans and flew back to her room, wriggling out of them. Then she pulled the rest of her clothes off and tossed them into the closet. Naked, she grabbed a tube of black body paint and began drawing greasy black arrows pointing to all her anatomical areas of interest. Next she grabbed the tube of red and wrote "No Parking" across her butt. Then she grabbed a tube of taxi yellow and wrote "This Way" above the arrow pointing down between her legs.

Beep beep!

Blair checked out the result in the mirror. The paint was garish and spooky in the candlelight. Her skin was still nice and tan from the summer, but now it was impossible to tell. Adding insult to injury, her unbrushed hair stuck up in a halo of frizz from the rain. Oh well, Nate was always horny. He wouldn't mind.

The doorbell rang.

"Hold on!" she called out, carefully drawing little red hearts on all four of her cheeks.

Serena let Chuck kiss her for a while because he was heavy and she couldn't get him off her. She wanted to kill him, but she was too drunk. As he explored the inside of her mouth with his tongue, she continued to watch TV. Jason's heart had just turned into a demonic baby and crawled out of some guy named Randy's neck. Serena turned her head away and closed her eyes.

"Chuck, I really don't feel so well," she said. "Do you mind if I just lie here for a little while?"

Chuck sat up and wiped his mouth with the back of his hand. "Sure, that's cool." He stood up and cleared his throat. "I'll go get us some water."

Chuck went over to the wet bar and filled up two glasses with ice and Poland Spring.

When he turned around, Serena was already asleep. Her head had fallen back against the cushions, and her long legs twitched. Chuck sank onto the couch beside her, grabbed the remote, and changed the channel. To be honest, he hated slasher films, and oh look, his favorite show: *Glee*.

"Hi," Blair said, opening the door a crack.

"Hi," Nate said, panting. His hair was wet from the rain and the cold sweat of fear.

"I'm naked," Blair told him. "Sort of."

"Really?" Nate said, barely absorbing the information. He couldn't wait to get inside and away from the vultures. "Can I come in?"

"Sure," Blair said, opening the door wide.

Nate stared at her, frozen in the doorway. She looked like a map of the London Underground.

Blair blushed and hugged her painted arms around herself. "I told you I was naked." She grabbed Nate's hand and pulled him inside.

"I'm all wet," he said shakily, kicking off his shoes.

Blair laughed. Nate sounded nervous, even more nervous than she.

"Hurry up and take your clothes off then." She started toward her bedroom, the red NO PARKING sign on her butt waggling with each step.

Nate followed, not doing any of the things a boy would normally have done under the circumstances. Like throw Blair down on the bed, or worry about condoms or bad breath. He was barely thinking at all.

Blair's room was a blaze of red candles. Weird Hawaiian ukulele music played softly from her iPod. A bottle of red wine was open on the floor, with two glasses beside it. Blair knelt down and poured each of them a glass. She felt more comfortable naked in the darkness of her room.

"Do you want me to paint you too?" she asked, handing him a glass.

Nate gulped the wine, swallowing noisily. "Paint me?" he repeated. "Sure."

Blair had made and remade the movie of this moment in her head so many times she felt like an actress who was finally getting her big break, playing the role of her career.

"Take off your shirt."

Nate took off his shirt and tossed it on the floor.

Blair picked up the tube of black body paint, ran a caressing hand over Nate's shoulder blades, and wrote the first thing that came to mind across his strong bare back: *My girlfriend got in early to Yale and all I got was this lousy T-shirt.*

"What're you writing?" Nate asked. He shivered. "It tickles."

Blair finished writing and turned Nate around to face her. "Take off the rest of your clothes," she whispered.

Nate did as he was told, trying not to look as she drew arrows, exclamation points, and asterisks all over him. Finally he couldn't help himself. She was naked and she was beautiful. She was a girl and he was a boy. And he was naked too. And they were both covered in body paint.

There have been plenty of songs written about this.

There have?

Maybe after we do it, I'll tell her, Nate thought. *I'll tell her everything.*

That didn't seem completely fair, but still, he kissed her. He kissed a red heart on one cheek, and then another red heart on another. And another. And another. Their body paint began to mingle and smudge. Outside, the vultures beat their jealous wings against the rain-streaked windows. But now that he'd started, he just couldn't stop.

When Serena woke up a little while later, Chuck was wearing her Pucci dress and her blue suede knee-high boots and was singing Madonna's "Express Yourself" along with Gwyneth Paltrow, who was guest-starring on *Glee.* The brightly patterned silk jersey stretched taut across his hindquarters as he strutted and vogued.

Serena propped herself up on her elbows and wiped the lip gloss scum out of the corners of her mouth. "What time is it?" she yawned.

Chuck glanced at her. "Time for us to get naked," he said impatiently. He'd been waiting long enough.

Serena's head felt thick. She was dying for a glass of water. "I feel awful." She sat up and rubbed her forehead. "Give me back my dress. I want to go home."

"Come on," Chuck said, flicking off the TV. "We could take a hot tub first. That'll make you feel better."

"No," Serena insisted.

"Fine," Chuck said angrily. He pulled off the dress and flung it at her. His chest hair had been shaved into bat wings and his silk boxer shorts were black and tiny. Still wearing her tall blue boots, he looked like a superhero gone completely wrong.

Jumpin' juju beads, Robin, it's Bat-Chuck!

He unzipped the boots and threw them at her too.

"It's raining," Serena observed as they both got dressed.

Chuck tossed her a scarf, his trademark cream-colored cashmere, monogrammed in gold with the letters *C.B.* "Wrap it around your head," he said. "It's okay. I wear a new one every single day." He shoved on his loafers. "Come on, let's go."

They rode down the elevator in silence. Serena knew Chuck was disappointed, but she didn't care. She couldn't wait to get out into the fresh air and into her own bed.

A cab pulled up, the Remi brothers' poster in the box on the cab's roof. Serena thought it looked like a close-up photograph of lips puckered into a kiss.

"What's that? Mars?" Chuck joked, pointing at it. He glanced at Serena without a trace of humor in his eyes. "No, it's your anus!"

Serena blinked at him. She couldn't tell if Chuck was trying to be funny or if that was what he actually thought the picture was. He held the cab door open for her, and she slid into the backseat.

"Thanks, Chuck," she said gratefully. "I'll see you soon, okay?"

"Whatever." Chuck leaned into the cab and pressed Serena against the seat. "What's your problem anyway?" he hissed. "You've been fucking Nate Archibald since tenth grade, and I'm sure you did just about every guy at boarding school, and in France, too. What, are you like, too good to give me some?"

Serena stared directly into Chuck's eyes, seeing him as he really was for the first time. He'd always been hard to like, but she'd never actually hated him before. Again the murderous montage of killings played before her eyes. She fumbled in her purse for something, anything that could be used as a weapon. BlackBerry, keys, iPod microphone cord. Grasping the BlackBerry in one hand, she unzipped her little Louis Vuitton cosmetics pouch and pulled out her eyelash curler with the other. They would have to do.

"That's okay, I wouldn't want to do it with you anyway," Chuck spat into her face. "I hear you have diseases."

"Get away from me," Serena hissed and whacked his left temple as hard as she could with her BlackBerry. With her left hand she clipped the eyelash curler over Chuck's right eyelid and pulled back *hard*.

"Fuck me!" Chuck cried out. He stumbled backward. The cab door slammed shut and the driver pulled away.

Serena couldn't exactly tell the driver to stop and wait while she finished Chuck off, so she decided to let it go. Chuck's bloody eyelid drooped from the eyelash curler. She opened the window and tossed it into the gutter. Within seconds two well-fed baby vultures were fighting over it, squawking.

Some endangered species.

Staring straight ahead through the taxi's rain-spattered

windshield, Serena wiped her bloody fingers on the ends of Chuck's cream-colored scarf. When the taxi stopped at a light on the corner of Broadway and Spring, she opened her door, leaned out, and threw up into the gutter.

That will teach her not to drink on an empty stomach.

Chuck's creamy cashmere scarf swung from her neck and dangled in the puddle of pink vomit on the pavement.

"Yuck." Serena pulled off the scarf, wiped her mouth on it, and stuffed it into her bag. She slammed the cab door closed again.

"Tissue, miss?" the cab driver offered, passing a box of Kleenex back to her.

Serena pulled one from the box and wiped her mouth with it.

"Thanks," she said, grateful—as always—for the kindness of strangers.

"What about a condom or something?" Blair murmured, gaping at Nate's body paint–smeared hard-on. It looked like it was going to take over the world.

They'd been fooling around for almost an hour, their bodies tacky with black paint. Blair picked up a candle. She was running out of foreplay ideas. It was about time they did it.

Nate rolled onto his back while Blair poured hot red candle wax all over his empty stomach. Man, was he hungry. Maybe when he went home he'd pick up a burrito from the Mexican place on Lexington Avenue. That's what he wanted, a chicken and black bean burrito with extra guacamole.

Blair grabbed his hand and stuck his pinky into the flame.

"Ow," Nate said, his hard-on deflating as if pricked with a pin. He sat up and blew on his hurt hand. "I can't do this," he muttered under his breath.

"What?" Blair said, tossing aside the candle. "What's wrong?" Her heart fell. This wasn't in the script. Nate was ruining a perfect moment.

Clumsily, Nate took Blair's hand and looked into her eyes for the first time all night. Her face was black and red and creepy-looking, like some tribesgirl from the movie *Avatar* except not blue. "I have to tell you something," he said.

Blair could tell by the look in Nate's eyes that the moment wasn't just ruined—it was killed. "What?" she said softly.

Nate reached down and gathered up the edges of the quilt. He draped one end around Blair's shoulders and wrapped the other end around his waist. It didn't seem right to talk about this when they were both so naked and covered with black gunk. He took Blair's hand again.

"Remember the summer before last when you were away in Scotland, at your aunt's wedding?" Nate began.

Blair nodded.

"It was so damned hot that summer. I was in the city with my dad, just hanging out while he went to some meetings and stuff. I got bored, so I called Serena in Ridgefield, and she came down." Nate noticed Blair's back stiffen when he mentioned Serena's name. She removed her hand from his and crossed her arms over her chest, her eyes suddenly distrustful.

"We had some drinks and sat out in the garden. It was so hot, Serena started splashing around in the fountain, and then she started splashing me. And I guess I got kind of carried away. I mean—" Nate fumbled. He remembered what Cyrus had told him about girls liking surprises. Well, Blair was about to be very surprised, and he didn't think she was going to like it.

"And what?" Blair demanded. "What happened?"

"We kissed." Nate took a deep breath and held it. He couldn't just leave it at that. He blew the breath out. "And then we had sex."

Blair threw the quilt off her shoulders and stood up. "I knew it!" she shouted. "Who *hasn't* had sex with Serena? That nasty slut. Sure she wants to be friends again. I'll fucking kill her. I'll rip her heart out and eat it and then throw it up and make you eat it and then make you throw it up and make *her* eat it!"

"I'm sorry, Blair. It wasn't like, planned or anything," Nate said. "It just happened. And then it sort of happened again, earlier this week, right after she got back." He swallowed, realizing how totally lame he sounded. "I just wanted you to know this wasn't my first time."

Blair stomped into her bathroom and snatched her pink satin bathrobe off its hook. She put it on, cinching the belt tight. Her graffitied skin shone in the candlelight. Angry tears sluiced her painted cheeks in greasy gray rivulets.

"Get the fuck out of here, Nate," she sobbed. "Before I kill you."

Her blue eyes widened as the notion hit her with extreme clarity, like a dim bulb that has finally been properly screwed in.

It wasn't Nate she wanted to kill. It was Serena.

"Blair—" Nate pleaded. Then he noticed the same crazed look on Blair's face that he'd hallucinated when she killed the L'Ecole girl outside the pizzeria.

Blair slammed the bathroom door in his face.

Nate stood up and pulled on his boxers. Kitty Minky poked his gray, furry head out from under the bed and stared at him accusingly, his golden cat eyes glowing eerily in the dark. Nate left the rest of his clothes on the floor and headed for the front door. Fuck Blair's creepy cat. Fuck the vultures. Fuck the rain. He was going to run, barefoot, in his underwear, all the way home.

The front door closed with a hollow bang. Blair remained locked in the bathroom, glaring at her tearstained, paint-smeared reflection in the mirror. The tube of Serena's lip gloss was still lying on the sink where she'd left it. Blair picked it up with trembling fingers. *Gash*, it was called. What an ugly name. Of course Serena could wear lip gloss with ugly names, and tights with holes in them, and dirty old boots, and never cut her hair, and kill anyone she felt like killing, and still get the boy. Blair grunted at the irony of it all and opened her bathroom window, tossing the lip gloss out into the night without waiting to hear the pained squeals of the rat it killed on the pavement below.

Her head was too full of the new movie she was working on. The movie in which she pushed the fabulous Serena van der Woodsen in front of a speeding bus with Serena's stupid picture plastered on the side of it. Serena would flail and flop on the pavement like a dehydrated mermaid while Blair watched. Then Blair would shave off all of Serena's annoying blond hair for the pigeons and vultures to use in their nests, gouge out her bluer-than-blue eyes with quarters, and leave her ugly, maimed, and smushed carcass there to rot as she died.

a diptych

Jenny had gone to bed hours ago, still recovering from her invitation-making all-nighter. Rufus had fallen asleep in front of the Food Network. He liked to laugh at the so-called gourmet chefs struggling to make simple dishes like risotto with aspara-gus and poached salmon. His own specialties included curried crab apple soup made with apples picked fresh from Riverside Park and onion bagel peanut butter pie using bagels from the Dumpster behind Zabar's. Hence Jenny's taste for uncooked ground beef.

It was Friday night. The apartment was quiet.

Friday the thirteenth,
full moon—how appropriate.
Boy, man. Scarf Boy, dead man.

When Dan really took a good look around, he saw that his apartment was an arsenal of weaponry. Fire pokers. Handsaws. Corkscrews. Meat cleavers. Carving knives. Razor blades. Ice skates. A baseball bat. A hatchet. A bottle of paint thinner. His dad even owned a blowtorch, which he used for cooking his inventive, if inedible, dishes.

If only Serena hadn't taken the knife he and Vanessa had bought at Paragon. It would have been perfect. Dan decided on a meat cleaver. He could imagine throwing it at Chuck, ninja style, and watching Chuck's shocked expression as it cleaved his rotten heart in two. He'd bleed to death slowly, from the inside out. A little coughing up of blood would be nice too.

Dan had heard about Chuck's suite at the Tribeca Star, and because it was Friday night, he was pretty sure that's where Chuck would be. He took a cab downtown, the meat cleaver wrapped in a kitchen towel and stuffed into the front pocket of his gray Gap hoodie with just the wooden handle sticking out.

Made up almost entirely of prewar residential doorman buildings, the stately inclines of West End Avenue after dark were always elegantly somnolent. Tribeca, on the other hand, was a mash-up of blocks of shuttered boutiques, spanking new glass-fronted condos, and hot new restaurants, hotels, and bars with bouncer-manned velvet ropes and red carpets outside their doors.

The Tribeca Star was such a place. The entrance to the bar was to the right of the hotel's main entrance, nondescript, unmarked, and totally unnoticeable, save for the line of people outside it, which went around the corner and halfway down the block. Of course this was what every establishment in town craved. The more people came, the more people would come. An ambulance with its lights flashing was parked outside the hotel's main entrance, boosting the sexiness of the place a millionfold. Was there a celebrity inside? What had happened? An overdose? A bar fight? A suicide attempt?

An eyelash curler accident?

Overhead in the hotel eves the vultures roosted, their red-rimmed eyes only half-closed, dreaming of the next delicious carcass.

Dan had never been anywhere this exciting. He joined the long line, already feeling like a murderer in his shabby corduroys, too small hoodie, and dirty sneakers, surrounded by pretty, tall girls wearing shiny lip gloss and expensive-looking high-heeled shoes. The damp sidewalk actually smelled like perfume.

An hour passed before he reached the enormous bouncer at the door. The bouncer wore a puffy black leather jacket and looked like he could bench press two hundred pounds using only his neck. The beat from that Rolling Stones song Dan's dad liked thrummed loudly from inside the bar.

"Uh-ah uh-ah-ah uh-ah-ah-ah
You will be mine, you will be mine, all mine."

Dan stuffed his hands into the front pockets of his hoodie, doing his best to conceal the meat cleaver. He was Serena's knight in shining armor, he reminded himself. Coming to her emotional rescue.

"Hello," he greeted the bouncer nervously.

"Can I see your ID, please?" the bouncer replied.

Dan was prepared. He handed the bouncer his Riverside Prep ID card.

The bouncer handed it back. "You're only seventeen. Get the fuck out of here."

"But I don't want to drink anything. I'm here to see Chuck

Bass." Dan's tongue was basted with bitter bile as he said the words. "He's a friend."

The bouncer just stood there, huge and unmovable. "Get the fuck out of here," he said again.

Dan stepped out of line, his hand clutching the meat cleaver in its kitchen towel bunting. He could just kill the bouncer. His eyes roved down the line of gorgeous, happy bargoers. He could just kill them all. But he wasn't insane. He didn't even wish them ill. Chuck Bass was the one he had it in for. He turned and started for the hotel's main entrance.

The ambulance was still parked outside, lights flashing, its back doors slightly ajar. Inside Dan could just make out the tips of two wildly annoying pigskin shoes, bespoke-cobbled in England by dapper elves for none other than the mighty wanker himself: Chuck Bass.

Dan's heart soared. Chuck was lying on a stretcher. Was he already dead, having been pecked to death by those big scavenging birds that seemed to be everywhere these days for the simple reason that he was a custom-made-pigskin-shoe-wearing scumbag?

Dan could only hope.

He turned away from the hotel and flagged down a cab, relieved of his duties as an assassin, at least for tonight.

Blair was just getting started.

The Remi brothers were happy to meet her at their gallery.

"I'm Serena's best friend. We grew up together," Blair told their gallerist over the phone. "Serena wants to do our portraits together. You know, like with both of us in one picture?"

The Remi brothers were wearing matching navy blue silk

Hugo Boss suits with matching navy blue silk skinny ties and matching matchstick-thin black mustaches. Their hair was shaved to a short black fuzz. One of the brothers, the shorter and gayer one, actually clapped when Blair arrived at the gallery. She hadn't even bothered to put on clothes—she'd simply thrown her coat on over her body paint and pink satin bathrobe. "I absolutely *adore* your little figure," he said. "All that body paint. It's so modern. So buon giorno!"

And you, my dear sir, are so arrivederci.

The gallery was on the ground floor, huge and white, with ceiling-high windows facing the deserted Chelsea street. The walls were hung with the enormous perforated rosebud "portraits" of the Remis' "Behind the Scene" show. Blair recognized Serena's right away, displayed on its own, opposite the gallery's entrance. While Blair pretended to be waiting for Serena, the Remis popped open a bottle of champagne and made a toast.

"To beautiful girls!" they cried in twinly unison.

They were on their second bottle when Blair pretended to receive a text from Serena.

"She says she's in a cab and she'll be here in five minutes." She rolled her eyes dramatically. "Serena's always late."

She excused herself to go to the restroom.

"Ah yes," one of the Remis said. "We always ask that our subjects freshen up before we photograph them."

Next door to the ladies' room Blair discovered a closet. In the closet were all sorts of art-hanging supplies and hardware. She found just what she needed to do what she needed to do.

She always does.

The Remi brothers were fiddling with their tripods and

cameras and lights in a small anteroom—their studio—where they photographed their subjects.

"Do you mind removing your clothes so we can adjust the lighting?" one of the Remis asked.

Blair polished off her champagne and smiled obligingly. She made as if to untie her bathrobe, instead reaching in the pocket for the coil of picture wire she had hidden there.

"Wait, do I have something in my teeth?" she asked, walking toward the Polaroid camera on its tripod and jutting out her chin.

The Remis leaned their heads in close to look.

"It doesn't matter," the less gay one said. "We're not photographing your face."

"I'm aware of that."

Blair unfurled the coil of wire and wrapped it tightly around both the Remi brothers' skinny necks. In her deft, perfectly manicured hands the wire became a garrote, crushing their delicate windpipes and choking them in unison. The perky black dashes of their mustaches withered as they gasped their last gasps.

As they died, Blair admired their dedication to wearing only navy blue. She thought she might try it out herself in the spring, variations on a sailor theme from A.P.C., Agnès B, J.Crew, and Armani, with a pair of cute white Christian Louboutin ankle booties to match.

The Remis fell in a lifeless heap at her feet. Their necks still wrapped in wire, Blair dragged them over to the far wall of the gallery and strung them up from the same nail on which Serena's portrait hung. She turned their dead heads to face each other, their twin bodies dangling—a diptych—over their masterpiece: Serena's nostril or navel or whatever orifice it was.

Blair stood back to admire her work, a masterpiece in itself. She was pleased she'd stuck with her tennis and was fit enough to kill two grown men at the same time with her bare hands.

And she was only just warming up.

will *s* & *n* hook up again?

Just before midnight, the taxi pulled up at 994 Fifth Avenue. Across the street, the steps of the Metropolitan Museum of Art were deserted, glowing eerily white in the light of the streetlamps. Serena stepped out of the cab and waved to Roland, the old night doorman, who was dozing just inside the lobby. One of the cast iron and glass double doors to the apartment building opened, but it wasn't Roland who opened it. It was Nate, wearing only a pair of boxers and some weird black paint on his face and chest, and looking sort of freaked out.

"Nate!" Serena squealed, genuinely surprised. "Hey, silly. Could you loan me five bucks? I haven't got enough cash. Usually the doorman helps me out, but I guess he's asleep."

Nate gave his credit card number to the bemused taxi driver. He put his finger to his lips and crept up to the front door of the building. Then he knocked loudly on the glass door. "Hello?" he shouted.

"Oh Nate." Serena laughed. "You are so mean!"

Roland snapped his eyes open and nearly fell off his chair. Then he opened the door for them, and Serena and Nate ran inside and rode the elevator up to Serena's apartment.

Serena led the way to her room and sat down heavily on the bed. "Did you get my message?" she yawned, pulling off her boots. "I thought you'd come out tonight."

"I couldn't." Nate picked up the little glass ballerina perched on top of Serena's mahogany jewelry chest. She had the tiniest toes, like little pinpoints. He'd forgotten about her.

"Well, it wasn't worth it anyway," Serena sighed.

She lay down on the bed, wondering if Chuck had gone to the hospital with his missing eyelid or if—fortuitously—he'd staggered into the road and gotten hit by a speeding limo.

"I'm so tired. And really drunk." She patted the bed next to her and slid over to give Nate room. "Come lie down and tell me why you're not wearing any clothes."

Nate put the ballerina down and swallowed. Breathing in the scent of Serena's room with Serena in it made his heart hurt. He lay down next to her, their bodies touching. Nate put his arm around her and she snuggled close and kissed his paint-smeared cheek.

"I was just over at Blair's," Nate said.

Serena didn't answer. She was breathing noisily. Maybe she was already asleep.

Nate lay still, his eyes wide open, his mind racing. He wondered if he and Blair were officially broken up now. He wondered if he kissed Serena right now, full on the lips, and told her he loved her, how she'd respond. He wondered if he'd just gone ahead and had sex with Blair if everything would have been all right. He wondered if this frigging body paint was ever going to wash off his skin and if those creepy vultures were ever going to stop following him.

He cast his eyes around the room, taking in all the familiar well-loved objects that he'd grown up seeing and had forgotten all about. The kilt-wearing teddy bear from Scotland that sat aristocratically on Serena's little dressing table. The big mahogany armoire with its drawers half-open and all her clothes spilling out. The little brown burn mark he'd made in ninth grade on the white eyelet canopy hanging from her bed.

On the floor by the door was Serena's red velvet bag. The contents had spilled out of it. A blue pack of Gauloises cigarettes. A one-hundred-dollar bill. Her BlackBerry. And a cream-colored cashmere scarf with the letters *C.B.* stitched on it in gold, covered in blood and vomit.

Why had she needed to borrow money from him when she had one hundred dollars with her? Nate wondered. And what the hell was she doing with Chuck's bloody, vomit-soaked scarf?

Nate turned over on his side and Serena moaned softly as her head sank into the pillow. He studied her critically. She was so beautiful, but so full of surprises. It was sort of easy to believe some of the things people said about her.

She slid her arms around Nate's neck, pulling him toward her. "Come on," she murmured, her eyes still closed. "Sleep with me."

Nate's whole body tensed. He didn't know if Serena meant just go to sleep, or *sleep with her*, but he was definitely aroused. Any boy in his right mind would be, which is exactly what turned Nate off.

There was something so careless about the way she'd said it. Nate suddenly had no trouble imagining her doing everything he'd heard she'd done. Sex. Murder. Cults. Drugs. With Serena, anything was possible.

A glint of chrome on the floor caught his eye. The clasps of a black violin case. Since when did Serena play the violin?

Nate rolled off the bed and opened the case. An expensive-looking hunting knife lay on the plush blue velvet interior. Dried blood mottled the blade. Beside the hunting knife was a bone-handled switchblade, the kind made it Italy, custom fit for a small hand.

He shuddered. Were the so-called lies and vicious rumors about Serena all true? At least the vultures were scavengers, preying on the already dead. Serena was . . . Nate didn't know exactly what she was, but he knew he didn't like it.

He snapped the violin case shut, stood up, and tossed Chuck's stained scarf on the pillow beside Serena's sleeping head. Then, without even looking at her again, he left, slamming the door behind him.

At the sound of the door closing Serena opened her eyes and breathed in the scent of her own barf. Gagging, she threw the covers back and ran to the bathroom. She clutched the rim of her white porcelain sink and heaved into it, her sides aching with the effort. Nothing came out. Serena turned on the shower as hot as it would go and ripped off the clammy multicolored Pucci dress. All she needed was a good hot shower with her favorite Biotherm Aquathermale Spa body scrub, followed by a rubdown with Decléor Aromessence Baume Spa Relax. Tomorrow she'd be good as new.

And ready to kill again.

gossipgirl.net

Disclaimer: All the real names of places, people, and events have been altered or abbreviated to protect the innocent. Namely, me.

topics   sightings   your e-mail   post a question

hey people!

BREAKING NEWS

The Remi bothers—those French, navy blue–wearing pretty boy geniuses of the art world—were found hanging by their necks in mute argument over one of their masterpieces in their gallery in Chelsea early this morning, where their latest show, "Behind the Scene," has been all the rage. It is unclear whether the artists' deaths were caused by suicide or murder. One thing is certain—the Remi brothers join Keats and Basquiat in the sad fate of doomed young brilliance: They will be even more famous now that they are dead.

BASQUIAT

CLOSE BUT NO CIGAR

Can you believe **N**? He was *thisclose* to getting a nice slice of **B** pie, if you know what I mean. I guess we're supposed to admire his self-control, his ability to keep the old hot dog in the bun, his savoir faire, his game-for-anything half-naked sprint up Fifth Avenue. Was that a lacrosse team thing?

I was wrong about him. He has a freaky streak.

Ooh, that makes me like him even more. He can let his freak flag fly with me anytime.

YOUR E-MAIL

q: hey gossip girl,
i saw **S** go upstairs with some dude at the Tribeca Star. she was wasted. so was i. i was kind of tempted to knock on the door and see if there was a party going on or s/t, but i chickened out. i just wanted your advice. do you think she'd do me? i mean, she looks pretty easy.
—Coop

a: Dear Coop,
If you're the type of guy who has to ask, then probably not. **S** may be a dangerous ho, but she has excellent taste.
—GG

SIGHTINGS

N at the burrito place on Lexington late last night, chatting up the cute girl behind the counter. She gave him extra guacamole for free. Yeah, I bet she did. And **C** out for his Saturday morning stroll, sporting a tan leather eye patch freshly flown in from Italy by Hermès' leather artisans and stamped in gold with his initials. How eye-catching!

You know you love me,

westsiders go bonkers for barneys

"Dan," Jenny whispered, poking at her brother's chest. "Wake up."

Dan flung his hand over his eyes and kicked at his sheets. "Go away. It's Saturday," he mumbled.

"Please get up," Jenny whined. She sat down on the bed, poking him repeatedly until he removed his arm to glare at her.

"What's your problem?" Dan said. "Leave me alone."

"No," Jenny insisted. "We have to go shopping."

"Right." Dan rolled over, turning his head toward the wall.

"Please, Dan. I have to get a dress for the party on Friday and you have to help me. Dad gave me his credit card. He said you could get a tux too." Jenny giggled. "Since we're turning out to be the type of spoiled rotten kids that will need tuxes and dresses and all that crap. Besides, I need to do something to get my mind off all the murders I keep reading about. It's giving me the creeps."

Dan rolled over, thinking of Chuck. He hoped he was dead, even though he hadn't gotten the satisfaction of killing him himself. "I'm not going to that party," he insisted.

"Shut up. Yes you are. You're going and you're going to meet

Serena and dance with her. I'll introduce you. She's totally cool," Jenny burbled happily.

"No," Dan said stubbornly.

"Well, you can at least help me pick out a dress," Jenny pouted. "Because I'm going. And I want to look nice."

"Can't Dad go with you?"

"Yeah, right." Jenny scoffed. "You know what Dad said? 'Go to Sears, it's the *proletarian* department store.' Whatever that means. I don't even know where Sears *is*, if it even exists anymore. Anyway, I want to go to Barneys. I can't believe I've never even been there. I bet Serena van der Woodsen and Blair Waldorf go there every day."

Dan sat up and yawned loudly. Jenny was all dressed and ready to go, with her curly hair pulled back into a ponytail. She even had on her jacket and shoes. It would be kind of hard to say no.

"You're a pain in my ass," Dan said, standing up and stumbling toward the bathroom.

"You know you love me!" Jenny called after him.

As far as Dan was concerned, Barneys was full of assholes, down to the dude who opened the door for him, smiling in the cheesiest way possible. But Jenny loved it, and even though she had never been there, she seemed to know everything about the place. She knew not to bother with the lower floors, which were full of designer clothes she could never afford, and headed straight to the top floor Co-op. When the elevator doors rolled open, she felt like she had died and gone to heaven. There were so many beautiful dresses hanging on the racks it made her salivate to look at them. She wanted to try them all on, but of course she couldn't.

When you're a 32DD, you're kind of limited. And you definitely need *help*.

"Dan, will you go ask that woman to help me find this in my size?" Jenny whispered, fingering a purple velvet empire-waist sheath with beaded straps. She pulled out the price tag. Six hundred bucks.

"Whoa," Dan said, looking at the price over her shoulder.

"Shut up. I'm just trying it on for fun," Jenny insisted. "I won't buy it." She held the dress up to herself. The bodice would barely cover her nipples. Jenny sighed and put the dress back on the rack. "Would you please ask that lady if she'll help me?"

"Why can't you ask?" Dan shoved his hands in his corduroys and leaned against a wooden hat rack.

"Please?"

"Fine."

Dan strode over to a haggard-looking woman with frosted blond hair. She looked like she'd been working in department stores her entire life, only taking one vacation a year in Atlantic City, New Jersey. Dan imagined her chainsmoking Virginia Slims down on the boardwalk, worrying about how the girls back at the store were managing without her.

"Are you lost, young man?" the woman asked. Her name tag read MAUREEN.

Dan smiled self-consciously. "Hello. My sister over there needs help." He pointed at Jenny, who was studying the price tag of a red silk wraparound dress with ruffles on the sleeves. Jenny had taken off her jacket and was wearing a too small white tank top.

"Certainly," Maureen said, striding purposefully toward Jenny.

Dan stayed where he was, glancing around the room and feeling completely out of place. Behind him, he heard a familiar voice.

"I look like a nun, Mom, I swear. It's just completely wrong."

"Oh, Serena," another voice said. "I think it's darling. What if you just unbutton the collar a bit. There. See? It's very Jackie O." Dan spun around. A tall, middle-aged woman with Serena's coloring was standing half in, half out of a curtained dressing room. The curtain was slightly parted, and Dan could just see a bit of Serena's hair, her collarbone, her bare feet with the toenails painted dark red. His cheeks burned and he bolted for the elevator.

Last night—knife in hand—
sidewalk stank of piss and fear.
I sleep perchance to dream.

"Hey Dan, where're you going?" Jenny called over to him. Her arms were already piled high with dresses while Maureen flicked efficiently through the racks, giving her all sorts of advice about support bras and the latest figure-enhancing underwear. Jenny had never been happier.

"Gonna check out the men's stuff," Dan mumbled, glancing nervously toward the side of the store where he'd spotted Serena.

"Okay," Jenny said gaily. "I'll meet you down there in forty-five minutes. And if I need your help, I'll call you on your cell."

Dan nodded and leapt onto the elevator as soon as the doors opened. Down in the men's department, he shuffled over to a counter and spritzed his hands with Gucci cologne, wrinkling his nose at the strong, Italian male scent. He looked around the intimidating, woody department store for a bathroom where he could wash it off. Instead, he found a mannequin in full evening dress and, beside it, a rack of tuxedos. Dan fingered the luxurious material of the jackets and looked at the labels. Hugo Boss, Calvin Klein, Donna Karan, Yves Saint Laurent, Armani.

He imagined stepping out of a limo wearing his Armani tux with Serena on his arm. They'd stroll down the red carpet leading into the party, music thumping all around them. People would turn and say "*Oh*," in hushed voices. Serena would press her perfect mouth to Dan's ear. "I love you," she'd whisper. Then Dan would stop and kiss her and pick her up and carry her back to the limo. Screw the party. They had better things to do.

"Can I help you, sir?" A salesman asked.

Dan turned abruptly. "No. I—" He hesitated and looked at his watch. Jenny was going to take forever upstairs, and why shouldn't he, now that he was here? He picked up the Armani tux and held it out to the sales guy. "Can I try this on in my size?"

All that cologne must have gone to his head.

The salesman taught Dan how to tie a perfect bow tie before leaving him alone in the dressing room to admire his reflection. He looked older and cleaner and super sharp. Amazing how a tuxedo could instantly turn you into James Bond. Dan posed in front of the mirror, pretending to whip out a gun and fire at foreign double agents.

"Friggin' silk fucking bow ties," he heard a familiar assaholic voice intone from the next dressing room. "I hate these fucking things."

Dan pressed his back against the dressing room wall, holding his pretend gun aloft. So Chuck Bass was still alive. If only he had a real gun.

"Fuckingchristshitmotherfucker!" the asshole continued to swear.

Dan took a deep breath, parted the velvet curtain, and stepped out of his dressing room.

"Hey, is that you, Chuck?" he called cheerfully. "It's Dan, your classmate? I could probably give you a hand."

Jenny and Maureen had completely scoured the racks, and Maureen had filled a dressing room with dozens of possibilities in assorted sizes. The problem with Jenny was she was only a size two, but her chest was a size twelve at least. Maureen thought they'd have to compromise and go for a six, letting it out in the bust and taking it in everywhere else.

The first few dresses were a disaster. Jenny nearly busted the zipper of one trying to unsnag it from her bra. And the next one didn't even make it over her boobs. The third one was completely obscene. The fourth one fit, sort of, except it was bright orange and had a ridiculous ruffle running across it, like someone had slashed it with a knife. Jenny poked her head out of the curtain to look for Maureen. Next door, Serena and her mother were just heading out of their dressing room to the cashier's desk.

"Serena!" Jenny called out without thinking. Serena turned around and Jenny blushed. She couldn't believe she was talking to Serena van der Woodsen while wearing a bright orange dress with a stupid ruffle on it.

"Hey Jenny," Serena said, beaming sweetly down at her. She walked over and kissed Jenny on both cheeks. Jenny sucked in her breath and gripped the curtain to steady herself. Serena van der Woodsen had just kissed her.

"Wow, crazy dress," Serena said. She leaned in to whisper in Jenny's ear. "You're lucky you don't have your mom with you. I got suckered into buying the ugliest dress in the store."

Serena held the dress up. It was long and black and completely gorgeous.

Jenny didn't know what to say. She wished she were the kind of girl who could complain about shopping with her mother. She wished she were the kind of girl who could complain about a beautiful dress being ugly. But she wasn't.

"Is everything all right, dear?" Maureen strode over and handed Jenny a strapless bra contraption to try on with her dresses.

Jenny took the bra and glanced at Serena, her cheeks burning. "I'd better keep trying this stuff on. See you Monday, Serena."

She let the curtain fall closed, but Maureen pulled it open a few inches. "That looks nice," she said, nodding approvingly at the orange dress. "It suits you."

Jenny grimaced. "Does it come in black?"

"But you're too young for black," Maureen said, frowning. She swept into the dressing room and yanked up the dress's back zipper, which was only partially zipped.

The dress had no give and no room to spare. Jenny felt like she was being squeezed from all sides, suffocated, tortured. She glared suspiciously at Maureen's reflection in the mirror. How did she know this Barneys saleswomen wasn't a total psychopath? For all she knew Maureen could be the freakish murderer responsible for all the killings she'd read about online.

She pulled away from Maureen's abusive hands and yanked the orange dress off over her head. "Thanks for your help," she said, stuffing the dress and the horrible flesh-colored strapless bra device into Maureen's arms. She pushed the saleswoman out of the dressing room and closed the curtain in her face. "I'd like to finish trying these on in private, please."

Whipping off her bra, she reached for a black stretch satin dress she'd picked out herself. She pulled the dress on and felt it ooze all over her in a comfortable yet sexy way. It even had hidden pockets.

In case she needed to carry a weapon?

When she looked up, little Jenny Humphrey had vanished from the dressing room. In her place was a gorgeous goddess who looked like she could fire real bullets out of her sizable breasts.

Down in men's evening wear, Dan was hoping Chuck would deign to speak to him, given that Dan was wearing a very expensive Armani tux.

Chuck yanked open his dressing room curtain. A tan leather eye patch with the letters *C.B.* monogrammed on it in gold covered his right eye. Dan couldn't believe it. That's all the ambulance had been for—Chuck had hurt his eye?

"The Barneys guy just taught me how to do this." Dan gestured toward Chuck's lamely tied bow tie, which was dark purple silk and had a black tag dangling from it that said Yves Saint Laurent. "It's actually pretty easy," he added, trying and failing to keep the condescension out of his voice. Chuck's family probably employed nannies or slaves to tie his bow ties for him, which was why he didn't know how to do it himself.

Chuck shrugged his shoulders and stuffed his hands into his sleek YSL tuxedo pockets. "Go ahead. It's not like it could look any worse."

Dan reached out and yanked on the purple silk bow tie until it untied and dangled loose from Chuck's white tuxedo shirt neck. He moved behind Chuck and put his arms around him to retie it.

The boys faced the mirror. Dan glared at their reflection. Chuck's hair was slicked back in a particularly annoying fashion and with Dan's arms around Chuck's neck it looked like they were hugging.

"First you make a loop," he instructed. "Then you make another loop, wind it around, and push it through—"

"Like this isn't totally gay," Chuck commented with a smirk.

Dan ignored him. "Then you pull it tight." He tightened the bow tie and kept on tightening and tightening it. He stood on tiptoe and tightened it some more.

> *Taut silk round your neck.*
> *Let's hope that was your last breath.*
> *No one knows I'm here.*

"Hey," Chuck gasped. "Hey!"

The salesman parted the curtain and poked his head into the dressing room.

"You boys okay?"

He frowned when he saw Chuck's red face and Dan's look of guilty consternation. The bow loops of the tie were Minnie Mouse huge.

"Oh dear, let me." The salesman swept in and untied the purple bow.

Chuck doubled over and sucked in his breath. "Fucking idiot asshole!"

But Dan, foiled again, had already vanished.

she's come undone

"Shut up! Shut up! Shut up, shut up, shut up!"

Blair threw her laptop across her room, smashing it against her closet door. Shoes toppled willy-nilly from the shoe rack. Kitty Minky jumped off his pillow and hid under the bed. Blair ripped off her red velvet Natori dressing gown and threw that across the room too. If she had to read one more word about how famous the Remi brothers were now that they were dead, and how valuable their portraits were going to be, she was going to throw herself out her penthouse window, and the corpse would be anything but pretty after those foul, totally unendangered birds were done pecking at it.

But that would be giving Serena exactly what she wanted.

Blair's old Barbies dangled from their nooses, blond and dead and sad. She'd tied them to the chandelier over her bed so she could lie beneath them, plotting and scheming with morbid dedication. But killing her Barbies had given her no more satisfaction than killing the Remi brothers. She couldn't rest until Serena was dead and gone and out of her life. In fact, Blair was so completely obsessed with murdering Serena that she thought she might have to kill Serena not once, but twice, just for the thrill of it.

Coming soon, a new society lifestyle cookbook: *The Joy of Killing*.

Blair pulled on a pair of stretchy black Topshop leggings and a murderously soft black Tse cashmere tunic. Then she began to search for just the right weapon to execute the execution of her former best friend.

The penthouse was deliciously deserted. Eleanor and Cyrus were away until Sunday, and her little brother, Tyler, was at a friend's house. Tyler had taken fencing a few years back. She padded into his room and began to dig in his stinky little brother closet for his old fencing foil. The foil was tucked behind a hockey stick and a golf club. It was disappointingly bendy and not sharp enough at all. That would never do.

She moved on to her mother's medicine cabinet. The shelves were laden with a shocking number of prescription bottles with names that she vaguely recognized as potentially harmful—Valium, Percocet, Ambien, Xanax—but she didn't want to kill Serena with pills. She wanted to kill her in cold blood.

And so it went. Blair spent the entire day wandering from room to room, plotting Serena's dire end with any number of fire pokers, letter openers, nail scissors, the cook's meat carving and bread slicing collection, the maid's ironing equipment, and the nail gun and electric drill that were stashed in the hall closet for uses unknown.

She was in the living room, standing in the window and passing from hand to hand a Japanese sushi knife she'd found in the pantry, when she spotted a blond girl down below on the street, turning off Fifth Avenue and entering the park.

A day's worth of adrenaline pumped through Blair's veins. Not bothering with a coat or her bag, she headed for the elevator, sushi knife in hand.

No one seemed to mind the sight of a half-crazed almost-seventeen-year-old girl brandishing a large, sharp knife, brunette mane flying, as she ran after her prey.

"Serena!" Blair shouted, chasing the blonde up a tree-lined path headed north.

The girl glanced behind her and started to run.

Blair ran faster. She'd been pent up in the house all day. It felt good to run. They ran down the path and through a field and over a bridge and up another steeper path through the woods. As the gap between them closed, Blair raised the knife up, bracing for the kill.

But the girl kept running and running, all the way to the obelisk behind the Metropolitan Museum of Art, where the path ended abruptly. She had nowhere to go.

The blonde turned back toward Blair just as Blair swung the knife, holding it in both hands for extra head-chopping power. Serena was born on Bastille Day. It seemed especially fitting for her to lose her head; although a guillotine would have been best.

The girl's head separated from her neck with a satisfying slicing sound. Her body fell, while her head soared through the air, landing with a splash in a puddle at the base of the stone obelisk. Blair stared at it as she caught her breath. The hair was long and blond, but the staring, terrified eyes were a muddy brown, not navy blue. The head wasn't Serena's, but at least she'd had a good workout.

Beheading works all the muscle groups.

Blair knew this spot well. Each May, when the cherry blossoms were in full bloom, the Constance Billard girls marched down Fifth Avenue to picnic at Cleopatra's Needle, as the obelisk was called. Their art teachers made them sketch it, their history teachers made them write reports about it, and their gym teachers used it as the halfway mark for relay races.

The obelisk was the oldest man-made object in Central Park, one of a pair of obelisks commissioned by an Egyptian pharaoh back in 1500 BC. It had taken workers one hundred and twelve days to move it from the banks of the Hudson River, where it was delivered by ship from Egypt, to its spot on Greywacke Knoll in Central Park. People came from all over town to watch the raising of the obelisk by the light of two huge bonfires on a snowy night in January 1881. The other obelisk was in London. Blair had gotten extra credit in fifth-grade History for taking a picture of it and e-mailing it to her teacher.

Twilight was setting in and the park was pungent and peaceful. Blair looked up at the looming, pearly expanse of the Met. A host of vultures peered down at her from their perch on the roof ledge. With so much to feed on lately, the birds were content to wait until Blair had gone before claiming their bloody prize.

Blair headed back down the path toward home. She'd be back here soon enough. Tomorrow her family and her friends and their families would all gather for the annual fall brunch beside the reflecting pool in the Sackler Wing of the museum, where the Temple of Dendur was housed. Her family had been benefactors of the museum for over a century. In fact, the Arms and Armor collection had been donated in the Waldorf name. The Arms and

Armor collection happened to be right next door to the Temple of Dendur.

As she walked a slow, wicked smile spread across Blair's face. Enjoy your eggs Benedict, S. It may be your last meal.

an ellipsis

That evening Vanessa Abrams patrolled Madison Square Park, filming more background shots for her remake of *Natural Born Killers*. She sighed, weary of the same old Manhattan sights—a bum with his penis out, a three-legged dog, a little boy selling yellow boxes of stolen peanut M&M's. She needed more stuff like the body outside the pizzeria and the drowned girl in the darkroom. If she got enough footage she could turn the whole movie into a documentary and forget about casting it altogether. She'd call it *Naturally Born Killers: A Sickeningly Addictive High School Movie Without Music, a Prom, Cars, or Blue Jeans.*

The sun had just set. Vanessa decided to sit down on a bench and wait for something interesting to happen.

She didn't have to wait long.

Three young vultures swooped down from the sky and dropped three small objects on the pavement. The objects rolled until they came to a stop in front of Vanessa's bench. Two human eyes and a human nose stared up at her, all in a row, like an ellipsis.

Vanessa zoomed in on them excitedly.

Talk about found art.

sunday brunch

Late Sunday morning the steps of the Metropolitan Museum of Art were crawling with people. Tourists mostly, and locals who had come for a brief visit so they could brag about it to their friends and sound cultured.

Inside, brunch was being served in the Sackler Wing for all the museum's board members and their families. The wing was a superb setting for nighttime parties—glittering gold and exotic, with the moonlight shining dramatically through its modern glass walls. But it was all wrong for brunch. Smoked salmon and eggs and mummified Egyptian pharaohs really don't mix. Plus, the morning sun shining so brightly through the slanting glass walls made even the slightest hangover feel ten times worse.

Who invented brunch anyway? The only decent place to be on a Sunday morning is in bed.

The room was filled with large round tables and freshly scrubbed Upper East Siders. Eleanor Waldorf, Cyrus Rose, the van der Woodsens, the Basses, the Archibalds, and their children were there, all seated around one table. Blair sat between Cyrus Rose and her mother, looking grumpy.

Nate had been intermittently baked, drunk, or passed out since Friday night, and looked woozy and rumpled, as if he'd just woken up. Serena wore a pretty yellow dress she'd bought shopping with her mother the day before, and she'd had her hair cut, with soft layers framing her face. She looked even more beautiful than ever, but felt nervous and jumpy about being seated with Blair and Chuck. Only Chuck seemed at ease, happily gulping his Bloody Mary and looking rather dapper in his Hermès eye patch.

Cyrus Rose sliced his salmon and leek omelet in half and plunked it on a pumpernickel bagel. "I've been craving eggs," he said, biting into it hungrily. "You know when your body tells you you need something?" he said to no one in particular. "Mine's shouting, 'Eggs, eggs, eggs!'"

And mine's shouting, "Shut the fuck up before I ram that omelet down your windpipe," Blair thought.

She winced and pushed her plate away from her. "I hate eggs."

Cyrus pushed her plate back. "No, you eat. All you girls are dying because you're way too thin."

"That's right, Blair," her mother agreed. "Eat your eggs. They'll keep you strong for tennis."

And other strenuous activities.

"I hear eggs make your hair shiny," Misty Bass added.

Blair shook her head. "Eggs make me gag."

Chuck reached across the table. "I'll eat them, if you don't want them."

Blair handed her plate over, careful not to look at Serena or Nate, sitting on either side of Chuck. Instead she watched the table's centerpiece, a fishbowl terrarium full of electric blue poison dart frogs, frantically hopping around their round glass prison.

Jacked up on strong coffee, Serena was busy cutting her omelet into little squares, like Scrabble pieces. She began building tall towers of them.

Out of the corner of his eye, Nate was watching her. He was also watching Chuck's hands. Each time they slid underneath the tablecloth and out of view, Nate imagined them all over Serena's legs.

"Anyone see the Styles section of the *Times* today?" Cyrus asked, looking around the table.

Serena's head shot up. Her picture with the Remi brothers. She'd forgotten all about it.

She pursed her lips and slunk down in her chair, waiting for an inquisition from her parents and everyone else at the table. But it never came. It was part of their social code not to dwell on things that embarrassed them.

"Pass me the cream, Nate darling?" Serena's mother said with a smile.

And that was that.

Nate's mother cleared her throat. "How are the preparations for the *Kiss Me or Die* party going, Blair? Are you girls all ready?" she asked, swigging her Seven and Seven.

"Yes, we're all set," Blair answered politely. "We finally got the invitations cleared up. And Kate Spade is sending over the gift bags after school on Thursday."

"I remember all the cotillions I used to organize," Mrs. van der Woodsen said, with a dreamy expression. "But the thing we always used to worry about most was would the boys show up." She smiled at Nate and Chuck. "We don't have to worry about that with you two, do we?"

"I'm all over it," Chuck said, scarfing Blair's omelet.

"I'll be there," Nate said. He glanced at Blair, who was staring at him now.

Nate was wearing that same green cashmere sweater she had given him in Sun Valley. The one with the gold heart.

"Excuse me," Blair said. Then she stood up abruptly and left the table.

Nate followed her.

"Blair!" he called, weaving his way around the other tables, ignoring his friend Anthony, who was waving to him from across the room. "Wait up!"

Without turning around, Blair began walking even faster, her heels clacking on the white marble floor.

They reached the hallway to the restrooms. "Come on, Blair. I'm sorry, okay? Can we please talk?" Nate called.

Blair reached the door to the women's room and turned around, pushing it halfway open with her rear end.

"Just leave me alone, okay?" she said sharply, and went inside.

Nate stood outside the door for a moment with his hands in his pockets, thinking. That morning, when he'd put on the green sweater Blair had given him, he'd found a little gold heart sewn into the sleeve. He'd never noticed it before, but it was obvious Blair had put it there. For the first time, he'd realized that she really meant it when she'd said she loved him.

It was pretty intense. And pretty flattering. And it kind of made him want her again. It wasn't just any girl who'd sew a gold heart into your clothes. Or cover her body in paint and greet you naked at the door.

He had that right.

Serena had to pee desperately, but Blair was in the bathroom.

After Blair and Nate had been gone for five minutes, though, she couldn't hold it any longer. She stood up and headed for the ladies' room.

Familiar faces gazed up at Serena as she passed their tables. A waitress offered her a glass of champagne. But Serena shook her head and hurried down the marble hall to the bathrooms. Quick, heavy footsteps smacked on the floor behind her. She turned around. It was Cyrus Rose.

"Tell Blair to hurry if she wants dessert, will you?" he told her.

Serena nodded and pushed open the door to the ladies' room. Blair was washing her hands. She looked up, staring at Serena's reflection in the mirror over the sink.

"Cyrus says to hurry if you want dessert," Serena said abruptly, walking into a stall and banging the door shut. She sat down on the toilet, but nothing happened. Her bladder was full, but nothing came out.

Serena couldn't believe herself. How many times in the past had she and Blair gone to the bathroom together, talking and laughing while they peed?

There was a quiet, awkward pause.

Don't you just *hate* awkward pauses?

"Prepare to die," Serena thought she heard Blair whisper in a low growl before she left the bathroom.

The door swung shut, but even with Blair gone Serena couldn't relax. Like Diana, goddess of the hunt, she was the huntress. She wasn't used to being hunted.

Cyrus caught Nate in the men's room.

"You and Blair have a fight?" Cyrus asked. He unzipped his pants and stood at the urinal. Lucky Nate.

Nate shrugged as he washed his hands. "Kind of."

"Let me guess. It was about sex, right?" Cyrus said.

Nate blushed and pulled a paper towel out of the dispenser. "Sort of . . ." He really didn't want to get into it. He certainly wasn't going to mention the body paint.

Cyrus flushed the urinal and joined Nate at the sinks. He washed his hands and began fussing with his tie, which was bright pink with yellow lions' heads on it. Very Versace.

Read: *tacky*.

"The only things couples fight about are sex and money," Cyrus observed.

Nate just stood there with his hands in his pockets.

"That's all right, kid. I'm not going to give you a lecture or anything. This is my future stepdaughter we're talking about. I'm sure as hell not going to tell you how to get into her pants."

Cyrus chuckled to himself and left the bathroom, leaving Nate to stare after him. He wondered if Blair knew Cyrus was planning on marrying her mother.

Nate turned on the tap and splashed cold water on his face. He studied himself in the mirror. He'd been up late last night with the boys, playing stupid drinking games to *Tomb Raider*. Every time they saw Angelina Jolie's nipples, they had to drink. He'd tried to drown his worries about Blair and Serena in as much booze as he could swallow, and now he was paying for it. His face was pale, there were brownish-purple circles under his eyes, and his cheeks were still sort of gray from the paint. He looked like shit.

As soon as this damned brunch was over, he was heading into the park for a smoke in the sun and a can of whiskey and Coke. The perfect cure-all.

But first he'd have to flirt with Blair a little bit. If she would let him.

Instead of returning to her table when she left the ladies' room, Blair made her way across the Sackler Wing, toward Arms and Armor. She'd waited long enough. It was time.

Rain and Laura spotted her first.

"Blair! Over here!" Rain called, patting the empty gold chair next to her. Their parents and friends were working the room, socializing, so the girls had the table to themselves.

"Here," Laura said, handing Blair a glass full of champagne and peach puree.

"Thanks," Blair said, taking an impatient sip.

"Anthony Avuldsen just came over and tried to get us to come to the park with him." Rain giggled. "He's kind of cute, you know, in a Waspoid kind of way."

Hey, cool word!

Laura rolled her eyes. "Isn't this boring? How's your table?"

"Don't ask," Blair said. "Did you see who I'm sitting with?"

The other two girls sniggered. "Have you seen that billboard of her by those dead artist guys?" Laura said.

Blair nodded and rolled her eyes.

"What's it supposed to be, anyway?" Rain asked. "Her belly button?"

Blair had gotten awfully close to having her own Remi brothers portrait done, but she still had no idea. "Who cares?"

"She has no shame," Laura ventured. "I actually feel kind of sorry for her."

"Me too," Rain agreed.

"Well, don't," Blair said fiercely before making her escape.

Nate pushed open the men's room door at exactly the same time that Serena pushed open the ladies'. Together, they walked down the hallway back to the table.

"Nate," Serena said, smoothing her new yellow Marni dress over her legs. "Can you please explain why you're not talking to me?"

"I'm not not talking to you," Nate said. "See, I'm talking to you right now."

"Barely," Serena said. "What happened? What's wrong? Did Blair say something to you about me?"

Instinctively, Nate reached into his jacket pocket and fingered the silver flask of whiskey that was hidden there. He looked down at the marble floor, avoiding Serena's beautiful sad eyes.

"We should get back," he said, speeding up.

"Fine," Serena answered, trailing after him.

Chuck smirked at them knowingly as they returned to their chairs. *How was it?* his face seemed to say.

Serena wanted to rip off his other eyelid. She ordered another cup of coffee, dumped four teaspoons of sugar in it, and stirred and stirred, wondering where the hell Blair had gone.

Nate ordered a Bloody Mary. Chuck followed suit.

"Bottoms up!" Chuck cried cheerfully, banging his glass against Nate's and taking a big gulp. Blood red tomato juice sloshed on the white tablecloth. Blue frogs hopped crazily in their round glass cage.

Serena pushed her chair back and stood up to hunt for Blair.

A Kentucky rifle. A double-barrel breechloading pinfire shotgun. The crossbow of Count Ulrich V of Würtemberg. The rapier of Christian II, Elector of Saxony. The flintlock gun of Louis XIII, King of France. The flintlock pistols of Empress Catherine the Great. Rowel spurs. A powder horn. The smallsword of Colonel Marinus Willet.

Blair browsed the displays, finally deciding on a pretty Colt third model Dragoon percussion revolver inlaid with tiny golden animals and displayed in a nifty blue velvet–lined wooden box. A life-sized oil portrait of the proud Revolutionary War leader Colonel Marinus Willet himself looked on as she wrapped her fist in her lavender Lutz & Patmos cashmere cardigan and broke the glass.

Serena heard the alarm. Instinct told her to run toward the sound, sure that Blair was up to something. She dashed across the sun-dappled Charles Engelhard Court in the American Wing and through the glass doors to Arms and Armor. The doors swung shut and locked behind her. Before her stood the collection's central exhibit, a lifelike display of four mounted knights and their horses. The alarm pealed loudly. Tourists ambled around the display, unfazed. Blair was nowhere in sight.

"Miss, you can't do that!" a suited security guard on the other side of the display shouted at Blair.

Blair pointed the revolver at him. "Oh, shut up," she snapped. "My family basically owns this entire wing."

Serena shot around the mounted knights and across the main hall. She ran up behind the quavering guard under Blair's arrest and stopped short. "I doubt they'd put a loaded gun in a display case, Blair."

Blair pulled the trigger, hoping to blow a large hole through the guard's chest and then through Serena's. The trigger clicked. Nothing happened. Fuck. Serena was right.

Both girls dashed away to arm themselves. Serena broke a glass case and chose the saber of Sultan Murad V. It was long and sharp and perfectly arched, with a gorgeous gold-tassled jade hilt, encrusted with gold and precious jewels. Blair broke another case and chose a yataghan from the court of Süleyman the Magnificent, a gleaming sword-machete-spear combo with a nearly three-foot-long blade that looked sharp as hell and was decorated in gold with a fight scene between a dragon with ruby eyes and a phoenix with silver teeth.

The weapons were so heavy the girls had to use both hands to wield them. The security guard had disappeared, either afraid for his life or calling for backup, or both. The alarm was loud. It rang in the girls' ears. But that didn't stop the tourists.

Nothing ever does.

"Do you girls know how to get to the Arts of Africa, Oceana, and the Americas?" a ditzy bald man wearing half-glasses asked them.

"Shut up!" Blair shouted at him, and sliced him in half.

"Blair!" Serena scolded while taking a stab at Blair with the saber.

"Like you're so perfect," Blair scoffed, leaping away with balletic grace.

Serena drew back the saber and prepared to strike again, accidentally disemboweling a tour of matriarchs from the Cosmopolitan Club while she was at it.

Whoops.

Blair swung at Serena with the yataghan's gleaming blade. Two security guards ran in to stop her, losing their legs as Serena swung back with the saber to defend herself.

Whoops again.

Besides the now-locked doors to the American Wing, Arms and Armor had only two methods of egress—the main entrance, and a stairway in the far right-hand corner of the hall. Serena sprinted toward the stairs, her breath coming short and fast, her arms aching as she ran with the heavy saber.

Blood dripped from Blair's weapon onto her gunmetal Miu Miu mules.

"Oh, no you don't!" Blair cried, giving chase.

The girls' footsteps echoed in the cavernous hall. A display of armor for a mounted Japanese samurai warrior looked on in delight, his cricket bat of a sword remaining sheathed in its leopardskin scabbard.

Running up stairs with a long, heavy saber was hard work. Plus, Serena didn't play tennis. With aching legs and arms she labored, sweating and panting, to the top of the stairs, headed for Musical Instruments on the second floor.

Next thing you know they'll be going at it with cellos.

Far fitter, Blair took the marble steps two at a time. Soon she was right behind that familiar blond swath of hair. Blair squared her shoulders and took aim. She drew her arm back like a bow and hurled the yataghan at Serena's straining form, catching her between the shoulder blades. Blood blossomed on the yellow dress. Slowly, like a slain warrior in a movie, Serena dropped her saber, staggered, and fell.

Blair wished she had a chainsaw. Somehow she'd expected Serena's death to be grisly, gruesome, and *noisy*. But the stairwell was quiet. She waited for Serena to rise up and strike again like Glenn Close in the bathtub at the end of *Fatal Attraction*, but nothing happened, not even a twitch of Serena's bloody hand. Blair turned and headed back downstairs again, feeling slightly ripped off. At least Serena was dead now, but her new shoes were totally fucked.

Security was busy locking down the area. No one was allowed in or out while the murderers ran amok. Blair returned to her table and began to devour her crème brûlée. It was full of eggs, but she didn't care—she'd throw it all up soon anyway.

"Hey Blair." Nate came up behind her and put his hands on her shoulders, causing Blair to drop her spoon with a clatter. He smiled and leaned over her. "That looks awesome. Can I have a bite?"

Blair's hand fluttered nervously to her heart. Sexy Nate. Her Nate. God, she still wanted him—so, so much. But she wasn't going to give up that easily. She had her pride. Regaining her composure, she reached for her Bloody Mary and downed the entire drink in one big swallow, including the poison dart frog Chuck had thrown in just for fun.

"You can have the rest," she belched and pushed her chair back. "Excuse me."

Outside the Met the ambulances were just arriving. There would be quite a commotion once they figured out that Serena van der Woodsen was dead.

Blair clacked away on her soiled mules to the ladies' room where she could stick her finger down her throat *and* hide from security.

Some lady.

gossipgirl.net

hey people!

I thought **S** looked cute in her picture in the Sunday *Times* Styles section. Although her teachers probably weren't thrilled to see her double-fisting martinis on a school night. To tell you the truth, I'm kind of over the whole thing. I mean, isn't it enough that we have to see that picture of her every time we use public transportation? Obviously *you're* not over it yet, though.

YOUR E-MAIL

q: hey gg,
i went to the show at the gallery and looked for ur picture. very sexy. i like ur column too. u rule.
—Bigfan

a: Dear Bigfan,
As long as you are not a stalker, I guess I'm flattered.
—GG

q: Dear Gossip Girl,
When I saw **S**'s picture in the paper, I had an idea!! Are you **S**? If you are, you are very sneaky. Also, my dad loves you and wants you to write a book. He's got lots of connections. If you tell me who you are, he can make you famous.
—JNYHY

a: Hey JNYHY,
You are very sneaky yourself. And not to brag or anything, but I'm already

kind of famous. Infamous is more like it. All the more reason for me not to tell you who I am.

—GG

SIGHTINGS

D returning a gorgeous **Armani** tux at **Barneys** and renting a much less gorgeous one at a formal store. His sister **J** buying underwear at **La Petite Coquette**, although she chickened out on the thong. **N** buying a big bag of pot in Central Park. Tell me something new. **B** in the **J. Sisters** salon getting waxed, buffed, and shined. And **S**? **S** has gone missing. Not in school, not anywhere. There certainly were a lot of ambulances at the Met yesterday. Say it isn't so . . . ?

A THONG

MUSEUM NEWS FLASH

First, a valuable seventeenth-century Indian dagger with a very sharp blade forged of watered steel and a hilt made of engraved gold encrusted with emeralds remains missing from the Metropolitan Museum of Art's recently ransacked Arms and Armor collection. Know anyone with a thing for emeralds or sharp knives?

Secondly, the Frick, that famously beautiful old home of industrialist Henry Clay Frick on Seventieth and Fifth, now a museum and home to so many of our best parties, has been renamed the Katherine Farkas and Isabel Coates Memorial House in honor of our slain sisters. Can't wait to raise a toast to them on Friday!

TWO QUESTIONS

First: If you knew about a party that you weren't invited to, wouldn't you go, just to piss people off? I would.

Second: If you'd made up your mind to go to the party, wouldn't you want to really rub people's noses in it by appearing out of nowhere looking completely gorgeous and stealing everyone's boyfriends? *Definitely*.

But who knows what **S** will decide to do, if she's even with us anymore. That girl is full of surprises. . . .

At least I've given us all something to think about while we're getting our pedicures, plucking our eyebrows, and concealing our blemishes and stab wounds.

See you at the party!

You know you love me,

gossip girl

s, the resurrection

"Ugly, ugly, ugly," the tall blonde muttered, wadding her new black dress into a ball and tossing it onto her bed.

A gorgeous black crepe de chine Tocca dress? Come on, how ugly can it be?

All week long she'd been in an induced coma at Clinic Schloss Mammern in Switzerland, healing. The wound was sealed, but Serena still felt only half-there, a ghostly shadow of her former self, a girl people had known once, but couldn't quite remember anymore. And for the first time in her entire life, she felt ugly and awkward. Her eyes and hair looked dull, and her beautiful smile and cool demeanor had been roped off until further notice.

Now it was Friday, the night of the *Kiss Me or Die* party. And the question she couldn't answer: to go or not to go?

It used to be, before fancy parties like this, Serena and her friends would spend half the night getting dressed together—swilling gin and tonics, dancing around in their underwear, trying on crazy out-fits. But tonight she rummaged through her closet alone.

There was the pair of jeans with the rip in the leg where she'd snagged them on a barbed wire fence in Ridgefield. There was the white satin dress she'd worn to the Christmas dance in ninth grade. Her brother's old leather jacket. Her moldy tennis shoes that should have been thrown out two years ago. And what was this? A red wool sweater—Nate's. Serena held it to her face and smelled it. It smelled like her, not him.

Toward the back of the closet was a black velvet flapper dress that Serena had bought with Blair at a vintage store. It was a dress to wear while drinking and dancing and lounging around decoratively in a huge house full of people having a good time. It reminded Serena of the good-time gal she'd been when she bought the dress—her old self, the girl she'd been up until two weeks ago. She let her robe drop to the floor and slipped the dress on over her head. Maybe it would give her back some of her power.

Barefoot, she padded into her parents' dressing room, where they were getting ready for their own black tie affair.

"What do you think?" Serena asked, doing a little twirl in front of them.

"Oh, Serena, you're not wearing *that*. Tell me you're not," her mother exclaimed, fastening a long rope of pearls around her neck.

"What's wrong with it?" Serena demanded.

"It's an old ratty thing," Mrs. van der Woodsen said. "It's just the sort of dress my grandmother was buried in. Besides, it droops in the back. Your scar shows."

"What about one of those outfits you bought with your mother last weekend?" Mr. van der Woodsen suggested. "Didn't you buy anything to wear to the party?"

"Of course she did," Mrs. van der Woodsen said. "She bought a lovely black dress."

"That makes me look like the Bride of Frankenstein," Serena said grumpily. She put her hands on her hips and posed in front of her mother's full-length mirror. "I like this dress. It's got character."

Her mother sighed disapprovingly. "Well, what's Blair wearing?"

Serena stared at her mother and blinked. Under normal circumstances she would have known exactly what Blair was wearing, down to her underwear. And Blair would have insisted on going shoe shopping together, because if you bought a new dress, you had to have a pair of new shoes. Blair loved shoes.

But last weekend Blair had almost killed her.

"Blair told everyone to wear vintage," she lied.

Her mother was about to respond when Serena heard her phone ring in her bedroom. Was it Nate calling to apologize? Blair? She raced down the hall in her bare feet, scrambling to pick it up.

"Hello?" she said breathlessly.

"Yo, bitch. Sorry I haven't called in a while."

Serena took a deep breath and sat down on her bed.

"Hey," she said. Erik didn't know about Switzerland. About her almost dying. Her mother wanted as few people to know as possible.

"Saw you in the Styles section last Sunday. You are crazy, aren't you?" her brother laughed. "What did Mom say?"

"Nothing. It's like I can do whatever I want now. Everyone thinks I'm like, *ruined* or something," Serena fumbled for the right words.

"That's not true. Hey, what's up? You sound sad."

"Yeah." Serena's lower lip started to tremble. It wasn't a tantrum brewing this time, but actual tears. "I sort of am."

"How come? What's going on?"

"I don't know. There's this party I'm supposed to go to that everyone's going to. You know how it is," she began.

"That doesn't sound so bad," Erik said gently.

Serena propped her pillows against the headboard of her bed and wriggled under her comforter.

"It's just that no one's talking to me anymore. I don't even know why, but ever since I've been back it's been like I have Mad Cow disease or something." One by one, the tears began to fall.

"What about Blair and Nate? Those guys must be talking to you," Erik said. "They're your best friends."

"Not anymore," Serena said quietly. Tears were streaming freely down her face now. She picked up a pillow and dabbed it against her cheeks to stem the flow.

"Well, you know what I say?" Erik asked.

Serena swallowed and wiped her nose on the back of her hand. "What?"

"Fuck 'em. Totally. You don't need them. You're like, the coolest chick in the Western Hemisphere. Fuck 'em, fuck 'em, fuck 'em."

"Yeah," Serena responded doubtfully. "But they're my friends."

"Not anymore. You just said so yourself. You can get new friends. I'm serious," Erik said. "You can't let assholes turn you into an asshole. You just have to fuck 'em."

It was a perfect Erikism. Serena laughed, wiped her runny nose on a pillow, and threw it across the room. "Okay," she said, sitting up. "You're right."

"I'm always right. That's why I'm so hard to get ahold of. There's a huge demand for people like me."

"I miss you," Serena told him, chewing on her pinky nail. Her knuckles were still sore and bruised from last weekend.

"Miss you too," Erik said.

"Serena? We're leaving!" she heard her mother call from out in the hall.

"Okay, I better go," Serena said. "Love you."

"Bye."

Serena clicked off. On the end of her bed was the invitation to the *Kiss Me or Die* party that Jenny had made for her. She snatched it up and tossed it in her wastepaper basket.

Erik was right. She didn't have to go to some stupid benefit just because everyone else was going. They didn't even want her there. Fuck 'em. She was free to do what she pleased. Besides, if she went to the party she and Blair would just try to kill each other again, and she was sort of tired of that game. Enough was enough. It was time to move on.

She carried her phone over to her desk and shuffled through a pile of papers until she found the Constance Billard School student directory, which had arrived in the mail on Monday. Serena read through the names. She wasn't the only one skipping the party. She could find a new friend.

Serena dialed a number and the phone began to ring. She ducked down beneath her bed and pulled out the violin case. Snapping it open, she withdrew the bloody hunting knife.

the red or the black

"Hello?" Vanessa said, picking up the phone. She was getting ready to go out with her sister. Right now she was wearing a black bra, black jeans, and her Doc Martens. She didn't have any clean black shirts left. Her sister was trying to convince her to wear a red one.

"Hi. Is this Vanessa Abrams?" a girl's voice said on the other end of the phone.

"Yes. Who's this?" Vanessa stood in front of her bedroom mirror and held the red shirt up to her chest. She hadn't worn anything but black in two years. Why should she start now? *Please?*

"It's Serena van der Woodsen."

Vanessa stopped looking at herself and threw the shirt on her bed. "Hey. I thought you were dead. Where the fuck's my knife, bitch?"

"That's why I'm calling. I'd like to return it."

"Uh-huh," Vanessa said, trying to figure out why Serena van der Woodsen of all people would be calling her up on a Friday night. Didn't she have a ball to go to or something? Some fête?

"I could bring it over now. Tonight. If that's okay."

"Sounds good." Vanessa frowned down at the pale roll of flab above her waistband. She sucked her stomach in. "Although I'm going out pretty soon."

"Okay." Serena paused. She didn't seem very eager to hang up the phone.

"Hey, isn't tonight that big party at the Frick or whatever the fuck they're calling that place now?" Vanessa said. "Aren't you going?"

"Nah," Serena responded. "I wasn't invited."

Vanessa nodded, processing this information. Serena van der Woodsen wasn't invited? Maybe she wasn't so bad after all.

"Well, do you want to come out with us tonight?" Vanessa offered before she could stop herself. "Me and my big sister are going to a bar here in Williamsburg. Her band is playing. It's sort of a headbanging slam-fest type thing. People always get hurt or arrested or trampled to death."

"Sounds great!" Serena cried. "I'll bring the knife."

Vanessa gave her the address of the Five and Dime—the bar where her sister's band played—and hung up the phone.

Life was so strange. One day you could be picking your nose and plotting to blow up your school with everyone in it, and the next day you could be inviting Serena van der Woodsen to hang out and talk knives. She picked up the red shirt, pulled it on over her head, and looked in the mirror. She looked like a tulip. A tulip with a stubbly black head.

"Dan will like it," her sister Ruby told her, standing in the doorway. She handed Vanessa a tube of dark red lipstick. *Vamp.*

"Well, Dan's not coming out tonight." Vanessa smirked at her sister. She dabbed on the lipstick and rubbed her lips together. "He has to take his little sister to some fancy ball."

She checked herself out in the mirror once more. The lipstick made her big brown eyes look even bigger, and the shirt was kind of cool, in a loud, look-at-me way. She stuck out her chest and smiled invitingly at her reflection. *Maybe I'll get lucky*, she thought. Or maybe not.

"I have a friend coming to meet us," she told Ruby.

"Boy or girl?" Ruby asked, turning around to check out her butt in the mirror.

"Girl."

"Name?" said Ruby, rubbing hair gel into her thick black bangs.

"Serena van der Woodsen," Vanessa mumbled.

"The girl whose picture is all over town?" Ruby said, clearly delighted. "The girl who may or may not have murdered those twin artists?"

"Yeah, that's her," Vanessa said.

"Thought she'd kicked it," Ruby said.

As if any legend ever really dies.

kiss me or die

"What fantastic flowers," chirped Becky Dormand, a junior at Constance. She kissed Blair on both cheeks. "And what a hot dress!"

"Thanks, Beck." Blair looked down at her simple dark green satin Prada gown. The emerald-encrusted dagger she'd stolen from the Met was strapped to her thigh, concealed beneath the ankle-length gown. Call her paranoid, but ever since her battle with Serena inside the Arms and Armor collection she'd decided to stay armed, just in case.

You never know when your best friend is going to rise from the dead and stab you in the back.

A waiter walked by with a tray of champagne. Blair whisked a flute off his tray and downed it in a matter of seconds. It was her third so far.

"I love your shoes," Blair said. Becky was wearing black high-heeled sandals that laced all the way up to her knees. They went perfectly with her short black tutu dress and her super-high ponytail. She looked like a ballerina on acid.

"I can't wait for people to open the gift bags," Laura Salmon squealed.

"I can't believe we put glow-in-the-dark condoms in them," Rain Hoffstetter giggled. "And those little pen knives! Are we crazy?"

"Not that you'll be needing them," Laura quipped.

"How do you know?" Rain huffed.

"Blair?" Blair heard someone say in a tremulous voice.

Blair turned around to see little Ginny Humphrey standing behind her, looking like a human Wonderbra in her black stretch satin dress.

"Oh, hello," Blair said coolly. "Thanks again for doing the invitations. They really came out great."

"Thanks for *letting* me do them," Jenny said. Her eyes darted around the huge room, which was throbbing with people and music and smoke. Black three-foot-high candles in tall glass beakers trimmed with peacock feathers and fragrant white orchids flickered everywhere. Jenny had never been to anything this cool in her life. "God, I don't know anyone here," she said nervously.

"You don't?" Blair wondered if Ginny thought she was going to talk to her all night.

"No. My brother Dan was supposed to come with me, but he didn't really want to, so I just let him drop me off. Actually, I do know one other person," Jenny said.

"Oh," said Blair. "And who is that?"

"Serena," Jenny chirped. "Have you seen her?"

Just then, a waitress brandished a platter of sushi under Blair's nose. Blair grabbed a chunky tuna roll and shoved it into her mouth. The dagger dug into her thigh. It might be fun to kick off the party by slitting Ginny's throat.

"Serena's not coming," she said, chewing hungrily. *She's dead,* she added smugly to herself. *And you will be too, very soon, little Ginny. Just as soon as I eat a few more of these delicious hors d'oeuvres.*

Jenny snagged two flutes of champagne from a waiter's tray. She frowned as she handed one to Blair. "I know Serena's been out sick, but I didn't think she'd miss the party." She paused to take a tiny sip of champagne. Blair looked sort of angry for some reason. Maybe she should stop talking before something bad happened.

Blair burped queasily. The worshipful way Ginny talked about Serena was making her nauseous. She'd have to wait to kill her until after she vomited.

"I'll be right back," she said, practically running for the powder room.

Jenny polished off her champagne. Another waiter walked by with more full glasses, and she grabbed two. She'd never had champagne before. It tasted wonderful.

The party was crowded, but there was no one to talk to. Jenny carried her champagne over to the bottom step of a marble staircase and sat down. If only her dress weren't quite so tight. She continued to drink, taking in the sparkling room and congratulating herself for making it there.

Two pigskin-loafered feet appeared beside her on the step.

"Well, *hello*," a deep voice said, hovering above her.

Jenny looked up. Her eyes settled on Chuck Bass's handsome gold monogrammed eye patch–bedazzled face. She sucked in her breath. He was the most dashing boy she'd ever seen, and he was looking right at her.

"Aren't you going to introduce me?" Chuck said, staring at Jenny's chest.

"To who?" Jenny frowned in confusion.

He just laughed and held out his hand. The cleavage on her! "I'm Chuck Bass. Would you like to dance?"

Jenny hesitated, but only for a second. She wasn't wearing a sexy black dress just to sit on the steps by herself all night. She stood up, feeling a little wobbly after all that champagne.

"Sure, let's dance," she slurred, falling against Chuck's chest.

He slipped his arm around her waist and squeezed it tight. "Good girl," he said, like he was talking to a dog.

Jenny stumbled and swayed against Chuck as they danced. This boy was so handsome, so debonair. The music was amazing. This party was amazing. This would definitely go down as one of the most memorable nights of her life.

If she survived.

the five and dime

"Have whatever you want," Vanessa told Serena. "It's on the house."

Ruby took their order. Because she played bass in the band, she got drinks for free.

"And don't forget my cherry!" Vanessa yelled after her as Ruby left to get the drinks.

"Your sister's awesome," Serena said, admiring Ruby's cool black bob and dark green leather pants.

Vanessa shrugged her shoulders. "Yeah," she agreed. "It's a pain in my ass. I mean, everyone's always like, 'Ruby's so cool,' and I'm like, 'Hello? Fuck you.'"

Serena laughed. "I know what you mean. My older brother— he goes to Brown, and everybody loves him. My parents are always so into everything he does, and now that I'm back from boarding school it's like, 'Oh, we have a daughter?'"

"Totally," Vanessa agreed. She couldn't believe she was having such a ridiculously normal conversation with Serena van der Woodsen, psycho killer.

Ruby brought them their drinks. "Okay guys, I gotta go set up."

"Good luck," Serena told her.

"Thanks, sweetie," Ruby said. She picked up her guitar case and went to find her bandmates.

Un-fucking-believable, Vanessa thought. Ruby never called anyone sweetie except for Tofu, her parakeet. Serena certainly had a way of melting people's hearts. Vanessa was even starting to like her a little herself.

She picked up her drink and clinked her glass against Serena's. "To coolass chicks," she said, knowing it sounded seriously gay, but not really giving a shit.

Serena laughed and tossed back her shot of Stoli. She wiped her eyes and blinked a few times. A scruffy-looking guy wearing an oversized tuxedo was walking into the bar. He stopped in the doorway and stared at Serena as if he'd seen a ghost.

"Hey, isn't that your friend Dan?" Serena said, pointing.

Dan was wearing a tuxedo for the first time in his life. He'd felt pretty sharp when he first put it on, but not sharp enough to deal with *Kiss Me or Die*. After dropping Jenny off he'd asked the cab to head over to the Five and Dime, hoping Vanessa would accept his apology for being such a dick about the movie.

On the ride over he'd tried to convince himself that it didn't matter that he'd probably never see Serena van der Woodsen again. He'd heard a strange rumor that she was dead anyway.

> *The meter ran out.*
> *Life is fragile and absurd.*
> *This love never dies.*

Life was absurd all right. Because *there Serena was*. Alive, and in Williamsburg, of all places. His dream girl.

Dan felt like Cinderella, in a tuxedo. He shoved his hands in his pockets to keep them from shaking, and tried to plan his next move. He would walk over and suavely offer to buy Serena a drink. Too bad the only suave thing about him was his outfit. And it was only half as suave as it would have been if he'd kept the Armani from Barneys.

"Hey," Dan said when he reached their table, his voice cracking.

"What're you doing here?" Vanessa demanded. She couldn't believe her luck. Did it have to be quite this bad? Was she going to have to sit there for the rest of the night watching Dan drool over Serena? The bowie knife was still in Serena's pretty black patent leather clutch. Vanessa had told her to keep it in there until it was time to part ways. She could whip it out now and put Dan out of his drooling misery.

"I blew off *Kiss Me or Die*," Dan explained. "Not my thing."

"Me too." Serena smiled at Dan like he'd never been smiled at before.

Dan clutched the back of Vanessa's chair for balance.

Heart!
You there.
That wasn't life—this is.

"Hey," he greeted her shyly.

"You remember Serena," Vanessa said. "She's in my class at Constance."

"Nice tux," Serena said.

Dan blushed and looked down at himself. "Thanks." He looked up again. "And that dress is . . . looks . . . pretty also," he stuttered. He hadn't thought it was possible to sound so idiotic. When had he forgotten how to talk?

When he stopped talking and starting writing depressing haikus instead?

"What about *my* shirt?" Vanessa said loudly. She stood up and twirled around. "Have you ever seen me look this hot?"

Dan stared at Vanessa's red T-shirt. Not very exciting. "Is it new?" he asked, confused.

"Never mind." Vanessa collapsed in her chair, her eyes on Serena's purse. Who to stab—Dan or Serena? Both?

"Come, sit." Serena moved over to make room for Dan. "The band is going to start soon. I hear it gets pretty rough."

The rumors couldn't possibly be true, Dan thought. Serena didn't act like a sex-crazed, drug-addicted, maniacal murderess. She looked delicate and perfect and exciting, like a wildflower you stumble upon unexpectedly in Central Park. Dan wanted to hold hands with her and whisper love poems in her ear all night.

> *Sweet forget-me-not.*
> *I'll slit my throat now, smiling.*
> *Forget me—never.*

He sat down next to her. His hands were shaking so badly he had to sit on them to keep them still.

The band started to play. Ruby let out a bloodcurdling yowl and slammed heads with the drummer. Serena finished her vodka.

"Want some more?" Dan offered eagerly.

She shook her head. "Let's just listen to the music for a while."

She sat back in her chair. Their elbows touched. Ruby let out another yowl and threw her black steel-toed combat boots into the audience.

Dan pressed his elbow against Serena's as hard as he dared. She could kill him now and he would die happy.

as usual, *b* is in the bathroom and *n* is stoned

"Let the festivities commence!" Anthony Avuldsen cried, throwing open the doors to the Katherine Farkas and Isabel Coates Memorial House.

As always, Nate, Anthony, and Charlie had smoked a big fattie before the party. Nate was silly high, and when he walked through the door and saw Blair pushing her way through the crowd with her hand clapped over her mouth, he started to giggle. Rumor had it that Blair had stabbed Serena, which was why Serena had been out of school all week. And Serena hadn't responded to either one of his two stoned texts. But sometimes you just had to laugh. Blair, with her weak stomach, actually stabbing anyone? Ha!

Ha!

"What're you laughing at, jackass?" Anthony said, shoving his elbow into Nate's ribs. "Nothing's even happened yet."

Nate wiped his hand over his face and tried to look serious, but it was hard to keep a straight face in a room full of boys dressed like penguins, and girls in sexy dresses. Blair was probably already in the bathroom. The question was, should he go and rescue her? It was the type of thing a good, concerned boy-friend would do.

"Bar's over there," Charlie said, leading the way.

"I'll catch you guys later," Nate called. He ducked around Chuck in his eye patch, gyrating his crotch against the ass of a short girl with curly brown hair and insane cleavage, and headed for the ladies' room.

But Blair hadn't made it there. She'd been stopped by a middle-aged woman in a red Chanel suit with a "Save the Birds" button pinned to it.

"Blair Waldorf?" the woman said, smiling her best fundraising smile. "I'm from the Birds of Prey Foundation."

Talk about bad timing.

Blair stared at the woman's outstretched palm. Her own right hand was clapped over her mouth, holding in the vomit that threatened to spew out at any moment. She started to remove it, but then a waiter walked by with sizzling skewers of chicken satay, causing her to gag.

Blair squeezed her lips together to keep the puke from seeping out the sides of her mouth. She held out her left hand. It would have to do.

"It's so wonderful to finally meet you," the bird woman said. "Although I do have a little confession to make." She took a step closer, still holding Blair's hand. "Our birds aren't really endangered anymore. In fact, the mayor wants to start euthanizing them. Which, of course, we're against."

Blair snatched her hand away, unsure of whether to puke all over the woman or stab her with one of the chicken skewers. Both would be messy, and it was such a nice party. Her eyes darted around the crowded room, desperate for help.

There were Rain and Laura, dancing with each other. There was Anthony Avuldsen, handing out tabs of E. There was Charlie Dern, trying to teach a group of Seaton Arms girls how to blow smoke rings by the bar. There was Chuck, holding that little Ginny girl so tight it looked like her boobs might explode.

All the extras were there, but where was her leading man, her savior?

"Blair?"

She turned around and saw Nate pushing his way through the crowd toward her. Nate's eyes were bloodshot, his face slack, his hair uncombed. He looked more like a forgettable supporting actor than a leading man.

Was this all there was? Was Nate *it*?

Blair didn't have much choice. She opened her eyes wide, silently asking him for help and praying he'd be up to the job.

The bird woman frowned and turned to see what Blair was staring at. Blair made a dash for the ladies' room, and Nate stepped in just in time.

Thank God he was so stoned.

"Nate Archibald," he greeted the woman, shaking her hand. "My mother is a huge fan of birds."

The woman chortled. What a charming young man. "Well. Perhaps your family would like to make a donation."

Nate plucked two flutes of champagne off a passing tray. He raised his glass and drank up. Then he raised his other glass and drank that too. "To the birds," he said, trying to fend off another outbreak of the giggles.

Rain and Laura stood on the edge of the dance floor, tossing their hair around, useless as usual. Nate waved them over.

"Hello, Nate," said Rain, tottering on five-inch stilettos.

Laura had taken some of Anthony's E. "I *love* your red suit," she told the bird woman and gave her a hug.

"Excuse me," Nate said, and slipped stealthily away.

"Blair?" Nate called, cautiously cracking open the ladies' room door. "Are you in there?"

Blair was crouched in the end stall. "Damn," she murmured, wiping her mouth with toilet paper. She stood up and flushed. "I'll be right out," she said, waiting for him to leave.

But Nate pushed the ladies' room door open the rest of the way and stepped inside. On a counter by the sinks were little bottles of Evian, perfume, hairspray, Advil, and hand lotion. He unscrewed a bottle of water and shook a couple of Advil into his palm.

Blair opened the stall door. "You're still here."

Nate handed her the pills and the water. "I'm still here," he repeated.

Blair sipped the water and swallowed the pills. "Thanks. I'm really fine. You can go."

"You look nice," Nate said, ignoring her. He reached out and rubbed one of Blair's bare shoulders. Her skin felt warm and soft, and Nate wished they could just lie down on the cold marble bathroom tile and fall asleep together. And then maybe have sex.

"Thanks." Blair bit her lower lip. She didn't want to stab Nate anymore, she wanted to kiss him. "So do you."

"I'm sorry, Blair. I really am," Nate began.

Blair nodded and began to cry. Nate pulled a paper towel from the dispenser and handed it to her.

"I think the only real reason I did it . . . I mean, that I did it with Serena . . . is because I knew she'd do it," Nate said, grasping for the right words. "But it was you I wanted all along. It's always been you."

Aw.

Blair swallowed. He'd said it just right, exactly the way she'd written it in the scripts in her head. The ones without any brutal stabbings or decaying corpses or severed heads hanging from trees. She put her arms around his neck and let him hold her. His clothes smelled like pot.

Nate pushed her away and looked down into her eyes. "So everything is okay now?" he said. "You still want me?"

Blair caught the reflection of the two of them together in the bathroom mirror. She turned to gaze up into Nate's gorgeous green eyes and nodded yes.

"But only if you promise never to mention Serena," she sniffed.

Nate wound a strand of Blair's hair around his finger and breathed in the scent of her perfume. Behind them a vulture beat its wings against the bathroom window. Nate ignored it. It felt okay, standing there, holding Blair. It felt like something he could do. For now, and maybe forever. He didn't even need to think about Serena, especially not if she was dead.

"I promise," Nate said.

And then they kissed—a sad, soft kiss. In her head, Blair could hear the swell of music signaling the end of the film. It had started out a little gory and half the cast was dead, but at least the finale was romantic. The vulture pecked at the glass, staring at them with its beady black eyes.

"Come on." Blair pulled away and wiped the mascara smudges from her eyes. "Let's dance."

Holding hands, they left the ladies' room. Rain Hoffstetter smiled knowingly as she tottered past on the way in.

"You guys," she scolded. "Get a room!"

s and d and j and c body slam

"This band rocks!" Serena shouted at Vanessa over the pounding drum and bass. She wriggled her butt from side to side in her chair, her eyes shining. Dan was having trouble breathing normally. He'd barely touched his drink.

Vanessa smiled, pleased that Serena liked the music. Personally, she hated it, although she'd never tell Ruby. She'd rather lie by herself in the dark listening to Gregorian chant.

Yeehaw!

A girl wearing a red leather vest and black lace leggings was being tossed in the air by the pulsating crowd. Something about her legs looked wrong, like they'd been pulled off and stuck on backwards.

"You're such a creep I hate my life you're such a creep I hate my life you're such a creep I love your lies!!!!" Ruby growled into the mic.

"Come on." Serena stood up. "Let's dance."

Vanessa shook her head. "That's okay," she said. "I value my life."

"Dan?" Serena tugged on his tux sleeve. "Come on!"

Dan never, ever danced. He glanced at Vanessa, who raised

her black eyebrows, challenging him. *If you get up and dance right now, you will go straight to the top of my loser list,* her look said.

Dan stood up. Serena grabbed his hand and pushed her way into the throng. Suddenly she whipped around and slammed her whole body against his.

Dan stood there for a moment, unsure how to respond. Then he began to nod his head up and down in time to the beat. All around him people were jumping straight up into the air and slamming into each other. Dan took a deep breath and slammed Serena back, laughing. Serena raised her arms overhead, closed her eyes, and let out a wild banshee yell. Dan closed his eyes too and howled into the din.

The music was so loud, the crowd so crazy, it didn't matter what they did. It didn't matter that he couldn't dance, or that he was the only one in the room wearing a tuxedo—probably the only one in Williamsburg.

He opened his eyes. Serena was smiling at him. She stuck out her tongue and slammed her perfect body into his once again. Dan stumbled backwards, grinning. What mattered was *he was with her.* And he was alive.

Alone at the table, Vanessa finished first her drink and then Dan's. Finally she got up and went to sit down at the bar.

"Nice shirt," the bartender remarked when he saw her. Her sister was always talking about how cute he was—early twenties, red hair, long sideburns, and a sly smile.

"Thanks." Vanessa smiled back. "It's new."

"You should wear red more often." He held his hand out. "I'm Clark. You're Vanessa, right?"

Vanessa nodded. She wondered if he was just being nice to her because he liked her sister.

"Can I tell you a secret?" He dumped a few different things into a martini shaker and shook it up.

Oh, fuck, Vanessa thought. *Here's when he pours out his heart and tells me all about how he's been in love with Ruby forever, but she doesn't seem to notice him, and he wants me to play Cupid and blah, blah, blah. Or he's going to tell me he killed someone once, which would be equally boring.*

These days, who hasn't?

"What?" she yawned, feigning disinterest.

"Well," Clark said, "I see you and Ruby come in here all the time."

Here he goes, Vanessa thought.

"And you never come up to the bar and talk to me. But I've kind of had a crush on you since I first saw you."

She stared at him. Was he joking?

Clark poured the drink out of the martini shaker into a short little glass and squeezed a few limes into it. He pushed it toward her. "Try that," he said. "It's on the house."

Vanessa picked up the glass and tasted it. It was sweet and sour at the same time, and she couldn't taste any alcohol.

"I could drink about ten of these," she admitted.

"Don't," Clark warned.

Vanessa put the empty glass down. Serena and Dan could slam their pretty asses off for all she cared. "Why the fuck not?"

Clark replaced the glass with a bottle of water. He leaned toward her and whispered softly in her ear. "Because I want to kiss you and I want you to remember it."

The *Kiss Me or Die* DJ had a thing for Celine Dion. Gorgeously dressed couples held on to each other and swayed slowly to the diva's yelping cries, barely moving beneath the soft lights. The air smelled of candle wax, raw fish, and cigarette smoke. The party wasn't the rocking slam-fest that some had hoped for, but it wasn't too terribly dull. There was still plenty of booze, nothing had caught fire, no one had been murdered, and the cops hadn't shown up to card people. Secretly everyone in attendance felt they had something to celebrate—that they had survived.

Eyes closed, Nate and Blair held each other, her cheek against his chest, his lips brushing the top of her head. Blair had put her brain on pause and her head was full of static. She was tired of dreaming up movies and killing people. Right now, real life suited her just fine.

A few couples away, Chuck had his hands full of Jenny Humphrey. Jenny wished the DJ would bring up the tempo. She bobbed up and down, trying to dance as fast as she could to keep Chuck from groping her, but when she moved her shoulders just so, her boobs bounced out of her dress and bumped against Chuck's chin.

Chuck was delighted. He wound his arms around her waist and shimmied her off the dance floor, straight into the ladies' room.

"What are we doing?" Jenny demanded, confused. She gazed up into his eyes. She knew Chuck was friends with Serena and Blair, and she wanted to trust him. But he still hadn't asked her what her name was. In fact, he'd barely spoken to her at all.

"I just want to kiss you." Chuck bent his head down and enveloped her mouth in his. His leather eye patch dug into her cheek. His muscular tongue rammed against her teeth with such force that Jenny let out a little cry.

Relenting, she opened her mouth and let him thrust his tongue deep into her throat. She had kissed boys before, playing games at parties. But she'd never tongue-kissed. *Is this what it's supposed to feel like?* she wondered, frightened. She reached up and pushed against Chuck's chest, pulling her head away, desperate for air.

"I have to go to the bathroom," she mumbled, stumbling backwards into a stall and locking the door.

She could see Chuck's feet, standing outside the stall. "All right," he said. "But I'm not finished with you yet."

Jenny sat down on the toilet seat without pulling up her dress and pretended to pee. Then she stood up and flushed.

"All done?" Chuck called.

Jenny didn't answer. Her mind was racing. What should she do? Anxiously, she reached inside her little black handbag for her phone.

Chuck crouched down to look under the stall door. What was she doing in there, the little tease? He crawled forward on his hands and knees. "All right," he said. "That's it, I'm coming in."

Jenny closed her eyes and backed against the stall wall. Quickly, she pressed the buttons for Dan's number into her cell phone, praying that he'd answer.

Ruby's band was on their last song. Serena and Dan were slick with sweat. Dan had some new moves down. He was in the middle of a hip jab to the side with a squat-jump slam into his neighbor when his cell phone vibrated in his pocket.

"Damn," he said, pulling it out.

It was a text from his sister.

Bad bad party. Please take me home!

Dan tapped Serena on the arm and pointed to his phone. "Sorry," he shouted over the music. He pushed his way through the throng, putting his hand over his free ear as he called Jenny back.

"Dan?" Her voice sounded very small and scared and far away. "I need your help. Please come get me?"

"Now?" Dan shouted. He looked up. Serena was pushing her way toward him, looking beautiful and sweaty and perfect and gorgeous, the spattered blood of the other slam dancers smeared like rouge on her cheeks.

"Please, Dan?" Jenny pleaded.

"What's wrong?" Dan asked his sister. "Can't you take a cab?"

"No, I—" Jenny's voice trailed off. "Just please come *now*," she said and hung up.

Ruby let out a final orgiastic siren wail, threw her bass at the lead guitarist's head, and cannonballed into the headbanging crowd.

"Who was that?" Serena shouted over the howling mob.

"My little sister," Dan told her. "She's at *Kiss Me or Die*. She's having a bad time."

"Are you going to pick her up?"

"Yeah, I think so. She sounded weird," he said, thinking of all the murders on the Upper East Side. That neighborhood was bad news. Brooklyn felt like a sheltered paradise in comparison.

"I'll come with you," Serena offered. "Just let me get my purse and say goodbye."

"Good." Dan grinned. "Great."

She found Vanessa at the bar. "Hey," Serena said, touching her arm. "We're going to get Dan's sister."

Vanessa turned around slowly, waiting for Clark's eyeballs to enlarge and register "beautiful girl" in bold black letters like the cherries in a slot machine. But Clark only glanced at Serena like she was just another customer.

"Later, Vanessa!" Dan called from over by the door.

Vanessa glared at him. She wished Clark would stop slicing limes for just a second so she could kiss him right in front of Dan.

Serena held up her purse and leaned in to whisper in her ear. "I know you want your knife back, but can I borrow it, just for tonight?"

Vanessa shrugged her shoulders. Clark rolled an olive across the bar and picked it up with his teeth. She giggled. "Go ahead."

Serena tucked the purse under her arm. "Okay. See you. Tell Ruby she rocks!"

Vanessa turned back to Clark without a word.

"Who were they?" He picked an olive out of a dish and held it just in front of Vanessa's lips.

Vanessa bit into the olive and shrugged. "Just some losers from uptown."

the couple that kills together stays together

Dan hailed a cab and opened the door for Serena. The October air was crisp and smelled of burnt sugar. Dan suddenly felt very elegant and mature—a man in a tuxedo out on the town with a beautiful girl. He slid into the seat beside her and looked down at his hands as the cab pulled away from the curb. They weren't shaking anymore.

Unbelievable as it seemed, he had touched Serena with those very hands while they were dancing. And now he was alone with her in a taxi. If he wanted to, he could take her hand, stroke her cheek, maybe even kiss her. He studied her profile, her skin shining in the yellow glow of the streetlights, but he couldn't bring himself to do it.

"God, I love to dance," Serena said, letting her head fall back on the seat. She felt completely relaxed. "I could seriously do this every single night."

Dan nodded. "Yeah, me too."

They rode the rest of the way in silence, enjoying the tired feeling in their legs and the cool air from the open window on their sweat-dampened foreheads. There was nothing awkward about the fact that they weren't talking. It was nice.

The cab pulled up in front of the Katherine Farkas and Isabel Coates Memorial House, formerly known as the Frick. Dan had expected to see Jenny waiting for them outside, but the sidewalk was empty.

"I guess I'm going to have to go in there and get her." He turned to Serena. "You can go ahead home. Or you can wait. . . ."

"I'll come with you," she said, clutching her clutch. "I may as well see what I missed."

They got out of the cab and headed for the door.

"I hope they let us in," Serena whispered. "I threw out my invitation."

Dan pulled the crumpled invitation Jenny had made for him out of his pocket and flashed it at the bouncer. "She's with me," he said, putting his arm around Serena.

"Go ahead," the bouncer said, waving them on.

She's with me?
She's with me.
She's with me!

Dan couldn't believe his balls. He'd had no idea they were that big.

"I'd better go find her," he told Serena when they got inside.

"Okay," she agreed, squeezing his arm. "Meet me back here in ten minutes."

The room was full of old familiar faces. So familiar that no one there was quite sure whether Serena van der Woodsen had just arrived or if she'd been there all night. They'd heard she was dead, but she looked healthier than ever. In fact, she looked like she'd been having a fantastic time. Her hair was windblown, her dress was slipping off her shoulders, there was a run in her tights, and her cheeks were dark pink, as if she'd been running. She looked wild, like the kind of girl who'd done everything everyone said she'd done, and probably a whole lot more.

Blair noticed Serena right away, back from the dead, standing on the edge of the dance floor in that funny old dress they'd bought together at Alice's Underground.

What the fuck? Of course she was alive. Serena was never going to fucking die.

She pulled away from Nate. "Look who's here."

Nate turned around, squeezing Blair's hand tightly when he saw Serena.

The hand squeeze was out of shock, but Blair took it as a demonstration of his devotion. She squeezed his hand back. "Why don't you go tell her?" she instructed. "Tell her it's over. You can't be friends with her anymore. You can't have anything to do with her." Her stomach rumbled nervously. After all the throwing up she'd done, she really needed another tuna roll.

Nate stared at Serena with grim, slightly stoned determination. If Blair thought it was crucial that he tell Serena to get lost, then he'd do it. He couldn't wait to get this all behind them so he could relax. In fact, after he talked to Serena he was going to head upstairs and find somewhere private to light up.

Waspoid rule #1: When things get intense, get stoned.

"All right," he said, letting go of Blair's hand. "Here I go."

"Hey." Serena greeted Nate with a kiss on the cheek. He blushed. He hadn't expected her to touch him. "You look mahvelous, darling," she said in a silly, hoity-toity accent.

"Thanks." Nate tried to put his hands in his pockets, but his tuxedo didn't have any. "You look . . . nice also. Are you . . . all better?"

"I'm great! I kind of blew off this party," she gushed. "I've been out dancing with this guy at this crazy place in Brooklyn!"

Nate raised his eyebrows in surprise. But then again, nothing Serena said should have surprised him anymore.

"So, you want to dance?" She put her arms around Nate's neck before he answered, and began to swing her hips from side to side.

Nate glanced at Blair, who was watching them carefully. "Look, Serena." He stepped back and removed her arms. "I really can't . . . you know . . . be friends . . . not like the way we were before," he began.

Serena frowned. "Why not?" she said. "Did I do something wrong?"

"Blair is my girlfriend," Nate continued. "I have to . . . I have to be loyal to her. I can't . . . I can't really be . . ." He swallowed.

Her knuckles white, Serena slipped her hand inside her black patent leather clutch and gripped the cold handle of the bowie knife. If only she could hate Nate for being so cruel and so lame. If only he weren't so good-looking. If only she didn't love him. She would kill him this time for being so mean. That was what she'd set out to do, when she'd first come home to New York. But she couldn't do it. She never could.

"Well, I guess we should stop talking then. Blair might get mad." She slipped her purse back under her arm and turned abruptly away.

As she crossed the room, Serena's eyes met Blair's. She stopped in her tracks and opened her clutch. Once again, her fingers closed around the large knife's handle. She pulled out the knife, ready to strike.

Blair hiked up her green dress. She reached down and withdrew the gold and emerald dagger from its solid gold sheath.

En garde.

Touché.

But instead of attacking each other, the two girls smiled.

It was strange smile, and neither girl knew what the other meant by it.

Was Blair smiling because she'd won the boy in the end and stamped all over Serena's party shoes, leaving Serena scarred and bruised? Because—as usual—she'd gotten her way?

Was Serena smiling because she admired Blair's taste in antique weaponry? Or was she was already plotting her revenge?

Was it a sad smile because their friendship was over?

Maybe they were smiling because they both knew deep down that no matter what happened next—what boy they fell in or out of love with, what clothes they wore or didn't wear, what their SAT scores were, who they incinerated or decapitated, or which college they got into—it wouldn't be worth killing each other over.

It's no fun kicking ass without a little competition.

Serena dropped the knife back in her bag and tucked it under her arm. She kept on walking, headed for the ladies' room to splash some cold water on her face.

Blair lifted up her dress and tucked the dagger back into its golden sheath.

Over by the door, the director of the Birds of Prey Foundation was just putting on her mink coat and kissing Rain and Laura good night.

Blair walked over and pressed a gift bag into her hand.

"Those birds are lucky you're alive," she said with a smile.

Serena turned on the tap and splashed her face over and over with cool, clean water. It felt so good she wanted to peel off all her clothes and jump in.

She leaned against the row of sinks, patting her face dry. Her gaze slipped to the floor, where she saw a pair of tan pigskin shoes, the fringed end of a cream-colored scarf, and a girl's purple patent leather H&M handbag.

Serena rolled her eyes and walked over. "Chuck, is that you?" she said into the crack in the door. "Who've you got in there with you?"

A girl gasped.

"Dammit," Chuck swore. He'd stood Jenny up on the toilet seat lid in the end stall and pulled her dress down so he could get at those massive jugs. Serena had come at the worst possible moment. He pushed open the stall door a few inches. "Fuck off," he growled.

Behind him Serena could see little Jenny Humphrey, her dress pulled down around her waist, arms hugging herself, looking terrified.

Someone pushed open the bathroom door. "Jenny? Are you in here?" Dan called.

Serena suddenly registered: Jenny was Dan's sister. No wonder she'd sounded scared on the phone. She was about to be mauled by Chuck Bass.

"I'm here," Jenny whimpered.

"Get out of here," Serena snapped at Chuck. She pulled the stall door open just wide enough for him to get past her without Dan having to see his own sister half-undressed.

Chuck shoved Serena against the stall door. "Well, excuse me, psycho bitch," he hissed. "Next time I'll be sure to ask your permission."

"Wait a minute, Scarf Boy," Dan snapped. If only he'd killed Chuck before, none of this would be happening. "What were you doing to my sister?"

Serena pushed the stall door closed and stood outside it, waiting for Jenny to step down from the toilet and fix her dress.

"Fuck off," Chuck said, pushing Dan out of the way.

"No, you fuck off," Dan's hands were shaking. Chuck was going to die. It was now or never.

Serena hated it when boys fought. It made them look so dumb. She opened her clutch and took out the knife.

"Hey Chuck." She poked him in the back with the point of the knife. "Nice eye patch."

"You bitch," Chuck hissed, whirling around to face her. Spit flew from his mouth as he spoke. "You think you can come back here and act all high and mighty after everything you've done?"

"What have I done, Chuck?" Serena demanded, the knifepoint pressed against his tuxedoed chest. "What is it that you think I've done?"

Chuck licked his lips and laughed quietly. A drop of sweat trickled out from underneath his eye patch. "What *haven't* you done? You got kicked out of boarding school because you are a perverted slut who made marks on the wall above the bed in your dorm room for every boy you did. You have STDs. You were addicted to all kinds of drugs and busted out of rehab and now you're dealing your own stuff. You were a member of some cult that killed chickens. You have a baby in France. And you kill people." Chuck took a deep breath and licked his lips. "You tried to kill me."

Serena smiled, knife ready. "Wow. I've been busy."

Chuck frowned. He glanced at Dan, who stood, watching silently, with his hands in his pockets.

Sniff, sniff.

Still locked in the bathroom stall, Jenny couldn't get control of herself. She just could not believe that of all the people in the universe, it had to be Serena van der Woodsen who'd found her like this. Serena must think she was so pathetic.

"Fuck off, Chuck," Serena whispered. She grabbed Chuck's scarf and yanked him toward her, holding up the knife.

Dan picked up a huge naked girl–shaped pink glass bottle of Dolce & Gabbana perfume and held it aloft. He was about to slam it down on the back of Chuck's head when Jenny burst out of the bathroom stall, clutching a white porcelain toilet seat in both hands.

"Don't kill him, he's mine!" she shrieked, holding the toilet seat out in front of her and running full tilt toward Chuck.

Serena and Dan stepped out of the way.

The toilet seat caught Chuck just below the waist, shattering his pelvis.

"Fuck me!" Chuck cried, doubling over and falling to his knees.

"Here," Serena said, offering Jenny the knife. "Watch out, it's pretty sharp."

Dan put down the perfume bottle and lit a cigarette. When would he get his turn?

Knife in hand, Jenny stood over Chuck's fallen form, feeling powerful and tall. "Look up," she commanded. "I want to see your stupid face while you die."

Chuck looked up, his forehead pink and damp with sweat. "Don't," he whined, struggling to rise. His pigskin shoes slipped on the damp tile. His scarf was tangled around his legs.

"Do it!" Serena urged. Her fingers itched to make the kill, but Jenny so deserved it.

Jenny took a step closer and held the knife out in front of her. "You know I'm going to."

"Don't," Chuck pleaded once more, his hands and feet scrambling on the slick tile. Half kneeling and half standing, he slipped and fell forward onto the outthrust knife. Jenny let go of the knife's blue steel hilt. It stuck out of Chuck's torso like a dart in a bull's-eye.

Serena lunged forward and grabbed the knife's hilt. She twisted it right and then left, gutting and disemboweling him. Chuck collapsed on the blood-spattered marble tile, smashing his skull. His guts were on the floor. His eye patch had fallen askew, revealing a lidless rolling eyeball. Serena raised her foot and crushed the good eye with the pointy red stiletto heel of her gold Louboutins.

"Asshole," she said.

Desperate to participate in the downfall of his most hated classmate, Dan lit a match and reached for an aerosol can of hairspray.

"I'm gonna burn you!" he bellowed, spraying hairspray directly into Chuck's face and holding the burning match in front of the spray.

Chuck's top half was momentarily bathed in fire. His black silk bow tie flared and shriveled. The mother-of-pearl buttons of his charred white tuxedo shirt blackened and turned to ash. Like melting wax, Chuck's cheeks and chin seemed to soften and slide away from the bone.

Pale nostrils flared, Dan stood over him, exultant. Doing it was way better than writing about it.

Hair smoking, guts pooling, lidless eyeballs rolling blindly back in his head, Chuck writhed on the floor in pain. His pigskin loafers kicked out with a final, valiant thrust. "But I'm Chuck Bass," he gasped, dying.

The stench of burnt flesh and hair, torched silk and leather, and fried hairspray was almost unbearable. "You know we love you," Serena said, spritzing the fallen body with the girl-shaped bottle of perfume. Chuck didn't respond. He seemed pretty dead. She spun around to open a bathroom window—to let the smoke out and the vultures in.

Jenny picked up the knife from the floor and ran her finger over the bloody blade. She'd skipped dinner. A little solid food would help soak up the champagne sloshing around in her stomach. Chuck's tongue lolled, pink and meaty, out of his mouth. She could cut it out, bring it home with her, slice it up, and eat it.

Dan lit another cigarette, enjoying the moment. He was the most suave and handsome man in the room. That line from Vanessa's screenplay echoed in his head: *Life is fragile and absurd. Murdering someone's not so hard.* In fact, it was ridiculously easy— even *fun*.

He wrapped a comforting arm around his sister's shoulders. "You all right?"

Jenny clutched the bloody knife, swaying unsteadily on her size-five feet. "I can't tell whether I'm still really drunk, or just tired and really hungry."

"Here, I'll take that." Serena removed the hunting knife from Jenny's hands and dropped it in her purse. She looked up at Dan and held out her hand. "Ready?"

Dan kept his arm around his sister and took Serena's hand. Together, they exited the bathroom and wound their way through the crowd and toward the door.

"Wait! Your gift bags!" Rain Hoffstetter squealed. She handed Serena and Jenny each a black Kate Spade tote bag. "There are glow-in-the-dark condoms. And knives!"

Dan pushed open the doors to the old mansion and ran out onto Fifth Avenue to hail a cab. They slid into the backseat with Jenny in the middle. She put her feet up on the hump in the floor and hugged her blood-spattered knees. Serena reached down and stroked her curly brown hair.

"You guys go home first," she offered.

Dan glanced at Jenny. She needed to wash off all that blood, drink a cup of warm milk, and go to bed. He gave the driver his address.

Serena leaned back, still stroking Jenny's hair. "Wow," she breathed. "I'm glad I didn't stay home tonight."

Dan stared at her. "So, those stories . . ." he said, and then he blushed. "I mean, did any of that happen, for real?"

Serena frowned. She fished in her bag for a cigarette, and then thought better of it. The blood from the knife had probably ruined them anyway. "Well, what do you think?"

Dan shrugged his shoulders. "I think it's a bunch of bullshit."

Serena raised her eyebrows playfully. "But how do you know for sure?"

Her mouth was open, the corners of it quavering up and then down. Her dark blue eyes glowed in the light of a passing car.

He'd just seen her disembowel the guy he most hated. She was carrying a very large, expensive knife. She could have been an angel or a killer, or both.

"You don't scare me."

The corners of Serena's mouth spread wide. "Good." She took a deep breath and let her head fall back against the seat.

Dan let his head fall back too, still wondering whether or not he ought to be scared.

As they sped down Central Park South and through Columbus Circle, Serena kept her eyes open. She'd always thought the rest of Manhattan was ugly and depressing compared to the quiet, manicured streets of the Upper East Side. But now the brilliant lights and loud noises, the steam rising from the grates on the corners of Broadway, were beautifully chaotic. The taxi rumbled over a bump. Her purse fell on the floor. The knife spilled out. In the darkness of the taxi, Serena, Dan, and Jenny all reached for it at the same time.

They couldn't wait to see what would happen next.

gossipgirl.net

Disclaimer: All the real names of places, people, and events have been altered or abbreviated to protect the innocent. Namely, me.

hey people!

Well, I had a great time at *Kiss Me or Die*. I must have lost fifteen pounds dancing—or maybe someone's chopped off my legs and I just haven't noticed.

Needless to say, I'm feeling good. I mean, I survived.

SIGHTINGS

B and *N* going into his townhouse together late Friday night. Hopefully she'll put her weapon away before he frisks her thigh. *C*, or what remains of *C*, getting wheeled into an ambulance—again. *D* and *J* and their scruffy dad eating a family breakfast on Saturday morning at that diner where they used to film **Seinfeld**. *V* snapping photos of her new boyfriend, modeling beside the decomposing bodies of a family of dead rats in a trash heap in Brooklyn. *S* handing a black Kate Spade tote bag to a homeless man feeding the vultures on the steps of the Met. One of the birds had what looked like a tan leather eye patch dangling like a medallion from its neck. And *V* at **Paragon Sports** on Broadway, returning a bunch of stuff and handing over a check for $4,500, engraved in gold with a long, vaguely Dutch name. Guess *S* wants to keep that pretty knife after all. Sure she'll put it to good use!

YOUR E-MAIL

q: Hey GG,
Just wanted to tell you that I'm writing my college thesis on you. You rock!
—Studyboy

BROOKLYN BRIDGE

a: Dear Studyboy,
I'm flattered. So . . . what do you look like?
—GG

QUESTIONS AND ANSWERS

Why worry about college? I'm having way too much fun right now. And there are so many questions to be answered:

Will **S** and **D** fall in love? Will **S** grow tired of his corduroys and cut them into strips along with his pale, skinny legs? Or is **D** already dead?

Will **J** swear off high society and fancy dresses and make new friends her age? Is she our new murderous heroine? Or is she dead too?

Will **V** ever actually blow up the school?

Will **B** stay with **N**? Will he live to tell the tale? Will he become a vegetable from smoking so much dope to calm his frayed nerves?

Will **C** come back from the dead with glass eyes, a prosthetic face, and a solid platinum cane, and haunt us like he always used to?

Will the mayor's office introduce some sort of predator to eat all the vultures? What's next—wolves?

Will Constance Billard's Phys Ed department update its curriculum to include knife-throwing, hand-to-hand combat, fencing, and jousting in order to keep up with its killer schoolgirls?

Will **S** and **B** maintain their truce?

Over my dead body.

Best keep a safe distance. Unless you're skilled with a knife. And—like me— you just can't stay away.

You know you love me,

Acknowledgments

Cecily von Ziegesar (author) and Cindy Eagan (editorial director, Poppy)

No one else was injured or maimed during the writing of this book, except Joelle Hobeika (editor, Alloy), Sara Shandler (editorial director, Alloy), Liz Dresner (designer, Alloy), Aiah Wieder (managing editor, Alloy), Josh Bank (president, East Coast, Alloy), Leslie Morgenstein (CEO, Alloy), Jeanne Detallante (illustrator), Andrew Smith (associate publisher, Poppy), Suzanne Gluck (WME), and the author's entire family. The author would like to thank them and Cindy from the darkest depths of her heart.